The RUTHLESS DICTATOR

RUMONT TEKAY

Murray Park Publishing
4230 East Towne Blvd, Suite 114
Madison, WI 53704
www.murrayparkpublishing.com
info@murrayparkpublishing.com

Cover design and layout: Marion Designs
Publishing Consultant: Nakea S. Murray, Literary Consultant Group
Editing: Tobias A. Fox and Keisha Caldwell
Typesetting: Shawna A. Grundy

Printed in United States

Library of Congress Catalog Number: 2008942836
    1. Urban, Chicago, Hip-Hop, African American, – Fiction

ISBN-13: 978-0-9821331-0-1
ISBN-10: 0-9821331-0-3

The RUTHLESS DICTATOR

Convolution
n: A complexity or intricacy, especially one of many.

Author's Note

The Convolution, a world-class crime syndicate, consist of a forty-three man assemblage that controls the twenty-two states of the Midwest. One man oversees a state while an underboss run the major city within the state and assumes responsibility for the surrounding cities as well. Their Chairman sits above it all, thus, taking the membership count from an even forty-two, to an odd forty-three. There are many street organizations, Cartels, and Cosa Nostras that co-exist on the Land Of Lincoln. But not in forty-seven years has there been any comparisons worthy to The Convolution. They were the undisputed throne holders. Their political influence has certified them a reckoning power of men beyond boundaries, without measure.

Throughout these series of events, it must be understood that Chicago is not a city; it is a nation.

My progress in life is dedicated to my beloved mother,
Mary Theresa Sims,
for being a single mother of three
and receiving little notoriety for doing the best she could.
Just know that the life I lived had nothing to do
with how you raised me.
I love you, Ma.

To my Great Grandmother and Grandmother Lorraine and Viola,
And my Uncles Edward, David and Tyrone—
May you all Rest in Peace.

ACKNOWLEDGMENTS

After traveling through a journey that took well over twelve years for me to make it to this date in time, I have no doubt that it's a blessing. Therefore, first and foremost, I'd have to give all praise to God; without him none of this would be possible. Next, I must acknowledge two beautiful hearted women, whom without their 'above and beyond' work ethic, I'll still be in a 6x8 cell; pining about this moment. Their names are Angela Wood and Amy Cramlet, Unit Manager and Social Worker at Oshkosh Correctional Institution. They knew my history, and, in spite of my past and their colleagues' disfavor, they pulled for me. I would like to thank you both for believing in me and for going against the odds. In addition, I'd like to thank the staff over at St. Croix Correctional Institution (Boot Camp) for challenging my mind and opening my eyes…there is a better way.

Then there's, Amy Taylor, who I can honestly say has believed in my dreams and me since day one. Even at times when I get frustrated about my writing flow or about the business in general, she's always there with genuine, encouraging words that'll get me back on track. I promise you, you're the very reason I've come this far in realizing my dream. I love you. To the Kerl family as a whole; Dan, Andrea, Aaron, as well as Dixie, Destiny Finley and Terry Moore; I would like to express my appreciation to you all for not pre-judging and accepting me for me.

I'd like to express a special thanks to my sister, Tisch Sims, for holding me down when I was behind the walls. Without you, family visits would have been non-existent and I appreciate the love! As for my younger brother, George E. Williams, I'm proud of you bruh! Get that education and keep your head above water.

To my Aunts Roslyn, Punkin, Beverly, Doris, Linda, Janice, and my Uncles Raydell, Clyde, Nick, and Robert; and of course my host of cousins including the Sims, Johnson, and Kirkpatrick family, thank you all for being a part of me! And I can't forget George and Melody,

Andre and Micheal, and the rest of the Williams family.

To my pops, Larry Kirkpatrick, whom I still haven't gotten the opportunity to get to know…I just want to say that although you weren't around when I was growing up, now that I'm a grown man and find myself in a similar situation, I'm not as critical. I want to assure you that there's no love lost, and when you're ready to build a relationship then let me know. And to my son, Marquise Ellison… your mother was five months pregnant with you when I went to prison, and now you're twelve years old. Wow! Because of the bad decisions that I made before your birth, I've been absent from you your entire life. I'm sorry, and I hope that you and I can build a relationship and move forward. I love you, son.

Victor L. Martin, you know that you're the last person that I'd forget. Over the years you and I have established a bond that symbolizes true friendship. I will never take that for granted, know that! I know that you're currently fighting an uphill battle, in a personal sense, with the courts, prison administration, and the business as a whole, but I know that you'll pull through as a shining example of what overcoming is all about. I'm your biggest fan homie, and know that we, the readers (your fans) are still out here supporting you!

To my Big Homie, the real BET's Ultimate Hustler, Mr. Dashawn Taylor: It's only been a little while since you and I initially crossed paths, but the real recognizes the real and I look forward to making Power Moves with you in the near future! 'Preciate you flying in to bring in the '2009 New Year' with yo' boy! These next shout outs go out to 33rd Street Media and 'Dutch' himself, Mr. Kwame Teague. 2009 is our year!

To the Queen Of Thug Love Fiction, Ms. Wahida Clark: I got love for you sistah and I'd like to thank you for both your time and insight. And to my consultant/publicist, Nakea Murray, I appreciate your bluntness. Don't change. Now let's get this book to the best seller's list!

I would like to acknowledge my advisory board: Jeffrey J. Bartzen (attorney), Wayne Hyler (accountant), Ron Brent, Keith Thomas, and Jerome Dillard. Speaking of Jerome Dillard, I will like to show a token of my appreciation to you and Voices Beyond Bars. You all have done more for the community and me than you'll ever know. Continue to give weary minds the direction they need. You all at MUM are doing phenomenal work and are instrumental in the reintegration process for ex-offenders. Last but never least, I'd like to say thank you to Heidi Schroeder for being understanding and flexible.

Shout outs to Larry Hoover, Jeff Fort, David Barksdale, Jerome Freeman, Gator Bradley, Mickey Cogwell, James Austin, Willie Lord, etc.

"Much luv to Eric "E The Exclusive" and Triumphant Entertainment for hosting the absolute best, major events in the Midwest region!" Keep it going, my nig.

Special shout outs to Andre Hamlin, Derrick Rose, Richard Greenlaw, Theodore Rush, Tom Niebuhr, Dawan Shelby, Koolaid and the Shelby family, Pierre Nettlesbay and Freddy and the entire Nettlesbey family, Rich and Frog at 'Divine Transformations', Deon 'Raekwon' Neighbors and LV, reppin' Raekwon Hair Designs, Cortez Shields, and the entire Murda Park outfit from old to new!

And for my nigs on lock: Darquice Streeter, Lamont Powell, Akeem Musa, Lamont Brown, Big D Brooks, Scrilla from the Mad, Latroy Harris, and everyone else who were a part of D-Block during the years 2005-2006. Hurry up home my niggas!

Now it's time for what you've all been waiting for…the most EXPLOSIVE novel of 2009, The Ruthless Dictator.

In the words of Wahida Clark, "Brace yourselves for the unknown."

PROLOGUE

Macklin Cutti's anger was boiling over. His ranting was heard throughout the house that he shared with his wife, Loretta, of five years and their two children; Natasha, age six and her two-year-old brother, Adon.

"It is 2:37 in the muthafuckin' morning and here you come waltzin' inside my muthafuckin' house like it's the thang to do," Macklin yelled as he followed Loretta from the foyer, through the hallway, and into the kitchen, turning on every light switch that she passed.

Natasha cautiously peeked around her bedroom doorpost and at Adon's partially opened bedroom door as the yelling continued.

Loretta stopped in her tracks, and spun around in her platforms to face Macklin. "Oh, so this is *your* house now," she said sarcastically, not taking him seriously.

"You muthafuckin' right this is my pad. I pay the cost to be the boss up in this here piece. And I can treat you like the bad habit you is and get rid of your ass!"

"Nigga please," Loretta tossed her hand into the air and began to walk away. "I'm one addiction that you can't shake," she said with confidence.

"What," Macklin grabbed her roughly by the arm and changed her entire direction. "You think I'm jiving?"

"I don't know," Loretta breathed into his ear. "*Are* you jiving, big daddy," she slowly reached below and gently caressed his dick. Her Tequila reeking breath only fumed him more.

He grabbed her by the throat and drove her to the wall. "Look bitch," Macklin seethed. "This is the second time this week that you've pulled this early morning shit, and it's not even payday yet. You have two children in this house to look after. You do this one more time and you gone!"

"Whatever you say, Daddy," Loretta conceded and dropped to her knees and swallowed Macklin's dick whole.

CHAPTER 1

A don Cutti, a twenty-three-year breadwinner, bolted from his laying position. He looked around in haste and checked his surroundings. Slowly, his erratic breathing became relaxed once he'd realized that he was in his bed and only dreaming. He reached for his BlackBerry on the nightstand and checked today's date and time.

"4:27A.M., June 14th, 2008," he uttered.

It clearly wasn't the year 1987 like his dream had tried to convince him. He put his cell back on the nightstand and reached inside its drawer, pulling back a bottle with a label that read PROZAC. He twisted the top, removed the white cotton, and turned it up. Not one pill fell into his palm. The bottle was empty. Adon jumped to his feet. He walked down the dark corridor of his home at a speedy pace, bypassing connecting rooms without a care. His nose started to bleed and heart rate climbed. He halted his steps in front of an Italian glass cabinet. There, he pulled out a .357 revolver. He wiped his nose with his forearm and resumed down the corridor.

Suddenly, he froze in his steps.

"Lights," he said as the voice activation setup illuminated the corridor. He found himself in front of a floor to ceiling, high definition mirror; outlined with an antique black pearl frame. He stared motionless at his reflection. His G-Unit tank top was speckled with fresh drops of blood. He shut his eyes.

In haste, he hoisted the .357 to his head and inhaled deeply.

Get it over wit' nigga!

He opened his eyes to face his murderer, before he murked himself. He strained his vision as if to see something far ahead; an object beyond his reflection. In the mirror, a transparent image began to take form right before him. It developed features, then an identity. It was his father, Macklin Cutti. He mimicked the same heavy panting as Adon. And he, too, held a .357 to his head.

Alarmed, Adon quickly turned the gun on his father, but that was one reaction his reflection didn't mimic. Instead it stood the same stance, never removing the gun from its own head. Adon took small steps toward the mirror; his own reflection; his father, until he was eye to eye with the man he never got a chance to know.

"Why did you throw Ma out on the streets, and why did you have to leave us? WHY!?" he screamed at the top of his lungs. For the first time in nineteen years, a tear rushed down his butternut complexion. "I love you, father, no matter what." He extended his arms to his sides while Macklin mimicked his every move. "I love you, pops."

He shut his eyes and leaned in to hug his father, but was cut short when his head slightly hit the mirror. He opened his eyes in dismay, and his father was gone. Adon was face to face with himself; the way it's been the whole time. He dropped the burna, and fell to his knees in anguish.

"Uggggg!" Adon woke up screaming. But this time he woke up to the stone-cold realities of his actual life. He was no longer having a dream within a dream. Sweating profusely, he reached over and grabbed his BlackBerry from the nightstand. It read, 4:27A.M., June, 14th 2008. He put it back and reached into the nightstand's drawer, pulling back a bottle of Prozac. He twisted the top, removed the white cotton, and turned it up. A pill fell into his palm, and he popped it into his mouth and swallowed. Adon put his sweaty hand on his sweaty forehead. His face bared a confused expression, for he had caught a case of déjà vu.

After falling head over hills in love with a generous and good man, who served in the United States Marines, Charlotte Cambray's mother, Pauline, packed their belongings and left their family behind in France, and migrated to America when Charlotte was all but four years old. The marine, named Robert Fitzgerald, was stationed in France for two hundred days when the two met. Sparks flew between them. A year after he returned to the U.S., he sent for Pauline and she came running with her daughter in tow. He set them up comfortably on the north side of Chicago. Pauline was ecstatic about her new life. She couldn't remember the last time she'd been more happier. For Robert, the feeling was mutual and even referred to Charlotte as his own. Their bond as a family had strengthened over the next few years until on one tragic morning, Pauline received a phone call detailing the event surrounding his untimely death. Another marine had accidentally killed him during a combatant training exercise. The news hit Pauline hard and Charlotte was affected a great deal. She was determined not to return home and viewed as a failure. Weathering the storm, Pauline acquired her first job in America and managed to raise an adorable young girl into an even more beautiful woman. Years later, Pauline was diagnosed with breast cancer. A week before Charlotte's high school graduation had went underway her mother lost the battle. Her boyfriend at the time, Adon, became her shoulder to lean on. Her rock. He helped her stay the course as her mother would've wanted, and financed her college education with the funds that he generated from the streets.

Charlotte now lived at 8853 South Luella, Southeast Side of Chicago. She woke up this morning thankful that she didn't have to rush out of bed and head to class. Her professors at Chicago State University were anal about being prompt and ready to digest knowledge from Monday through Friday. Having started college two years late because of her unplanned pregnancy, she compounded her classes and even took a few of them during the summer season. As she approached her third year, she was determined not to fall too far behind her high school graduating class.

With a 3.8 GPA, she was doing an outstanding job at staying true to her goal. She was majoring in Business Management and International Business, and the subjects became cryptic at times. Well, the International Business drained her most. But oddly enough, it was also the subject that captivated her interest. She had always dreamed of going back to France armed with an education and ambition. She hadn't any family in America. However distant he was, Adon was her financial lifeline and that's how she paid for the best daycare in the state. In the meantime, however, she looked forward to the weekend each time it came around. Her brain cells needed the break. Even though her five-year-old daughter, Joyous, didn't allow her much rest she still managed to find solace in being home. Joyous was her pride and joy.

Charlotte picked up her LG cell phone. In spite of it being out of service for the past few months, she kept it solely for the stored pics of Adon, which were taken before they had split six months ago. She stared down at the exquisite bone structure that defined his face as if she was seeing him for the first time. She was always fond of his smooth butternut skin tone and full, but naturally, well-shaped eyebrows. Joyous definitely inherited her cute little brows from him. Charlotte's cinnamon crumb cake complexion and superstar good looks, coupled with Adon's heart throbbing features, harmonized graciously in the making of Joyous. She resembled Raven Symone when she played Olivia, the "bundle of joy" on *The Cosby Show.*

Charlotte looked over at the blessing that both her and Adon shared while Joyous ate her breakfast quietly at the kitchen table like the good little girl she was. Charlotte smiled pleasantly as her five-year-old daughter pretended to read the side of the cereal box.

Charlotte lowered her eyes to the LG, then whispered, "Nia Long," and rolled her relaxed green eyes. Nia Long was a nickname that Adon had given to her in regards to the sexy actress, because he was convinced they looked alike. Charlotte didn't agree. She was more inclined to believe that she, not Nia Long was, in fact, the hotter of the two. She hated the nickname. Moreover, she hated when Adon would compare her to any female, celebrity or not. It only revealed his interest in the latter.

"But what I wouldn't give to hear 'Nia Long' roll off his lips now," she admitted with a sigh.

Charlotte relinquished the LG and reached for her pink Razr (her actual working cell phone) that was sitting on the island. She noticed that she had two missed calls.

"Um, okay," she mumbled sarcastically after reviewing the numbers from the missed calls, and sat back down behind the kitchen table.

Although she was longing to hear from Adon, she was curious as to why his older sister, Natasha, would call at 5:07 A.M., and then again at 6:01 A.M.? According to her message log, Natasha's last call attempt was made thirty minutes ago. She had never called at such an ungodly hour before. Charlotte thought the worst. She dialed Natasha's number when a beeping sound from her cell notified her that the battery was low. Not five seconds later the Razr went completely dead. Charlotte began to panic. She rose from the table in haste.

"What's wrong, Mommy?" Joyous asked, sensing trouble.

"Nothing's wrong, honey. Finish eating your cereal while Mommy uses the other phone," Charlotte said calmly and walked over to the far end of the kitchen where a house phone was situated. In view was a window that overlooked her side yard. She went on to dial Natasha's number.

"Hi, there."

"Natasha, this is Charlotte. Is everything okay?"

"You've reached the voicemail of Natasha Cutti—"

"Ahh," Charlotte murmured and hung up the phone. She picked it back up and dialed Adon's number and all she got was another voicemail. Charlotte sucked her teeth and threw her head in frustration.

"What the hell was that?" she thought aloud after seeing what she thought to be swift movements beyond her window.

Suddenly, a deafening bang came from the front room of her house. Charlotte nearly jumped out of her own skin.

"Come here, baby!" Charlotte ran in Joyous' direction before tripping over her long nightgown and falling to the floor. She crawled the distance.

Bang!

The second deafening sound forced Charlotte's front door to fly open, causing the warning notification of the house alarm to sound as three men clad in black, made their way to the kitchen. The men knew that they had a twenty-second window to deactivate the alarm before the siren goes off and the neighbors are notified, not to mention the local authorities. Their heads and faces were covered with hoodies and ski masks. Charlotte pulled Joyous down from her chair and engulfed her with motherly arms, shielding her from danger. Joyous' piercing scream was enough to break a father's heart.

"Shut her mouth!" One of the men said as he and his partners walked into the kitchen area pointing a gun in Charlotte's face.

"Please, take anything you want! The only money I have is in my purse...oh God! Please, just don't hurt us!" Charlotte pleaded hysterically from her knees while holding tightly onto a teary-eyed and screaming Joyous.

"Turn off that fuckin' alarm!" the smaller of the three yelled. Charlotte rose from the floor with Charlotte in her arms, and he followed her to the side door where the digital keypad was. After two attempts of nervous dialing, she finally punched in the correct code and deactivated the alarm before it could tip off local authorities.

"Let's go," he ordered and then followed her back into the kitchen while Joyous continued to scream.

"I'm not goin' to tell you again. SHUT HER UP OR I WILL!" The irate man demanded, his voice frightening Joyous even more so.

Charlotte turned to her daughter and gently stroke the side of her face with a visibly shaking hand.

"Honey, it's okay. Look at Mommy." Charlotte forced a smile when Joyous looked up at her. "Everything is fine. These are Mommy's friends. Remember how you said that you couldn't wait to play dress-up for Halloween later this year? Well, my friends have come over to play dress up with us early this year. See, honey?"

Charlotte turned her toward the three masked men as the leader raised his palm and displayed a jolly-false wave. Joyous looked into her mother's eyes with unyielding trust and begin to simmer down to a calm.

"See, baby, everything is fine."

"Mommy, can I play dress-up, too?" Joyous asked, but before her mother could respond, the leader spoke.

"Sure you can," he said and reached his arms out for her.

Charlotte was adamantly reluctant until the man with the gun raised it to the back of Joyous' head without the little girl seeing it.

"You have two choices," he said.

Joyous' body weight rested on Charlotte's protruding hip. Tears filled the wells of her eyes. Charlotte quickly used her free hand to wipe them away before Joyous spotted them. She leaned Joyous toward the man's extended arms. Joyous looked at the man's cold eyes, and then turned to look into the comfort of her mother's. Charlotte revealed an uneasy smile. Joyous didn't want to go.

"It's okay, honey. He won't hurt you," Charlotte said nervously and released her only child into the chilling arms of the unknown. She cupped her hands over her mouth and watched as Joyous was taken into the front room and out of her sight. She then turned to the man, the burly one, who hadn't said a word the whole time.

Very calmly Charlotte asked, "What is this all about?"

Without warning, he raised his over-sized hand and backhanded her with enough force to lay her out cold. The burly man caught her tumbling body before it crashed onto the tiled floor. He swooped her up in his tree stump-size arms and started for the front room. His partner followed closely.

Outside with Joyous, the leader waited patiently inside the backseat of a 1967 Lincoln with a cell phone to his ear.

"Mick and Mario is on their way out now. Okay, that won't be an issue," he intoned into the phone. "Just make sure Charlotte's front door gets fixed before anybody sees it...particularly, Adon."

The man shoved the cell into his pocket and removed his mask. He watched as his men walked out of the house.

Charlotte tried to adjust her eyes to the darkness. For a moment she laid in total dismay. The trunk was pretty cramp as she lay awkwardly on her side. With the constant engine braking and immediate acceleration, it didn't take her long to realize that she was locked inside the trunk of a car.

"Joy? Joy? Where are you, sweetie? Talk to mommy," she cried out, but there was no answer. She then yelled out, "JOY!" and flinched from the high-pitched music that was activated without warning.

Her shoulder scraped against the fresh blue-bruise that covered her cheek and she screeched in pain. The sound of subwoofers bumping in her ear explained the cramped space inside of the trunk. Charlotte attempted to scream over the music but it was useless. She was scared and without her little girl. "

"How could I have let this happen? I failed at protecting my little girl. Why!? Why!? Why!?" she cried.

In an attempt to feel around, Charlotte couldn't feel the left side of her body. Yet, with all of her might, she freed her sleeping arm before inadvertently striking her forehand against the trunk's hood that hovered closely above. Her hand awakened with pure hostility as the excruciating pain shot up her arm like a bolt of electric current.

"AAAHHHHhhhh!" she screamed at the top her lungs and then began to laugh as if the joke was on her. She didn't know rather to cry from the pain, or feel relieved that she was experiencing pain at all. She wasn't suffering from paralysis and that was definitely something to be relieved about, but her distressful laughter soon turned into loud, baby-like sobs, as her hand throbbed in agony. Charlotte's cries were muffled within the darkened depths of what she was convinced was hell.

CHAPTER 2

There was a knock at the door.

"I highly suggest that you don't disturb me during my reading hour," Nitty advised from the interior of his den.

"But, Mr. Calhoun, sir," the live-in maid said behind the closed door. "You have a visitor. Sir, it's, Adon."

"Well, where is he?" Nitty asked, never looking up from his *Chicago Sun Times* newspaper.

"He's right beside me, sir."

"Why do you have him out there? Let him in, would ya."

The door to the den opened slowly and the maid stepped aside, allowing Adon to enter. Once he was inside, she shut the door behind him.

"Wudup, Nitty?" Adon said as he removed a fresh, unlit Black and Mild cigar from his lips.

"That depends on you," Nitty replied, lifting his eyes up from the article he was reading. He folded the newspaper and tossed it on his modern-style desk. He removed his reading glasses and tossed them atop the newspaper. He then gave Adon a quick once-over from where he sat. "You sure love your urban wear don't you?" Nitty said in relation to his attire.

"I'ma urban nigga what'cha expect," Adon responded as he proudly popped the collar to his Pelle Pelle shirt and looked down at his crispy Air Force Ones. "So wudup, I hear you wanted to see me?"

Nitty rose up on the arms of his high-back leather chair and removed his Stacy Adams loafers that graced his feet from the top of his desk, placing them beneath him. He took hold of his desk phone and dialed one digit. "Casey, he's here," Nitty said sternly into the phone and hung up.

A minute later, an older man walked through the door and shut it behind him. At first glance he smiled. "How's it hangin', Young

Blood," Casey greeted Adon and shook his hand firmly.

"Enough of that shit," Nitty said irritably and addressed Casey directly. "Play the disc," he ordered and reclined behind his desk.

Casey obliged and grabbed a remote before aiming it at a 72-inch plasma screen that hung over a stone mantle. Casey sat down. All he could do was shake his head in anticipation of what Adon was about to see.

"You may want to have a seat as well," Nitty said.

"Naw, I'm cool like this," Adon said uneasy.

"Sit...your...ass...down," Nitty demanded and pointed to an area that was pre-arranged. Adon slowly accommodated the firm request.

Adon had no idea of what this was about and his patience was wearing thin. He slouched in the uncomfortable wooden chair in silence as the video begin to start. It was a recorded view of a neighborhood that looked familiar to him.

Oh, yeah, he mused. He recognized a spot where one of the Cabrini Green buildings were before a wrecking ball demolished it. *And?* he thought as if what relation did it have to him.

He turned around in his chair to address Nitty. "Is this what you called me here for?"

"Just turn around and keep watching," Nitty pointed to the screen.

Adon did as he was told, but he wasn't feelin' the vibes at all. The camera zoomed in after a white Dodge Charger came into view. It parked close to a curb and sat. Inside were three Caucasian males. Fifteen seconds later, a S600 Mercedes Benz pulled along side of it.

Adon's eyes widened. He recognized the whip. It was his homie, his main man, Shamrock. He remained there for all of three minutes, and from the conspicuous movements of their lips, Shamrock was exchanging words with at least two of the white men.

The S600 pulled off and so did the Charger. Adon's brows pointed inward as he watched the camera follow both whips in the distance before the two vehicles went in separate directions.

For a second or two the screen went black, and then it popped on again. The recorded date and time at the lower part of the screen told Adon that this second piece of footage was shot during a dissimilar period. On this occasion the camera man spotted Shamrock's S600 parked outside of Spiagga; a tri-level restaurant overlooking Oak Street Beach.

Inside, sitting incognito at a table for two was Shamrock. Across from him sat a different white male. He was older in age and had this authoritative look about him.

Adon sat up.

"Hold up. Hold up! Stop that right there!" he yelled out to Casey and Casey quickly paused the tape. "I know that white dude," he declared while throwing his finger at the screen. "That's the muthafucka who sat in during Folks-n-nem federal trial in '97. Plus, I remember seeing him on TV, giving interviews about that 9/11 terrorist act shit in New York!"

"His name is William Cunningham," Nitty offered calmly and continued. "And although he's a big part of the Federal Bureau of Investigations, he's also CIA affiliated."

"Well, what the fuck is he doing talkin' to my main man!?" Adon asked as he studied the still picture of both Shamrock and Cunningham on the screen. Adon turned to look at Nitty, who gave a stone-face stared back at him. Then he looked over to Casey, who, again, shook his head and hung it low. "Aww heellll naw!" Adon shouted loudly. "Not my nigga! Shamrock ain't no snitch. FUCK!"

"Continue the tape, Casey," Nitty said and that's when the audio started. Adon sat there and listened to his main man give up names and information on The Convolution and above all, on him.

Adon listened to Shamrock's voice: *"As far as The Convolution, Nitty Calhoun oversees Illinois, particularly Chicago. He got dis bitch locked and recently made Adon Cutti his underboss. Grant me immunity and I'll testify to dis shit and whateva else you want me to in court."*

Casey hit the stop button. Adon placed his head in his palms. He was crushed.

"Well, as it seems, your *nigga* has been participating in a lot more than what he's been reporting to you," Nitty said matter-of-factly. "I guess there *is* some jealousy there after all, and you know as well as I do, there's no room for that type of personality in *any* successful organization. As I stated to you before, you're 'one' with The Convolution now. A highly prestigious class of businessmen old enough to be your father; a paramount that controls Chicago's underworld and beyond. Do I have to remind you of these things?"

Adon sat in silence with his knuckles wrapped tightly under his chin. The veins in his arms swelled the width of extension cords from squeezing so hard as he rocked back and forth in the wooden chair.

Casey looked at attention as Nitty stood up and walked over to where Adon sat. "On the day that you took your 'Pledge Of Death,' you had to recite the Cardinal rules to me. I want you to repeat both Cardinal Rule numbers one and two to me right now," Nitty said calmly.

"What?" Adon hesitated.

"Repeat them to me, NOW!" Nitty shouted.

"Cardinal Rule number one, 'Death Before Dishonor,'" Adon recited. He raised his head and stood up. With angry mist in his eyes he continued. "Cardinal Rule number two, 'He Who Brings A Judas Inside The Mouth Of The Convolution, Will Be The One To Shit Him Out. No exceptions'."

Nitty placed his hands on Adon's broad shoulders and said, "Do we have an understanding, or need I say more?"

"Naw, I got'cha," Adon said hanging his head low.

CHAPTER 3

Charlotte prayed heavily as immanent visions of her kidnappers ripping Joyous from her hands played over in her mind. "I have to hold on for her…I just have to!" she screamed.

Adon prepared me for situations like this had they ever occurred. But what exactly did he instruct me to do!?

The three atrocious kidnappers continued to jump in and out of her rattled, racing mind; scaring her shitless each time. This made it impossible to focus on anything that Adon had taught her in the past. She trembled with panic and silently prayed for some sort of answer that would help in undermining her current oppressors.

Joy needs you Adon, we need you. So where are you? she mused.

The car made a sharp left turn throwing her body against its tail. Suddenly everything became calm, the car slowed down and the music stopped.

What's happening? What are they up to?

Charlotte was intimidated even more so by the unexpected silence. She frantically groped around the murky bondage, hoping to find something that she may have missed, maybe something small that would lead to liberation.

Meanwhile the kidnappers had a dilemma:

"Why in da hell did you slow down and shut off da music?" Mario asked in an objectionable manner.

"Ay, don't look now, but tha blue-n-whites just swooped down on us joe," Mick said in his very deep voice. He was careful to keep a reasonable distance between the Lincoln and the squad car, while maintaining the posted 35mph speed limit. The three men were alarmed, as Mario nonchalantly placed the seatbelt across his chest and clicked-it in.

"This crying bitch bet not make another sound, otherwise these pigs gonna find out why they call me Killa," Killa Mike spoke through clentched teeth and tugged on a concealed chopper that sat nose down between his legs. The three men looked ahead all, innocent-like, while their thoughts rested upon the human-cargo inside their trunk.

Charlotte began to have more visions of Adon salvaging the day. In the past he had always been their knight in shining armor. She thought of waking up from this horrible nightmare with Joy secured tightly in her arms, safely inside their home. "Please let me wake up. Please let me wake up from this." she babbled in a whispering tone.

She blindly gazed around, batting her eyelids, and tried in vain to adjust her eyes to the darkness.

"God, what am I missing? What should I do?" Charlotte hadn't a clue as to how close she was of being rescued, but something within her prompt her to scream out: "SOMEBODY PLEASE HELP ME!"

She squeezed her drowning eyes shut and bone-chilling screams soon followed as she burst into a child-like tantrum. The Lincoln was held up at a traffic light and the clamor didn't go unnoticed.

The cops caught an earful of Charlotte's desperate plea as both of them looked at each other. Unsure of where the screams were coming from, the cops slowly pulled forward until the front end of their squad car was nearly sitting on the Lincoln's back bumper. The cop leaned his chin over the steering wheel and observed a frightened little girl in the backseat crying her eyes out. Now he was sure of where the source of the screams was coming from.

"Someone is in that trunk!" He turned on his overhead lights and blared his siren.

The souped-up Lincoln fishtailed with speed! The subwoofers roared with deep, rich bass, as if dynamite was detonated. Charlotte's entire body shook! The terrifying levels of intensity seemed never-ending, until piercing sirens began to blare mildly over the ear-splitting music.

"Yes, God!" she praised after hearing the police-siren for a second time.

As the siren blared, Charlotte pounded on the trunk's hood. Pound after pound, she screeched from the pain that her injured hand endured while simultaneously impairing her other with each mighty blow she impinged. Out of nowhere she cringed as a variety of gunshots rang out. From years of visiting Adon when he lived in the Englewood District on Chicago's Southside, Charlotte knew that different pitch-tones of gunfire meant that either the aggressors were shooting more than one firearm, or the opposing side was shooting back, or both. There were too many loud bangs to count.

Unexpectedly, a thunderous, heart-wrenching crash of twisted metal had completely swallowed the echoes of the rapid gunfire. What was once a blaring police-siren now sounded more like a squawking malfunctioning outcry for backup assistance. Charlotte's hopes of being rescued had quickly diminished. She laid in the darkness as stiff as a board.

Twenty minutes later, the Lincoln came to an abrupt stop. She felt the vehicle's weight shift, as the kidnappers exited the car. The slamming of three doors sounded, along with scurrying footsteps. Charlotte could only think of Joy, as she anticipated what was to come. The jingling sound of keys pierced the heart-beat-silence that secluded her ears. Her body made spasmodic jerks. She was petrified with fear and wanted to submerge into the trunk's floor, or just disappear into thin air altogether. Instead, she involuntarily discharged from consciousness as the trunk opened from the outside.

Upon revealing the trunk's interior, the kidnappers grinned at the sight of Charlotte's unconscious condition.

"Look at da sleepin' beauty," the burly of the three men, Mick, gibed and hunched over Charlotte and elevated her body from the trunk.

Charlotte's fear mixed with the adrenaline rush of shooting out with the cops aroused Mario as Charlotte's silk nightgown tousled around her waist; exposing her Victoria's Secret.

WOW…I can't wait to get some of that coochie! he confided to himself, rubbing his crotch area.

The more interesting one, Killa Mike, walked casually with little Joy in his arms. He cradled her as if she was his own, and maintained a calculated distance behind the two men who led the way down a creepy street. Mick, with Charlotte in tow, and Mario at his side, made an inconspicuous right turn and suddenly disappeared. Killa Mike remained steady at his current pace, turned on the balls of his feet, and made the same right turn. They made their way through a dark, rat-infested passageway behind an EL station that led to a ducked-off apartment building.

Killa Mike whispered into Joy's tiny ear, "Don't worry little girl," he draped most of her small body with a small blanket to shield her from the small drops of rain that started to fall. "You and yo' mama gon' be alright," he added.

Joy stared up at him as she tore through the wrapper of a cherry Blowpop that he offered, unaware of what laid ahead for mommy and her.

CHAPTER 4

"Yes, hello," Divine, one of Shamrock's newest lovers, answered. "Put Shamrock on the phone," Adon insisted.

"Well, unfortunately, he's busy at the moment. May I ask who is this calling?" Divine inquired.

"Naw, you can't ask me a damn thang! And I don't give a fuck how busy you say he is. Place that nigga's ear to the phone!" Adon demanded.

Divine frowned at the phone and guided her pedicure toes to the customized bathroom where she knew to find Shamrock. An opened red silk robe draped over her shoulders and around her curvaceous temple. The bottom of it fluttered behind her as she walked.

Shamrock owned a luxurious home in the Country Club Hills. When Divine arrived to the bathroom, Shamrock was practically lying in his whirlpool with water up to his neck. He nestled with a long-term lover of his, a female named Fancy.

Divine made a conspicuous noise clearing her throat just before he penetrated Fancy's moist tunnel of warm embracement.

Shamrock gradually loosened his firm grip from the circumference of Fancy's globular ass and peered in Divine's direction. With a slight tilt of her head, she motioned toward the cordless phone that filled her hand while her other found a resting place atop her hip.

"Who it is?" Shamrock asked.

"I don't know," she said as Shamrock cupped his drenched hands and extended them in front of him. She tossed the phone and watched as he caught it.

"Who dis!?" Shamrock voiced into the phone.

"What it do, good buddy," Adon put forth.

"Oh shit! What's hatnin' playboy?" Shamrock returned in a jovial manner. He instantly placed a face with the familiar voice. He sat on the edge of the whirlpool, and Fancy guided her mouth to his erect manhood.

"You tell me pimpin', and I'll listen," Adon said and continued. "If I didn't know no better I'd think you was expectin' somebody else. Is there something I need to know? You cool?" Adon asked.

As cool as the central air blowin' outta my gold-plated vents," Shamrock boasted. "Playboy, I had to get my number changed 'cause some soft-hearted mafucka kept callin' da crib breathing heavy on da phone and screamin' idle threats. Apparently, I fucked his ho! I didn't think you had da new number yet," he explained.

"Yeah, I was wondering about that. But I got it from one of yo' lil' breezies so it wasn't no big deal." After a skeptical pause, "Haven't seen you in a few days. What cha got goin'?"

Shit, right now. Just doin' me. I know one thang though…"

What's that, pimpin'?" Adon asked attentively hoping he would offer an explanation as to why he's been moonlighting with the feds. Three days had passed since witnessing the video firsthand in Nitty's den.

"I can't wait fo' that statewide picnic you hostin' in August. That mafucka is gonna be off da chain my nigga! I'm countin' down da days. Ya'know what I'm sayin', gangsta?" Shamrock asked.

Yeah, yeah, no doubt," Adon continued. "Say…who was that breezy? The one that answered the phone when I called?"

"Oh, that there playboy is sumthin' brand new. Trust me, you'll meet her soon enough," Shamrock assured with a hint of lust in his voice.

"Hold up…let me guess…is she one of those Doberman pinscher-face, gigantic booty strippers that you usually go after?" Adon replied.

"Yeah, yeah, funny," Shamrock waved his hand. "Naw, fool. I ain't talkin' 'bout Miss Boo's dog-face ass," he paused and looked around to see if Miss Boo was nearby ear hustling. "Dis new lil' breezy is *right*! I'm talkin' right enough to settle down wit' right! And you know me, gangsta. I would be da last playa to ever mention anythang 'bout hangin' up tha prime playa's dobb that I received personally from da Bishop Don Magic Juan himself."

"Yup. But that's only because Don Juan wasn't aware of your little secret," Adon shot back.

"And what secret is that, playboy?" Shamrock asked without a care as he placed the palm of his hand atop Fancy's head.

"You've been known to pay hos for sex."

"Naw, see that's where you wrong, playboy," Shamrock said and wrapped his black lips around the rim of a Skyy Vodka bottle, downing what was left. "I don't pay hos to fuck. I pay them bitches to go home after I'm through fuckin' 'em, ya dig!"

The two of them erupted with laughter, and then Shamrock continued on a more serious note. "About the picnic, you not worried about dem pussy ass Vice Lords is you?"

Divine stood at the opposite side of the bathroom door, listening in on Shamrock's conversation before she decided to venture off into the master suite to eavesdrop on both sides of the dialogue. She was determined to find out exactly whom Shamrock was talking to.

"First of all, they ain't pussies. Them niggas got killers with choppers waitin' to chop shit like we do, cuz," Adon corrected. "Worried? No. But I'll be lying if I said I wasn't concerned," he kept it gutter.

"Concerned fo' what, my nigga!?" Shamrock was down for whatever.

"You wanna know *why*? And it's not like you don't all ready know, but okay I'll tell you why. Outta all the different mobs in Chi, the Vice Lord's newly appointed chief is the only one opting not to participate in the picnic. A statewide gathering that I'm responsible for; a gathering that I founded a year ago for the sole reason of keepin' peace on the streets while we rake in this bread...not to mention to keep yo' hog-wild ass from being found out."

"Okay, and..."

"And, that tells me they're not buying into that weak explanation of how Flukie Lord was killed," Adon said.

"Fuck 'em! That happened two years ago, they need to get over it."

"Fuck 'em!?" Adon responded as if he couldn't believe Shamrock's nerve.

"You heard me right. Fuck 'em! If the old head wasn't in my BI I wouldn't have murked his ass, period and point blank."

"He was their chief, nigga! You hear that? Their chief!" Adon achieved what he wanted and that was to get Shamrock to incriminate himself in case his line was tapped, but although it was planned he still couldn't help getting riled up. "Not to mention it happened during a peace treaty that was goin' strong for three long years, and you started a war all over a female," Adon lowered his tone and got a grip. "Listen, what's done is done. All I'm sayin' is now I have reason to believe they might target the picnic where they know all of the Gangster Disciples in the state will be. Hell, if I was them I would."

"You not thinkin' 'bout canceling the picnic…is you?"

"Never that," Adon continued. "We just goin' to have to strap-up heavy. I wish you could be their with me, cuz. I really do," Adon said solemnly and the hint of what was to come flew over Shamrock's head. It was similar to the Kiss of Death and Shamrock hadn't a clue.

"Oh, I'll be there my nigga," Shamrock assured unsuspectingly. "And my aid and assistance is what you'll get 100 percent of!"

"Shamrock," Adon calmly called out.

"What's good, my nig?"

"You know you can talk to me about anythang, right?"

"Fo' sho."

"Well is there anythang you have to tell me? I mean *anythang*?"

"Naw, playboy, e'vrythang is e'vrythang on my end," Shamrock said and instantly felt guilty for lying to his best friend.

"Silence and Secrecy is somthin' we die by, right?"

"Fo' sho, you know dat!" Shamrock responded with conviction.

Adon took the Blue Tooth earpiece away from his ear and inhaled a deep breath before putting the cell on speakerphone. He exhaled and said, "By the way, who all you got there with you?"

"Just three of my bitches," Shamrock confirmed what Miss Boo had reported to Adon only minutes before the call. Adon didn't have to search far to get help setting Shamrock up. He knew Shamrock had a thing for strippers, and Miss Boo was at the top of the pickin's.

"Aiight, in a minute. One."

"Before you go I wanna put sumthin' in yo' ear, playboy," Shamrock said.

"What's that?" Adon asked.

"No matter the season, you my N.F.L. (Nigga Fo' Life). We tackle haters, fumble hos, and touchdown money like da mafuckin' pros! Don't ever forget that, my nigga"

"Aiight. One."

"One."

A fingernail tapped rapidly against the wooden door. Divine jolted from the abrupt interruption. She carefully disconnected her intruding end of the line and slowly placed the telephone's receiver onto its cradle.

"Divine, are you in there?" A soft, feminine voice on the opposing side of the door uttered. Divine remained silent. The wooden door opened, but only barely. Miss Boo pressed the side of her ugly face against the doorpost and stuck her bugged eyes into the inner parts of the master suite.

I coulda sworn I heard somethin' in here.

She hesitated, then looked behind her and down the hall that led her there. She could no longer here Shamrock's loud voice and that worried her some, but not enough to divert her intent. She turned her attention back to the spacious room, and bit down softly on her bottom lip.

Ok, no one's in here.

A firm push from her forearm swung the hinged door against a filled "void" that stood perpendicular between the ocean printed wall, and the door itself.

That void was Divine.

Divine stood nervously behind it. She hoped that once Miss Boo seen that she wasn't there she would leave.

Miss Boo glanced around, making sure that the coast was clear. She dashed straight to the marble dresser and frantically searched drawer after drawer. Feeling that she was being watched, she looked over her shoulder nervously toward the bedroom door.

Divine just knew that her spot was blown. She relaxed when Miss Boo returned to the dresser.

"Hurry up," Miss Boo told herself.

Shit, that was close, Divine thought. *What is this ugly bitch up to?* Her mental inquiry was answered sooner than she realized she really didn't want to know.

Miss Boo hoisted a Glock .9mm handgun from the drawer and darted her eyes in the same direction as before, except this time she fixated directly on the door that Divine was hiding behind.

Divine's stomach twitched with nervous cartwheels, as they seemed to have locked eyes through the back slit of the door.

Oh shit!

With the Glock .9mm snuggled inside of Miss Boo's palm, she spurred towards Divine halting just inches before her. Divine inched backwards until her heels touched the bottom of the wall. Miss Boo quickly shoved the Glock inside the pocket of a leather Al Wissan jacket that hung carelessly from the door handle opposite of where Divine was standing. Miss Boo pulled on the door handle and fled the master suite, shutting the door behind her.

"Wheww!" Divine sighed in relief. She wasn't discovered. It was the jacket, and not her, that had the center of Miss Boo's last-minute attention. She placed the tip of her finger at the opening of her mouth and swayed her head in bafflement.

"Something ain't right," she said and left the master suite.

Divine stormed into the bathroom prepared to reveal her rattled thoughts to Shamrock. Once inside, she pumped her brakes as she witnessed Shamrock, head tilted back, watching the drizzle of the rain from his skylight while Fancy deep throated him. He looked to be on cloud nine. She sucked her teeth extra hard just to be heard.

"Baby," he looked over at Divine, "Do Big Daddy a favor and get my cush off the chess board. And bring sumthin' back to roll it up wit'."

"Can I talk to you a second?" Divine asked clearly viewing his recent request to be secondary, and with damn good reason. "I really need to talk to you. For real, for real," she was adamant.

"Don't mind this, baby," Shamrock pointed to Fancy's bobbing head as she began the vacuum effect of her oral performance. "What's on yo' mind? Talk to Daddy."

After what she had witnessed in the master suite with Miss Boo, there was no way in hell Divine was going to disclose the shady shit that she had encountered while Fancy was in the room.

I can't trust nann one of these jealous bitches, because whatever is going on her happy-ass could very well be in on it, too, Divine mused. She declared, "I need to talk to you in private, Shamrock…now!" then rested her French tips on her hips.

"Raise up a second, baby," Shamrock gently pulled Fancy by her wet hair. A loud sucking sound pierced the silence after she released his dick head from her juicy lips.

Fancy rose and rolled her eyes at Divine.

Divine turned up her nose and thought, *Look at this silly ho.*

Shamrock took notice to the cattiness between the two women and with his usual "big daddy" charm he handled it accordingly. "Baby, now if you wanted some one on one time with Big Daddy then you shoulda said sumthin'. Can't read no minds. But you can rest assure that it's enough of me to go 'round. You smell me?"

"It's not that—"

"I'll tell you what, 'lil mama," Shamrock interrupted. "Go get my cush and I'm all yours."

"But—"

"But my dick! Now go handle yo BI," he barked.

With reluctance, Divine slowly turned to walk away while Fancy shot visual daggers at her back.

The entire time while Shamrock conversed over the cordless phone, Adon was right outside of Shamrock's resting nest experiencing a mental struggle. Though he would not admit it to anyone else, he found that his conscience was second-guessing his better judgment; a trait that he tried to stay clear of. The more he reflected on Shamrock, the hardest nigga in his crew and godfather of his beloved daughter, the more he wanted to renege on the fatal plan altogether. But no matter how he felt, Adon knew that Shamrock's violation couldn't be rectified and he believed in the Pledge Of Death wholeheartedly.

Trust is not defined on who you are in the presence of a friend, but who you are when a friend turns his back. The streets were watching. And Adon knew what had to be done before the streets caught on.

Sitting between the luxuries of his brand-spanking-new Cadillac Escalade ESV, Adon shifted his transmission into drive. He let up off the brake pedal and pulled alongside of the car that was waiting on him. He lowered his tinted window halfway, showing himself barely and held up three fingers: indicating that there were three women inside Shamrock's crib. A customary, distinctive wink from his left eyelid followed and he raised the window back to its original mark. Amongst Adon's crew, it was understood never to break eye contact in tension-filled situations until a deciding signal was given. A right wink meant that all was good; and a wink from the left always alluded fatal action.

Adon curved the corner and hung his head in both anger and remorse upon realizing in great depth of what he'd just done. Killing Shamrock was a hard pill to swallow but apparently not impossible.

He stared blankly at his BlackBerry and cruised at a snail's pace. *Fuck! Should I stop the hit before it's too late?* he asked himself. After having come to a decision, he reached for his Blackberry.

The two henchmen that occupied a beat-up parked Buick caught notice to Adon's silent directive.

"Did Adon mean there's three people in total or three people plus Shamrock?" Tommy asked from the passenger seat.

A cell phone chimed.

"We'll find out once we get inside," Shakey Shawn said and answered his cell. "I'm here," he intoned.

"Is he sitting next to you?" Nitty's voice came through.

Shakey Shawn casually looked over at his partner with a fleeting glance and said, "Yeah."

"Need I say more?" Nitty made it short and sweet.

Once a hit was ordered there was no need to repeat it. Shakey Shawn had received fifty Gs in advance for the price of one head, and now Nitty just made it two. A kill was a kill to Shakey Shawn. As long as pre-payment was an option, he didn't give a fuck who the mark was. Besides, all he can think about was landing in sunny Miami after the hit went down. Both Nitty and Adon were aware of his immediate, scheduled departure following the murder. In fact, it was Nitty's idea. Shakey Shawn was so hot, Nitty wanted him out of Chicago.

"Say no mo'," he assured. "Consider it done."

"Enjoy your trip," Nitty said before the dial tone.

Shakey Shawn flipped his cell shut and looked over at Tommy. He envisioned a bullet wound gaping from his forehead. In his mind he was thinking one thing and said another. "Let's do dis."

He and Tommy reacted in haste. They vacated their jalopy and approached Shamrock's residence. They placed their rolled up ski mask around the tops of their heads to resemble the style of beanies. And thanks to Miss Boo, they made it on the other side of Shamrock's overrated security gate with ease.

The henchmen took the stairs by the twos until they met the top. They slowed their pace as they neared the front door and concealed their faces with weapons drawn.

Miss Boo heard the secret taps at the front door. She unsecured the maximum-security locks and opened it.

Back in the bathroom, Shamrock watched in silence as Fancy stepped outside of the spacious whirlpool. He stared at her exquisite body parts while she tended to the soaking water that dripped from her saturated body. Fancy locked her knees in place and skillfully curved over to dry her calves. By doing this, she exposed the lips of her vagina as the household lights shone ever clear through the gap between her glistening upper thighs. Shamrock heat swelled after witnessing the breathtaking moment from behind.

I'm convinced, there is a God, he mused and she smiled in the opposite direction as if she knew what he was thinking.

"Babygirl do Big Daddy a favor and pour me a glass of Remy and Sprite, and bring Divine slow ass back wit'choo wit' my cush."

"Okay baby," Fancy replied with a hidden frown.

"And bring sumthin' to roll it up wit' too, 'cause I see now that pretty bitch is real forgetful. I got sumthin' fo' her ass though."

"I don't know why you let that ho up in here anyway," Fancy took this opportunity to throw salt.

"Stop hatin' and go do what I ask *you* to do," Shamrock put her in her place quick.

Fancy envied Divine's natural beauty and felt threaten because of it. She hated the idea of the *new* girl getting all up on her man. She covered her hole-in-the-wall, strip club body with a heavy cotton robe, and exited the bathroom to carry out Big Daddy's request; and to set Divine straight once and for all.

Five minutes had crept by before Shamrock noticed that Fancy nor Divine hadn't returned with his drink or much-needed herb.

"Fancy! Miss Boo!" Shamrock shouted. "I know ya'll asses hear me. Then again, it's probably hard to hear when you freaky mafuckas SUCKIN' EACH OTHER DRY. You dike bitches!"

Shamrock overlaid his slim frame with a Hugh Hefner style smoker's jacket, except this one draped over his knees. He vacated the steamy bathroom and progressed down the corridor.

"Bitches 'bout to suck Daddy off," he sang.

Making his way to the master suite, he never took notice that his oil painting of the legendary Tupac Shukar was hanging crookedly.

Crossing the threshold, he said, "Here comes Daddy," before stopping cold in his tracks.

Miss Boo and Fancy lay in a pool of blood with their throats slit from ear to ear. Shamrock stood stunned for a few seconds before his reflexes kicked in. He quickly went to his marble dresser to retrieve his Glock.

"Uh-uh, sorry pimp it's not there," Shakey Shawn said, dangling his Glock off his index finger.

Shamrock turned to the voice. Two masked men stood behind him with weapons drawn. Thinking fast, Shamrock tried to punch the closest one to him but was cut off by Tommy with a crack to the back of his head with a Desert Eagle, causing him to fall on top of the bodies that laid across his bed.

"My bad," Tommy said referring to the girls' blood that now stained Shamrock's body. "Damn, and you jus' got outta da whirlpool too," the two shared a laugh. "So what it is, Mr. Infamous?" Tommy said after

Shamrock threw himself to the floor and away from the bodies of the deceased girls. "I thought you got down wit' that diabolic freaky-type shit; videotaping the ladies while they do the *damn thang* for you-n-shit. As a matter-a-fact, I believe I caught you in action wit' about ten hoes in one flick! Shittin' and pissin' on each other and gettin' off on the shit. You one nasty cat."

"At least they made the big screen," Shakey Shawn joked, referring to Miss Boo being on the sex tape.

"Who tha fuck are ya'll!? This shit—"

"Shut the fuck up!" Shakey Shawn bellowed and smacked Shamrock with the butt of the burna. Shamrock's head crashed into a floor to ceiling mirror. "I didn't tell you to talk!"

"Well damn, Shamrock, look at 'em. That there is a Kodac moment if I ever saw one myself," Tommy taunted and pointed to the bodies. "Well, ain't it?"

"Oh, yeah, you think so? Well how 'bout you go retrieve my camera and suck my dick while I film that shit too, you bitch ass nigga!" Shamrock spat out blood.

"Shut tha fuck up! I'm not gon' tell you again!" Shakey Shawn barked and out of the blue, broken mirror fragments fell from the high wall.

Shamrock quickly rolled over before landing on his stomach; missing the sharp sections of glass by inches. Tommy kicked him in the stomach, causing his robe to undo.

"Now turn yo' ass over! You betta cover that bullshit up before I remove those genitals from yo' body and feed 'em to you, nigga!" Tommy warned.

Shamrock's red-shot eyes became flooded with running blood that emerged from the deep gash atop his head. He could not believe what was occurring. Just moments ago he was soaking in his whirlpool, relaxing, chopping it up with Adon over the phone, and busting nuts.

It was becoming more difficult to breathe. He was certain that the last kick had broken some ribs. "What tha fuck do ya'll want from me!?" Shamrock yelled. His chest resembled a violent ocean of heavy panting. He swallowed both, his pain and fury, and spoke calmly. "I got bread, man, jus' take it," he plead with the henchmen, spitting out more blood.

Divine was watching the whole scene from the walk-in closet.

"Stand up," Shakey Shawn commanded.

Shamrock struggled to leave the floor, grabbing his ribs.

"Hurry up before I put a flame under yo' ass!" Shakey Shawn threatened with the burna angled at Shamrock's torso. "Now where's da safe?" He held the floor and nodded to his partner.

Tommy anticipated Shakey Shawn's last-minute decision of greed. Surely, that was the very reason Shamrock wasn't dead yet. He wasn't feelin' the sudden change in plans though, nor was he convinced by Shamrock's unusual willingness to cooperate. He looked over at Shakey Shawn and shook his head in a *let's do whut we came to do and get da fuck outta here* gesture.

"I said where's da safe, nigga!?" Shakey Shawn ignored his partner's gesture. In his mind, via Nitty's last minute phone call, Tommy was a dead man walking anyhow so muthafuck what he thought.

"All you have to do is escort me—"

"Escort you!?" Tommy shouted, cutting Shamrock short. "You ain't goin' no fuckin' where!" He looked over at Shakey Shawn, who was waving his free hand in a mild manner, gesturing Tommy to *calm tha fuck down.*

"Da safe is right over the marble headboard, behind the portrait," Shamrock said.

Shakey Shawn forced his leather covered claws around Shamrock's neck and pulled him forward. "Lead the way," he pushed Shamrock toward the king-size bed where the safe hovered above within the wall's interior.

As he walked up to the blood-drenched sheets, Shamrock looked on in contempt as he observed—in depth—the cruel, fatal wounds that were inflicted upon the late Miss Boo and Fancy.

These mafuckas gon' pay!

He glanced one last time over at the suspiciously opened drawer where his Glock use to be. It was evident to him that these fools either took his burna upon entry, or had it removed prior to their arrival. At any rate, Shamrock knew they had inside help. A half-grin graced his face. If there ever came a time where Shamrock had a chink in his armor, he would never show it.

"Where!?" Tommy barked.

Shamrock removed the framed portrait, exposing the titanium-steel safe. After placing the portrait on the Persian carpet, Shamrock punched in his code.

Without delay, Shakey Shawn shoved a stiff forearm to his chest, forcing him into the controlled possession of his partner across the room. Tommy buried his burna in his back waistband and grabbed a hold of Shamrock with both hands.

The henchmen knew Shamrock's work. The both of them had witnessed him in action first hand. But Shakey Shawn was undaunted. In his eyes, Shamrock's "last man standing" repertoire was nothing more than just luck. Hence, the reason his peers gave him the name "Shamrock." He was a human 4-leaf clover. In the past he was able to win his street battles because niggas underestimated his skinny build, his frame put you in the mind of Dave Chappel.

He looked over at Shamrock and searched his eyes for a hidden agenda that would have spelled out d-e-f-i-a-n-c-e. There was none.

He reached for the safe's steel handle and partially opened its door. He peeked in, conscious of any booby-traps. To his relief, there was nothing to fear. But just as he sensed, Shamrock was definitely up to one of his surprise schemes. Atop stacks of money was a Mac .11 semi-automatic. He hauled the weapon out of the safe and showed it to his partner. From across the room the henchman looked Shamrock square in the eye with a witty *I out-smarted-you* smirk. He extended his gun-filled hand and displayed an erect index finger, swaying side-to-side in a manner that Mutombo often demonstrated after sending his opponent's lay-ups into the bleachers.

Shamrock brandished another half grin for him to see. But in spite of his cockiness, Shakey Shawn was pleased. He had discovered Shamrock's ultimate survival scheme and incapacitated it. Or so he thought.

"Ay, Tommy," Shakey Shawn called out to his partner.

"Whut, man," Tommy answered, wondering why did he address him by name. Shamrock knew something was up.

"Did you actually believe that we wasn't gon' find out about yo' lil' habit?" Shakey Shawn placed a toothpick between his lips.

"Whut 'cha talkin', man?" Tommy said slowly, releasing one of Shamrock's arms and reaching around to his burna.

"Nigga, you been skimmin' off the top and feedin' yo' nose!"

Without notification, Shamrock rammed his head rearward, crushing Tommy's nose! Blood gushed from his cocaine-residue nostrils. He bowed over in pain as Shamrock simultaneously swept behind him.

Shakey Shawn let the Mac .11 loose. Bullets riddled Tommy's body as Shamrock used him for a shield. As Tommy's body hit the floor, Shamrock was hit twice; once in the arm and chest. Laying face up, he clutched his chest as he struggled to breathe.

Shakey Shawn stood over him, "You a gangsta fo' real, I gotta give it to you. You went out like a true soldier," he taunted.

Out the corner of his eye, Shamrock spotted movement in the walk-in closet and looked up at Shakey Shawn. "Mafucka," he struggled. "Before you pull da trigga show me da face of da nigga who got over on Shamrock," he coughed up blood, referring to himself in the third person

"That'll be my pleasure." Shakey Shawn took his free hand and grabbed a hold of the lower part of his woven black mask, revealing his identity. He confirmed what Shamrock had suspected. He knew who was responsible for the hit. In fact, he etched the culprit's face on the surface of his mind and screamed out his name in blood, "NITTY!" Shakey Shawn placed the nozzle between Shamrock's eyes.

Boom!

Divine, flinched but she held her composure.

31

CHAPTER 5

The Jay-Z blue Escalade ESV bent a corner referred to as 69th and Ashland; better known as the south side slums within the Englewood District.

Adon sparkled like a flawless diamond in the threatening eye of this concrete jungle. He was bred into it and touched every level the streets had to offer. But there was one sector of the game that dictated it all— The Convolution. And Adon was its youngest and newest member.

His BlackBerry vibrated as he sped through a red traffic light. He reviewed the small screen for caller ID purposes before answering. "Talk to me," he stated grimly.

"It's done," Shakey Shawn reported.

"Make sure you clean up your mess," Adon pressed down on the end button when his two-way chimed. He peered down at his hip and angled the gadget's screen upward. "Nitty," he uttered. He unclipped the two-way and read the message.

"Yay or Nay?" Were the words that Nitty put through indicating rather the hit was a success or not.

"Yay," was what Adon typed back implying that the hit was executed without incident.

Adon clipped the two-way to his hip and guided the truck up the southwestern strip of 79th Street, famously known as "Killa-Ward." As the rain began to pick up he pulled into the parking lot of Miss Muffet's Pancakes to gather his thoughts. This spot was a posttraumatic locality for him, especially on such a *familiar* rainy day as today. For, Miss Muffet's was his mother's, Loretta's, favorite place to take him; and also the lot where she was killed.

Back when he and his sister, Natasha, were much younger, it would upset her when little Adon would ask her to take him to Miss Muffet's. But what alarmed her more so than his eerie request, was his lack of memory of asking such a thing once she would later tell an adult about it. It was learned soon after, via psychologist, that he made such demands subconsciously. Now in later years, he took the liberty of escorting himself there during trying times, or when he just simply wanted to talk to Loretta.

Adon released a short chuckle after noticing a guy with a pimped out perm. The man failed miserably at avoiding the precipitation from sabotaging his over-relaxed hair as he sprinted through the rain. Suddenly, Adon's lips straightened. His conscience began to eat at him as he remembered when Shamrock use to rock perms back in the day.

Damn homie, why you had to go out like that, he thought, taking a swig from the Henny bottle that he had stashed under his seat.

"Whew!" The strong liquor burned his chest. His anxiety was progressing and he needed relief. He frantically searched the glove box for his pill bottle. Not finding it there, he checked his console. Inside was a bottle of 20mg Prozac. He was instructed by the psychologist to take one a day, but instead, he popped three at once and washed it down with the Henny, leaving just a small portion in the bottle. It wasn't long before the effects of the alcohol and medication mixed took place. Dropping the bottle, he became hypnotized by the rain that resembled giant worms across the windshield. Adon had passed out and his unresponsive mind began to roam:

"Mama, why can't I go to chool?"

Little Adon struggled to pronounce his words as he watched some bigger kids group-up with their book bags in tow.

"Oh baby, you're only four years old. You're not old enough yet," Loretta said to her child, and pulled into the parking lot of Miss Muffet's Pancakes.

"When the time comes for you to go to school, I'll let you go. Okay?" Loretta tried to let him down easy.

"But mama, sistah Ta-Ta go to chool. Why can't I go wif ha?" Little Adon asked.

Loretta couldn't help but to smile at how ambitious her little prince was. "You're definitely your father's son," she said, "Your sister, Ta-Ta, had to wait 'till she was five years old, and so do you. So for now I want you to spend some more time with me. Okay, boo boo?"

"Kay, you promise?" he asked.

"Yes baby, Mama promise."

Little Adon nodded and watched the bigger kids through the car window, wanting much to join them. He kept his eyes peeled on their independence.

Back inside the truck, Adon remained in his state of swoon and clung on to Loretta's every word. It had been such a long time since he had last seen his mother's angelic face, or heard her heavenly voice. If Adon could have it his way, he would discontinue all earthly affairs and be with his mother for all eternity.

"So my little prince," Loretta said. "Are you ready to go inside and eat some strawberry pancakes?"

Little Adon was too busy studying the characteristics of the school kids to even have noticed that his mother had said anything. Loretta turned to look in the backseat.

"C'mon now, boo-boo, I'm sure Miss Muffet will be so thrilled to see her little man," Loretta tried to persuade as the rain started to come down harder upon the roof and windshield.

Little Adon turned to his mother and suddenly became frightened by the man in the hooded raincoat. The evil man opened the car door, catching Loretta by surprise.

She screamed, "You don't have to do this! Be your own man for once and let go of me, Donald! Let me go!"

The evil man struck her in the face with a close fist.

"Get the fuck out of the car before I kill you in front of your boy!" the evil man threatened and dragged Loretta out of the car.

Little Adon, restrained to his car seat, reached out his hands and cried, "Mamaaa!"

Natasha was on her way home when she drove by Miss Muffet's Pancakes. "That looks like my brother's truck," she thought aloud. She made a u-turn and pulled into the parking lot, behind Adon's truck, blocking him in. The rain was coming down hard so she honked her horn a couple of times.

"Maybe he's inside," she said and got out of her car to investigate further. "I'll be right back, Vanity," she told her girlfriend who was sitting in the passenger seat and ran inside the restaurant.

A minute later, she walked out with a hood over her head and jogged over to the truck.

"Adon! Adon! Are you in there?" She banged on the window. The dark tint prevented her from even seeing a shadow. Natasha stopped banging and looked around.

"He's not inside the restaurant; he's not answering his cell, what's going on?" She heard a groan come from within and put her ear close to the black window. Adon continued to groan as he fought his nightmare.

"Adon! Adon!" Natasha yelled and banged on the window. She feared the worst. Suddenly the driver door slightly opened and she moved aside allowing it to swing open completely.

" Ahhh," he uttered and looked over at Natasha. "What 'cha doing here, sis?" He was obviously twisted. Natasha could tell he was kind of out of it. She hit the door locks on the side panel and ran around to the passenger side. She climbed in and removed her hoodie.

"Wassup, bruh, is everything okay?" Natasha was concerned.

"I'm good, Tash," he said rubbing his head.

"Well, you know you shouldn't be parked here, and sleeping of all places."

"Tru dat," Adon agreed. "I'ma 'bout to ride out now," he sat up in his Gucci interior and turned the ignition.

"Wait!" Natasha warned. "I'm parked behind you. Besides, you're not in any condition to drive. I'll drive you. Give me a sec. I'll be right back, okay?"

"Aiight," as shitty as Adon was feeling he didn't bother to argue. He climbed over into the passenger seat and reclined his head on the headrest.

Natasha opened the driver door and climbed in the truck. "Damn, it's coming down hard out there," she said removing her hoodie again and adjusted the seat to accommodate her hourglass, five-five frame. "Whats that?" She pointed to his pants leg.

"What?" Adon turned his attention to his Coogi jeans. "Oh, this shit? Ain't nothin. Probably spilled some Henny." Natasha adjusted the rearview mirror and watched as her Toyota Avalon backed up. She reversed the truck and then put it into drive as the Avalon followed. Adon spotted her car through the side mirror.

"Who dat driving your car?" he asked.

"Vanity," she said and halted at the outset of the parking lot.

"Who is she?" Adon had never heard her mention the name before.

"Vanity is one of my girls that I've known practically my whole life when I was living in Seattle. She just flew in. She said that she needed a vacation so I offered my place to her, considering she's never been to Chi before. I was coming back from picking her up from the O'hare when I recognized your truck, parked all suspicious-like."

She paused and checked the street lanes before leaving the parking lot.

"It was a good thing you had stopped by my house yesterday, after picking this bad boy up from Nondo's shop. Otherwise, you would've been on your own, because I would've drove right pass you. This is nice too, Adon. How much did it set you back?"

"I don't purchase setbacks," Adon shot back.

Natasha narrowed her eyes at him and then focused on the road.

"Is there any gas in the Vette?"

"How would I know bruh. It's been in my garage since you left it there. And how long has that been, about three weeks now? Besides, you're not in any condition to be driving that fast ass car or any vehicle for that matter, especially not in this weather. It's messy out here," she said while snatching a glimpse of her car through the rearview mirror. "Now, back to my original question: how much did this truck run you?"

"I paid about a yard for it," Adon answered nonchalantly.

"A yard, meaning?" Natasha didn't catch on to his lingo.

"A hundred thousand," he said.

"In cash?"

"Hardcore, sis."

"Boy, you're not going to learn until those feds—"

"What? You trying to do jinx a nigga? Besides, Siheed knows what he's doin'. Whatever don't cross over the table, makes its way under," Adon was becoming annoyed.

"But hell, I'm pretty sure he's under some type of investigation himself. Ever since 9/11, all of the rich Arabians in this country have been catching heat and…"

She discontinued her flow after acknowledging Adon's extended finger. She decided to ease up off the throttle some. "All I'm saying is be careful."

Adon had never flew off the handle toward her, or even in her presence. However, she was aware of his temper and kept her distance. She knew her limits. With that in mind, she continued on a lighter note.

"I was only asking the price because I'm thinking of getting a SUV, myself. Something cute but elegant. Maybe a Range Rover. I may even get a TV or two, but definitely not these many," she glanced at the flat monitors situated throughout the truck and in places that didn't make any sense to her, like on the side panels of all four doors.

"Bruh, why do you need a TV in the middle of your steering wheel?"

While Natasha continued to jabber, Adon was becoming sick to his stomach as nausea began to creep up his throat. Heavy perspiration spring boarded from his brow, landing in his eye. A dizzy spell came about. With limited sight ability, he reached into his glove box to retrieve paper towels, and clumsily caused an empty bottle of Prozac to fall onto his floor mat. He didn't even notice it.

Shit, that Henny crept up on me, something vicious!

His neck felt like flimsy rubber, while the inside of his head whirled in a rapid, non-stop fashion like a tornado. The combination was crucial.

I can pick myself up. This ain't nothing, he tried to convince himself. He used all of his mental strength to fight the feeling.

"Stop the truck!" he bellowed out of nowhere.

"What?" Natasha was alarmed and confused.

"Just pull it over…NOW!"

37

She made a reckless right turn, nearly side scraping a smaller vehicle while other drivers quickly veered off to either side or yielded.

"Sorry," she said to no one in particular and managed to restrain the truck at the curb of a sidewalk. Before she could come to a complete stop, Adon was all ready hanging his head out of the door throwing up his lunch. With spinning tops for eyes, he sat back down and braced his head inside of his palms.

He stared at the floor when, *"Shit!"*

He saw the exposed empty bottle of pills. He quickly darted his unsteady eyes in Natasha's direction. She was focused on her side view mirror, pulling back onto the road. Her cell phone chimed just as Adon reached down and grabbed a hold of the bottle. He placed it back inside his glove box without her noticing.

Natasha placed her cell to her ear. The caller was Vanity. "I'm sorry, boo. Yes, everything is fine. Stay close behind now," she ended the call and turned to Adon.

"What is it with you? Talk to me," Natasha pleaded.

"I'm straight. E'vrythang is e'vrythang with me, sis."

He paused to ignite the tip of his Black and Mild, not realizing that he just voiced one of Shamrock's favorite quotes. He inhaled deeply and took the cigar away from his dehydrated lips.

"I know you mean well Tash, but fact is you worry too much. Don't lean on the unnecessaries. Breathe easy for a change." He was beginning to feel somewhat better after vomiting.

"'Don't lean on the unnecessaries? Breathe easy?'" she mocked. "What!?" Natasha acted as if Adon was speaking a foreign language. "Well, you tell me, Adon, how can I not worry when you're playing Russian roulette with your precious life?"

"Freeze that shit," he sighed heavy releasing vapor from his lungs.

"I'm serious, Adon," Natasha tapped the steering wheel with her palm. "This type of lifestyle that you're living scares the shit out of me! You're involved with that gang nonsense, you're in the *game*, you rip and run these streets like the world is about to blow, and you host *these* statewide picnics and eat barbecue ribs and whatnot amongst gang leaders, cold blooded killers, and kingpin drug dealers."

She paused to catch her breath, then "And you take care of those half-slick-ass niggas that, to my bewilderment, you swear are your family. Who I may add, would not care two damns about you if you were broke, or in someone's jail cell."

Natasha focused on switching lanes as silence filled the air, but only briefly. She looked over at Adon and said, "God forbid, but what if you get killed out there? Or what if you *do* catch a case and have to do time? Who do you think will be there for you then, Adon? Them so-called mans-n-nem of yours? I think not!"

Natasha had been trying to lay down this righteous shit to him since their reunion two years back. Not until now did Adon feel the urge to defend his conviction to the streets.

"Contrary to what you think, my 'true niggas' is my family. Who do you think been watchin' my back all these years? When it's time to put in work, who do you think is on the front lines with me? Or how about when I was practically living in rat-infested alleys, serving dime rocks just to eat, buy decent clothes, and a pair of Jays for school. Don't get it confused, sis. That shit wasn't easy; on the daily I had to fight off bigger fiends who decided too quickly that I was an easy mark. Needless to say, they didn't make that same mistake twice and it was the OGs that aided and assisted me. Because of them, I was no longer the laughing stock of Harper High.

"But, let me take you back even further than that, when I had to duck and dodge bullets every five minutes of every day. All because my neighborhood bred a certain crew that the opposing side was at odds with. During those times I was an innocent lil'shit, just a shorty going to Randolph Elementary with typical hoop dreams like Derrick Rose. And one day out of the blue while Shamrock and I were walking home from school, a car drove by with a .357 Magnum pointing out of its window. Neither of us was in a gang, nor were we in the game, but we were forced to live everyday life like we were."

He paused and raised his pants leg, exposing his old bullet wound.

"When I felt the heat pass through my knee from a muthafucka that didn't even have the courage to get outta the car and off me, I knew what had to be done. It wasn't long before I realized there are no children in Englewood and innocence had no place. I was alone. I had no one to turn to. Pops and Moms were dead! You was gone! Shit, besides Shamrock all I had was self. Don't get me wrong, I'm thankful that Shamrock's mother prevented me from bouncin' around foster homes by takin' me in after our parents was murdered, but let's be real, she turned tricks 30 percent of the time and the other 70 she spent sticking needles in her arm.

"I had to get in where I fit in. Ain't no aspiring dreams here. Only the lavish realities of d-boys, and the pitiful existence of dope fiends. The Haves and the Havenots. And I'm not sorry to say that I wasn't cut outta my mama's wound to be no hype, nor to be no broke nigga. I figured it like this, Tash. I was Englewood stuck and Murray Park bound. So, why not capitalize?

"After I sought revenge on that coward who didn't have the nuts to finish the job, I promoted my last name, 'Cutti,' in the streets and it was a wrap after that. Niggas love Pops out here. It's been nineteen years since his death and niggas still breathe his name like it was yesterday. Now that's power, and the strength that I use to drive my aspirations of conquering this city."

By this time a steep fall of tears streamed down the flawless features of Natasha's face. While she was surrounded by a family that loved her as their own, Adon was thrown to a pack of wild wolves, only as a cub. Abandoned and left in the epicenter of a jungle where animals fed on their young. While she was placed six hundred miles away in Seattle, Washington, going on her first date, attending her senior prom, graduation, and enjoying the best life that a loving adopting family could provide, Adon was forced to adopt survival skills not meant to be practiced by a child.

She wished to turn back the hands of time and trade places with him. Maybe things would have turned out differently. Being that she was female and four years his senior, just maybe the obstacles that he faced would not have crossed her path. Natasha hated that they were separated at a time when they were inseparable.

Why couldn't they have kept us together? she often asked herself.

She knew that Adon had been shot before, but the notion of that God-awful incident being the mode responsible for which her brother was today, had never crossed her mind. Moreover, up until now, Natasha had failed to fully appreciate just how tough his upbringing was. For it had only been two years since they reunited, after being separated for nineteen years. It was clear that the streets of Englewood had raised her brother. It was the closest thing that Adon had to a *real* family.

Natasha wiped her tears and said, "Now I know throughout all of these years, you and Shamrock had each other's back and front. I see why the two of you are so close."

At that second Natasha had noticed something. It was in Adon's face. An expression that she had never seen before, and for that reason it was hard to decipher. It was quick in action, lasting an instant. But she knew what she saw, or what she thought she saw: A hateful grimace blended with heartbreaking sadness.

What was that about? Did he and Shamrock fall out, she pondered before Adon derailed her train of thought.

"Look, I don't need your pity, or no one else's," he hit the Black and Mild.

"And I don't know why I'm even wasting my time explaining this shit to you! I'ma grown ass man and have been for—"

Natasha interrupted with a compromising tone. "I know you have been taking care of yourself for a long, long time now, without any love or support from your *real* family. And I'm truly sorry for that. We're going to have to carry that burden for the rest of our natural lives, but you do not have to be alone with this. Please, do not shut me out nor push me away."

"It's simple, I never had hope until I sold dope."

"But how can you say that, Adon? What about, Joyous, your beautiful and precious daughter?" Natasha asked with great feeling.

"Look, I'ma money-getter. I get money, that's what I do. I'm not in love with the game, but I love what the game has done for me. My bottom line is this: Fuck how you feel I gotta eat!" Adon said with authority as Natasha guided the truck over the highway.

"I have a direction. Thanks to Nitty, I am a man who can hold his own in any situation known."

"What about the unknown? Are you prepared for that?"

Adon ignored Natasha's last two questions. "As for my baby girl, no matter what happens to me, Joyous is straight for life. Hell, even her kids are covered. The money ain't nothin'."

"When was the last time you've seen your daughter?"

"What!?"

"All I'm saying is that you should spend more of your time with Joyous, that's all I'm saying."

They had finally arrived to Palos Hills, Illinois, as Natasha detoured off the highway. Now only five minutes away from her suburban home, she observed a few of her white neighbors at a nearby grocery store. She made an estimated turn as she was still feeling out the vast size of the truck. She spotted Vanity in the rearview following close behind.

"Adon, I know you have money, I know that. But what you're failing to realize is that money isn't everything. That's what Mr. Nitty Calhoun isn't telling you, bruh. Joyous need her daddy, not her daddy's money."

"You know what? You right."

Just when Natasha thought she was finally getting through to him, his next words only proved her wrong.

"Money isn't e'vrythang…it's the only thing!" Adon declared.

"What!?" Natasha exclaimed with overwhelming frustration, and steered the truck across a deserted intersection that led to her home.

"You heard me," Adon shot back. "Now that's it! Look, Tash, you my sister and I got mad love for you, but I'm done talkin' 'bout this shit. So miss me with all that preaching, you ain't my fuckin'—" Adon abruptly cut his words short after realizing what he was going to say next.

"I'm not your what, Adon? Say it!" Natasha wheeled the truck to the left and stomped onto its brake pedal. The 26-inch Yokohama tires screeched as the chrome Devin rims remained in steady rotation.

Vanity veered to her right, barely missing the truck's back bumper. "What is going on in there?" She mumbled and looked up at the massive truck.

Natasha placed the gearshift into park. With her alluring, walnut-shaped eyes she compassionately demanded Adon's undivided attention, and in the softest tone she relinquished, "Is that why I found you there today…at Miss Muffet's?" her voice broke with emotion, her eyes filled with tears.

"I don't know," Adon admitted. "I mean, I wasn't even intendin' on takin' that route. But I kept driving, sippin' on Henny. Before I knew it, I had those pills in my hand."

"Pills? What pills, Adon?"

"You remember the medication that the shrink prescribed for me way back-n-da-day, before we were separated."

Natasha lost eye contact, and reluctantly took a trip down memory lane. It was true. However vague, but she did remember. After the brutal slayings of their parents, Adon, so young and fragile, fell into a consciousness coma. Though he was healthy, awake, and very much alive, Adon was numb. He would not talk, show any signs of emotion, or react to anything. It was as if he were born a mute. Before the tragic murders of their parents, no one could pay him to stop talking. It was said that he was being consumed by his dreams, his nightmares, his own world.

Trembling, Natasha slowly elevated her tear-soaked face, and glued her eyes to those of Adon. "So, is that what explains why I found you subdued like that? Bruh, you know you shouldn't take medication, especially not psych meds, and wash it down with liquor."

Adon nodded in agreement.

She reached for his hand and said, "I thought you stopped taking those pills when, you know, once your…your…" Natasha swallowed her next words as Adon broke his silence and revealed her fearful thought.

"Yeah, the dreams have come back, Tash."

Natasha's heart skipped a beat and her trembling increased. She threw her arms around Adon's broad shoulders and uttered, "Bruh please, just promise me that you will not let the streets do to you, what it did to our father. Don't go out like that. You promise?"

"Tash, I miss mama so much," he shedded tears over Natasha's shoulder as they held each other.

Natasha hated the fact that Adon had pledged his allience to Nitty Calhoun, and would be willing to lay his life on the line for Nitty if it came down to it.

CHAPTER 6

It was 5:33 A.M. and Adon found himself alone in bed.

He rose up, unsure of where he was until he caught a glimpse of the décor. Then he relaxed his back muscles and reclined onto the sheet-covered mattress. He was inside of Natasha's guestroom. He gazed at the ebony glass ceiling that hovered above. He had another dream about his past. He was troubled. And his penitent thoughts of Shamrock's murder only added to his anxiety.

Adon jumped to his feet and walked into the bathroom. He splashed his face with cold water and dried it with a towel. He felt a slight hangover. He left the bathroom and tiptoed down the carpeted corridor until he reached Natasha's bedroom. He smiled at the sight of her and wondered how was it that she can tuck herself in so neatly and not move a muscle all night? For a minute or two he examined her features. She was nearly identical to their mother, Loretta.

Adon quietly tugged on the doorknob and accidentally made a small noise as the door shut.

"Damn," he murmured, hoping that it didn't wake Natasha. He put his ear to the door and, with his fingers crossed, not a sound was heard.

She's sleeping like a baby.

He moved quietly passed his guestroom and further down the corridor in route to the family room. He was almost there when he passed the only other guestroom in the home and heard a distinctive sound come from within. He froze in his position and backtracked his steps, literally placing his toes in the exact places that he printed into the carpet only seconds before.

He thought about grasping his burna, but it was under the pillow back inside the guestroom.

That's way too far. What about a knife or something? he asked himself, before realizing that the kitchen was too far out of reach.

Fuck it, I'm here now.

Before he tore the door from its hinges, he shot a last look at Natasha's bedroom door, making certain that her area was clear of danger. He reverted to the door in question and noticed that it was partially opened. He decided to peek before entering.

The rays from the rising sun met his scouring eyes at the split of the door. Much too vigorous for the curtain to shield, the rising sun gradually illuminated the room. He pitched his hand to protect his eyes from the conflicting glare, while straining to see just beneath his six-point star diamond pinky ring. Adon was ready to defeat the unknown with his bare hands, but he was not at all prepared for what he was about to encounter.

At the foot of the bed laid a fine pair of pedicure feet. Confused, he pressed slightly against the door and caused it to part slowly, as he captured an eye full of a well-sculptured leg. Suddenly, he vaguely remembered the Vanity chick from yesterday.

He smiled and used his tongue to apply soft dampness to his lips. He began to play a one-sided game with her being an unknowing key participant, as the partially opened door acted as an imaginative go-between. Adon continued to press slowly upon the door.

The satin sheet hugged her curvy margin. Inch by inch, he revealed more of her Nubian Goddessship as he acquainted himself with the enticing curve that outlined her hip. He refused to blink. He followed that same enticing curve until it dipped low and disappeared into her thin waist. From that mouth-watering section, Adon ran his eyes up her toned arm; the sexy bone structure that made her shoulder. Her neck was slim, lips were kissable, and her face was lovely. The sun itself seemed to have spoken up for her as its rays started to embrace her exquisite body like caring arms. The illumination radiated more as the sun climbed the horizon. It did a wonder for Adon's sharp observation.

He leaned his lean, athletic frame against the doorpost, captivated by Vanity's motionless figure. He had to admit, the scenery that lay before him was not half bad.

Not half bad at all.

In fact, he found it incomparable to anything he had ever seen before. With Vanity's smooth coffee-brown skin, and wavy jet-black hair, she was definitely a "dime."

He didn't have the time to realize this the night before, because after making it to Natasha's home, the both of them rushed off to Natasha's beauty salon to check on things. Vanity didn't have a chance to step out of the car and flaunt her beauty. But Adon wasn't the least bit concerned about it then. The only things that were on his mind were two Aspirins for his migraine, and a big comfortable bed to lie in. However, Vanity had his undivided attention now.

In a rush to go nowhere, Adon allowed his eyes to drink her in, and noticed that the satin sheet was falling from her arm. He quietly walked over to her and reached for the slippery texture, and gently covered her. But not before he captured a glorious glimpse of her half of a dollar coin-size areola. Her nipples were standing at attention. He could only imagine what she was dreaming of.

Upon walking away, Adon turned one last time to take a mental picture of her sensational sleeping pose and mumbled, "Damn she fine," before leaving the room.

Not a minute later he reentered. This time Vanity's bedroom eyes were open. She anticipated his return. In fact, she had hoped for it. Adon stood at the door, waiting patiently for an indication.

Vanity sized him up, catching sight of the enlargement in front of his boxer briefs. She removed the satin sheet, revealing her naked body. She hadn't one stretch mark or blemish. Her body resembled the likes of Melissa Ford.

Adon waited patiently.

She raised her torso and scooted back against the headboard, and brought her knees to her chest. She smiled at Adon as he admired the view. She licked her index finger and placed it between her breasts. With her finger she slowly crawled down her flat stomach, leaving a damp trail that led to her pussy. She circled around it before her finger entered her flesh.

"Mmmm," she purred and crooked her finger from her free hand, inviting Adon to join her.

Adon shut the door behind him and freed the beast from its cage as his boxers fell to his feet. He stepped out of them and walked up to Vanity just as she pulled out a Magnum condom from her purse that she retrieved from the nightstand. She tossed the purse on the floor and tore through the little square package. She was now face to face with Adon's throbbing manhood. "Wow," she said, "niiccceeee." she was referring to his size. She placed the ring at the tip of his stiff dick and gently rolled it down the length of his shaft.

"Lay down," she mouthed and Adon obliged.

She straddled his hips, reached down between her legs, and guided his fat dick toward her wet pussy. She rubbed his dick head back and forth a couple times between her hot pussy lips and penetrated her slick tunnel.

Adon grasped with pleasure. He couldn't believe how tight she felt. She put all of her weight on him, pushing her well-proportioned ass cheeks firmly against his balls. She began to undulate her body making a wavelike movement that caused her ass to roll his nuts around pleasurably. As she rocked back and forth, she rolled her hips to the rhythm of his.

"Oh, my goodness!" she screamed. A soft "yes, yes…mmm…uh-huh" escaped her lips as they continued with their movements.

Vanity increased her pace, rocking the bed, and squeezing out sounds from the box spring. Her breasts were swaying enticingly in front of him as he smacked her ass.

"Get it! Get it, gurl!" Adon encouraged and moved his hands further up her back to leverage himself closer to her ripe tits. This maneuver put more pressure on his dick as she continued to grind steadily against him.

She lowered his back onto the bed and leaned over him with her hands beside his shoulders. She gripped the mattress and got crunk! He felt a surge start deep in his groin as he rose and clamped onto one of her solid nipples. He rolled her nipple around in his mouth and Vanity increased her speed, thrusting her hips forward. She began to groan and contract tighter.

Suddenly she tensed up, the jerking movements of her hips turned into a high frequency quiver and her breathing stopped! Then she started an up and down bouncing motion in his lap as she swallowed a deep groan. Ten minutes later, Adon felt her pussy muscles contracting through the condom and that put him over the edge. His stomach muscles flexed as he shot his nut into the condom.

Vanity couldn't believe what she'd done. This was her best friend's younger brother. In addition, the last thing she wanted was to appear loose. Promiscuity wasn't in her makeup, but for Adon she had made an exception. She could only hope that it won't come back to bite her on the ass.

The alarm clock went off at exactly 9:55 A.M. Natasha, half-asleep, searched the nightstand and deactivated the alarm. After stretching, she pushed her arms through the sleeves of her white robe and started for the restroom.

"Oh, I'm sorry, girl. I didn't know you were in here. I guess I'm just so use to being in this house all by my lonesome."

"That's okay, Tash. I'm on my way out anyway," Vanity said and patted her wet hair with a dry towel. "I can finish this in the bedroom."

"Girl, you better take your time and do what you have to do. Don't worry about me, there's three and a half bathrooms in this house, so do your thang girlfriend," Natasha insisted. "You should have waited until we made it to the salon and had your hair shampooed and conditioned professionally."

Vanity turned to her with a sheepish expression and said, "I didn't want to be a burden."

"If you don't stop playing. I own the damn shop, so how can you possibly be a burden to me? It ain't like I would be doin' it!" They both laughed at the truth. "But don't worry, we'll take care of it," Natasha reassured and started for the second bathroom. "Oh, and by the way, I love your robe. That color is cute!" she yelled before turning the corner.

On her way, Natasha decided to check on Adon.

"Rise and shine big head!" she said in a playful manner, and became puzzled by the empty bed. "How could he just leave like that without saying goodbye? That boy knows he stay on the move," she said aloud, to no one in particular.

Vanity left the bathroom wearing only a robe, matching slippers, and a towel wrapped around her head. While in route back to her guestroom she became aware of the fine art that streamed along the surrounding walls of the corridor. With every step, there was another piece worthy of admiration.

"Tasha was into art back in college, but damn. I never thought she had gotten this serious," she said as she spent around on the balls of her feet.

The paintings lured her to the stair casing like a fish to hooked bait. Once she reached the top, she noticed that the artwork had ceased where personal portraits begun. She came across an old fashion family photo of better times for Adon and Natasha. They were pictured with their father, Macklin Cutti, and their mother, Loretta Cutti.

At the last step her mood cheered up a little from the warm feeling that this next photograph brought to her. It was an enlarged representation of Nitty Calhoun's recent wedding. She acknowledged the date and year inscribed at the bottom right corner. She didn't recognize either the bride and groom, or the bridesmaids.

Then, suddenly, the deep dimples in her cheeks took form, and the lines on both sides of her succulent lips creased her skin. Unable to stop the urge, she took her finger and outlined a face that she was incredibly fond to see. That face bared the identity of Adon, looking splendid in his tux as he stood in the best man's position. She allowed her finger to linger on the photograph for a brief period before she decided to wander about.

"This girl knows she did a fabulous job with this house," she complimented after taking it upon herself to host her own grand tour.

She heard soft music. She followed the tune and began to quietly sing along with the lyrics to "Feelin' On Your Booty." She found herself standing just inside the entryway of the den. She blushed at the sight of Adon, nearly naked, with boxer briefs concealing his "goods."

"R. Kelly, huh…well, I see he has immaculate taste in music," she said and noticed that the Playstation 3 wireless controller was resting square on the "fly" of his boxers, as he leaned back in a velvet recliner, sleep with his lips slightly parted.

Vanity walked softly over to the entertainment center and shut off the wide screen. She then shielded Adon's athletic physique with a soft cotton quilt. Before she departed, Vanity blessed his lips with a soft sensual kiss. What she didn't know is that she gave him a sense of comfort while he fought the demon within his nightmare.

CHAPTER 7

Nitty Calhoun was a sagacious businessman who was viewed by his peers to be hard-nosed but vital to the commercial activity of Chicago. He was very influential in the world of business, and many in his field perceived it an honor just to be in the same room with him brainstorming lucrative ideas. His businesses ranged from gas stations, five construction companies, a host of property, the number one radio station WGCI, and he even had a large stake in the Bulls' very own United Center, just to name a few. He was undoubtedly at the top of his game. On the flip side, Nitty was a puissant drug lord who was responsible for the majority of cocaine that came into the Midwest. He was a powerful force to be reckoned with.

Out of his many businesses, Magic Hands was his baby; an upscale carwash on the Gold Coast of Chicago, just between the Bentley and Ferrari dealerships. It was the first business that he acquired over fifteen years ago, and had flourished tremendously over time. Nitty had added several additions to his establishment over the fifteen year span. The car wash area alone could fit seven of the local car washes inside. And Nitty employed the best of hands-on care that money could buy. Magic Hands was the undisputed "hot spot" for high-end ballers that either dribbled in the league, or played in the game. This place stayed busy, especially during the summer season, and today Mick and Mario used that to their advantage.

Although a ton of rain had drenched the once dry grounds for the past two weeks, by two in the afternoon the heavens displayed a sky brilliant with color and the sun was out blazing. The automatic garage door opened, revealing North Rush Street. Some of Magic Hands' employees quickly shielded their eyes from the blinding sun as the sweltering heat escaped inside. Balanced on Pirelli Tires, a Bentley Arnage Drophead Coupe drove inside with a pearl white Range Rover in succession.

Mick and Mario had much interest in the Bentley as the two of them blended with the atmosphere. The place was so crowded with people and high-end automobiles that no one paid the two of them any attention. Mick was certain of the person inside the Bentley. He quickly dialed seven numbers and put the cell to his ear. "Nitty just drove in," he said.

"Good, keep an eye on him," Killa Mike said and flipped his cell shut. He got off the couch a walked over to the bedroom where he was holding both Charlotte and Joy. He quietly unlocked the door and peeked inside. They were hunched together in a corner with their backs to him. He shut the door and locked it.

Behind the Bentley's tinted window, sat Nitty. He looked toward the south wing where his latest edition to Personal Touch was recently constructed. It was an extended compound that had a state-of-the-art recording studio that he named after his late mentor, Macklin Cutti. The studio contributed a great deal to Magic Hands' mass profits, and has hosted such names as Common, Lupe Fiasco, and Do or Die, just to name a few.

"It appears to be a slow day," Nitty commented after taking a visual account of the car wash area.

"Hell, any car wash in business would love to see this type of action on a wet Sunday," Casey reassured from the driver seat. He was Nitty's oldest and dearest friend.

"Sure, under those circumstances I'd be inclined to agree with you. But you see my good friend, this isn't just any car wash. This here is Magic Hands," Nitty declared boastfully.

"I hear that, Jack," Casey joined in with a chuckle, and just that quick, uneasiness suffused the Bentley with silence. He called everybody "Jack." Casey began to donate superficial attention to his twirling thumbs, when his pointed regards really rested on Nitty's sudden stillness. He's known Nitty for years on end, and one of the many things that he has picked up on was that Nitty became rather reserved when his thoughts are multifaceted. But Casey understood as his thoughts also bared a burden of its own. He searched his mind for some sort of logical reason as to why Shakey Shawn didn't report back like he was ordered to.

Nitty knew that the hit would be mentally difficult for Adon to see through, hence, the reason why he sent a trained henchman along.

Hell, why hasn't he contacted the either of us by now? Sumthin' is definitely not jivin' here, Casey wondered.

"Well the rain has just about dried all the way up," Casey said. "The way I fo'resee it, considering how feisty the sun has become, the pretty streets of Chi-town will be burning hot in no time. And you know what that means, Jack."

"And what is that, old man?" Nitty asked while throwing a wisecrack at his age, although they are only five years apart.

"Shoo, there's going to be more business starting at that big pretty glass door of yours, and ending three blocks away on Hermitage Street; out doing Heather Hunter and Vanessa Delrio combined, on their best gangbang day!" Both Casey and Nitty burst into laughter. Casey watched as Nitty guffawed, and silently commended himself for bringing his friend out of his worrisome shell. At least for the moment.

"Well", Nitty winded his laughter down, "I'm sure you know what comes next, right?" he asked, and wondered from which page of "Casey's Comedy" was his pal intending to quote from this time.

"If business picks up within the next hour as I so vividly predict, and I am usually pretty good with these types of formalities, I think that it'll be wise to drive the Bentley around front," Casey said, trying to sound all educated-like.

"Yep, we're going to need as much available space that we can squeeze," Nitty agreed.

Casey took the gearshift into his hand, just as Nitty threw up his index finger.

"Hold off," Nitty stated. "Before we move I'm going to try to contact Adon again, for the umpteenth time today."

Mick and Mario remained apart, but nearby. They were there only to monitor Nitty and nothing else. While Mick stayed keen, Mario covered his mouth with his palm and secretly popped a triple-stack X-pill. Before long, restlessness started to persuade Mario's anxious mind. He was playing mental tennis with foolish thoughts. He wanted to get into something.

At once, three doors of the Range Rover opened. Two middle-aged men climbed out.

Just like Mystery said, there goes Nitty's personal security, Mick mused and watched as a third man lingered inside the SUV, part of his lower leg hung from the driver's side.

The man rose up and placed his loafers on the pavement. He too had on a high-priced suit. He had a decent size going on, as if he worked out on the regular. It was evident that he was young enough to be in his mid-to-late twenties. A more suitable age for Adon's crew, and quite the opposite of the two fortyish men who traveled as passengers.

The two middle-aged men sprouted forth in their respective routes within the compound. The younger one visually swept the entire car wash area. He paused and stared toward the north wing for a distinctive second or two.

Now why is that still here? he wondered after spotting a particular automobile ducked-off in a corner stall.

Before Mario could turn away, dude glanced in his direction and turned for the Bentley in haste.

Mario became uneasy by his own foolish paranoia *Did he make me? Why is he walkin' to the Bentley like he's on sumthin'? Does he know? Is he goin' to warn Nitty?* Mario lost all self-restraint.

Casey turned to the swift sounds of intrusion coming from the Bentley's rear side. Quick on the draw, he aimed his palm-sized .32 revolver at the fatal parts of the unknown. He held back once he discovered that it was only Malcom, Nitty's stepson taking a seat and shutting the door. Casey shook his head and slid the .32 back down his Versace sleeve. It was something about Malcom's character that gave Casey bad vibes. Casey didn't trust him.

"What is it now, Malcom?" Nitty asked irritably.

"Everything's under control, pops. I was just wondering why was Shamrock's Six still here? It's been here for two weeks now. I called him over and over but he hasn't returned my calls. And his car is really holding up business," Malcom said and folded his arms.

"What in the fuck are you speaking on, boy?" Nitty said sternly, and turned to scrutinize the eyes of his stepson.

Malcom pointed his finger in the direction of the north wing and said, "Well, unless someone else has a charcoal grey S600 Benz, sittin' on the same 24-inch rims, and—"

Nitty interrupted Malcom with a look of disbelief. "Well, I'll be damned. That certainly is Shamrock's Mercedes," Nitty accorded. "Why didn't you tell me about this before now?"

"I didn't think it was that big of a deal," Malcom responded nervously.

"Are you not the newly appointed manager of Magic Hands?" Nitty asked.

"Yes, sir."

"Well, don't make me regret my decision. Do some fuckin' managing! Find out exactly how long that car been on the premises, who brought it in, and at what time! I want to know who was working that day and who did the services on it. Go now!" Nitty demanded.

"I'm on it, pops," Malcom opened the door and rose up out of the Bentley.

"That boy wouldn't happen to know about the hit on Shamrock, would he?" Casey asked, not feeling comfortable with Malcom knowing something about anything.

"Of course not," Nitty assured.

"I didn't think so. Just so you know, Shamrock's Benz has been here since the night before the hit. He brought it in for a wax-n-buff and got inside a decked-out Ford Excursion before pulling off. But correct me if I'm unjust. Wasn't Adon supposed to handle this whole Shamrock matter? His cars, the dead bodies, any evidence that could lead back to us Adon was suppose to take care of. And now he doesn't answer his phone for a full two weeks. This is not sittin' well with me, Nitty," he said and went on to adjust the side view mirror from the inside. Nitty used his mobile phone to blow-up every number he had on Adon. He wanted answers.

Malcom had made his way to the freshly buffed Mercedes Benz S600. He pulled on the door handle. "Shit, it's locked." He bent forward and peered into the heavily tinted window.

Mario was on his heels. His unwarranted paranoia had gotten the best of him. He pulled his weapon and caught a vague attraction out the corner of his eye. It was his crime partner, Mick, mouthing the words, "No fool, no!" Mario read his lips quite easily. With a disappointed frown, he put his eight-inch butterfly knife in his waistband, next to his .40 Caliber handgun and allowed his over-sized throwback jersey to drape over. Malcom turned around, spooked as he found himself face-to-face with a stranger.

"You gotta light, homie?" Mario asked playing it off, recognizing the fear written on Malcom's face.

Scary lil' bitch, he mused.

Malcom stood motionless, as if he had lost all direction. Mario raised his hand and snapped his thumb and finger only inches away from Malcom's face. He then pointed to the unlit Kool cigarette that sat between his yellow teeth.

"Oh, naw man, I don't smoke," Malcom said.

"You need to start," Mario replied and walked away.

Malcom stood there for a few seconds and gathered himself before he began to walk in the opposite direction. He wiped a nervous bead of sweat from his brow.

Casey scowled at the object in his side view mirror, and with a clinched fist he said, "Nitty, maybe you know something I don't know."

"And by that remark what could you possibly mean?" Nitty asked without looking up from his cell phone.

"The lowest of the low just stepped foot into your building," Casey said and continued. "I didn't think that such scum would be allowed inside of *Nitty Calhoun's Establishment.*" Casey knew that with this derisive approach he would grasp Nitty's much-needed attention.

"Now," Nitty started, "who or what are you referring to?" Nitty asked with undivided attention. Casey slowly veered his eyes to the rear of the Bentley. Nitty's eyes followed until he spotted the culprit standing several feet behind their immediate ground. "What in the blue hell—"

"Is Doe doing here?" Casey finished Nitty's sentence. "I could think of one damn good reason. He's lookin' to meet with Adon."

"When did he get out of prison?" Nitty thought aloud.

"Do you want me to take care of it?" Casey asked adamantly. He had unquestionable intentions of slumping Doe in cold blood. An action that, in his opinion, should have taken place two decades ago.

"Not right here, not right now. Too many witnesses."

"Well, we gotta do something, Jack, and fast, before he start running his mouth," Casey said.

"I know, I know. If you spot Adon before I do, direct him straight to my office. Do not, I repeat, do not let Doe talk to him. Understood? Another thing…I want you to stop by Shamrock's home and check things out. See if things are cleaned up and report back to me immediately after."

"I got 'cha, boss," Casey responded.

"I'll see you in say," Nitty looked down at his Presidential Rolex, "twenty minutes. During that time I'll be busy returning calls and initiating a couple of my own."

Nitty fell silent then looked into his side rearview. Through the deeply tinted windows, he sized-up Doe's scrawny build. He shook his head in disgust, gritted his teeth, and in a low stern voice he uttered, "Keep your eyes on that dead man walking, and as soon as he walks away from the grounds introduce him to his maker and be discreet about it. Thanks to Shamrock, we got enough heat as it is."

Nitty rose from the Bentley's interior and marked his way around the vehicle's front end. He acknowledged several "hellos" without losing a step.

Doe spotted Nitty and turned toward a wall as Nitty walked through a set of glass doors that led to his personal office.

Fuck, I can't let him see me. If he knows I'm outta prison, I'ma dead man.

Doe got out of there with the quickness. Casey had him in sight.

Nineteen years ago, Doe had the best of everything with a bright future in the making. This was during an era when Macklin Cutti was considered to be the King of Chicago's underworld, and surely on his way to becoming international. There was only one syndicate that could come remotely close to stopping Macklin in his tracks, and that was his worthy competitor, known simply as The Convolution.

Macklin had a navy of men that operated under the structured, "chain of command" system. After Nitty Calhoun, Doe was his second "go to" guy. Doe held his own and his contribution to Macklin's organization was priceless. He was certain to follow Macklin to the top.

In hindsight, he was loyal to a fault. He was content with staying in Macklin's shadow. Therefore, he left no legacy behind. And because of that, he had no status reserved in the street. He was a history lesson that the new generation of gangsters just didn't hear about. And the only OGs that knew the truth are the ones that want him dead.

Having been released from prison one week ago, after serving a nineteen year stint for murder, Doe had entered a new world order where Nitty Calhoun was the new dictator. He knew he had no chance of surviving his new placement. Not without the help of Adon. There was only one problem. Adon is as loyal to Nitty as Doe was to Macklin. If Doe had any chance of coming out of this with his life, he must expose the truth to the most intricate piece on the chessboard. That piece was, Adon.

CHAPTER 8

A don averaged 80 miles per hour on the Dan Ryan Expressway before detouring on the 71st Street exit ramp. A red traffic light caused him to bring his convertible Corvette Z06 to a smooth stop. Although its chameleon paint and 22-inch D'Vinci rims reflected his personality, the thick layer of dust that it accumulated from the three week stay inside Natasha's garage, and two weeks of sittin' up thereafter, described his present mood quite well.

The order was clear when he received his tenth text message all but five minutes ago.

"No later than right after you've received this message, contact me."

Though Nitty's voice held its usual placid demeanor, his anger was evident. A daily report to Nitty wasn't just a requirement, it was protocol. And could be considered a breach of security when a member of his organization failed to comply.

Although the circumstances were different, this was exactly where Shamrock's inconsistencies laid during the month that led up to the hit, and the reason a magnifying glass was placed on him to begin with. Adon, on the other hand, had never committed a violation, big or small. He lived for Nitty's approval, and for that reason he stayed ahead. But since Shamrock's murder, Adon's business has been in hiatus. Shamrock was his drop-off and pick-up guy. With him no longer in the picture, Adon had yet to pick up the slack. This in turn meant that Nitty was missing a profit.

The side effects from the Prozac wasn't pretty. Adon hadn't slept in days. Nightmares only got worst and jitters were constant. He'd break out in cold sweats for no apparent reason and had no control. He didn't want to be seen in his condition. He put down a cash advance for a suite in the Sybris Hotel & Resort that would cover a full month. And for the past two weeks he's taken advantage of that, cut off from the world and wasn't in any rush to pick things back up. Experiencing these drawbacks of his medical condition just after he'd been sworn-in into The Convolution, only deepened his depression.

Adon had spent the better part of his life dreaming about becoming "one" under the black umbrella of The Convolution. The work he's put in thus far was the groundwork toward achieving that goal. "Being set for life" had always been his motivation. Now he didn't seem to care as much.

The traffic light had let up as Adon's chrome pipes hollered. At the same time, "Put You On Game" by Lupe Fiasco blew from his fifteen inch Focal subwoofers. The lyrics brought about thoughts of his daughter, Joyous Cutti. He nicknamed her Joy for short and she bared his last name with pride as Charlotte was optimistic that he would wife her someday.

Adon knew that Natasha was right. Joyous needed him far more than his money, but his mind state would never have allowed him to adhere to that before.

Not right now, not while I'm on the grind, was what he'd tell himself.

He understood that the game was shitty, but it was fair. He was all too familiar with the risk and inside of his mind, distancing himself from the sweet innocence of his babygirl was *his* way of protecting her. He was convinced that occasional phone calls and brief visits would suffice.

Suddenly, he felt an urge. He guided the steering wheel with his knee and dialed seven digits into his BlackBerry. Charlotte's voicemail was all he tapped into.

"Damn, that girl knows she can sound sexy when she wanna. But where is she?"

Adon came up with an idea. Though he was careful not to keep tabs on her, he loved Charlotte. She broke it off solely because of his unwillingness to change his life for their daughter's sake. He knew she was justified for leaving and his dedication to the game justified his reason of not pursuing her. But he didn't let her go empty handed. He purchased her a four-bedroom house on the Southeast side, fully furnished and traded her '04 DTS Caddy in for a '08 ML 350 Benz truck.

Although Charlotte wanted to work, if for nothing else than to feel a level of independence, Adon made it clear that he was against it. He made sure that Charlotte didn't want for anything. Her responsibilities were to go to school and take care of their daughter. Period and point blank.

He reached her residential neighborhood and parked his Corvette in front of her home. Her platinum Benz truck was in the driveway. He tried her number again, but there was no answer. He started to feel something.

He glanced at her front door and thought, *She won't bring some other dude around my daughter, and in my house...would she?*

With some hesitation, he climbed out of the Vette and proceeded up the walkway. He slowed down to admire the landscape and how well the lawn was manicured.

Stepping on the doormat, he looked down and smiled as it read WELCOME TO THE CUTTI'S.

Maybe she don't have a man yet, after all, he mused.

Although he had been there once in the last month, they were broken up for six months and hadn't slept together in that time. So the strong possibility of moving on was there. He quickly wiped the smile from his face and took a deep breath as he came to terms with it.

He rang the doorbell. Thirty seconds had elapsed and there was no answer. Again, he looked over at her truck. It was Charlotte's only vehicle. She had to be there. He reached into a deep pocket attached to his Iceberg jeans and pulled out a set of house keys and used one to enter.

"Ay, Charlotte? Charlotte, are you here?" he called out as he walked in and noticed that the Brinks Security System had not been activated, as Charlotte usually does before she leaves her home.

He headed to check Joy's room first. Her cute little bed was empty and unmade. He turned on the heels of his Miu Miu shoes and pursued toward a closed door that secluded Charlotte's bedroom.

"Charlotte, are you in there?" He tapped on her door. "If you are, come on out so we can talk."

He understood that the two of them were no longer a couple, but he

61

acknowledged right then that it would be very difficult for him to see her with another man, especially like this, inside of her bedroom doing God knows what.

He continued to talk through the door. "Look, if you got company I give you my word that I won't hurt your little boyfriend. I just want to talk to you about, Joy...okay?"

He freed a concealed .45 auto from his shoulder-sling holster and pushed the door open, not knowing how far his next move will take him.

To his relief there was no man lying between the forest green lace canopy that suspended elegantly above and over the four sides of Charlotte's queen-size bed. And to his dismay, neither was she. Her bed was left in disarray.

This is not like her. What the fuck is goin' on?

Charlotte would never leave her home without making her and Joyous' bed. Since their daughter was still in the-making-her-own-bed-training, Charlotte made the chore an every morning ritual and Adon knew that.

He slid his burna back into his holster. He rushed to the bathroom and checked the soap, toothbrushes, and the bottom section of the sink's bowl. They were all bone dry. He raced to their closets and other places where they stored their cloths.

"Uggg!" Adon let out a loud grunt.

He interlocked eight of his fingers atop his head and paced up and down the floor. Their clothes were gone. Apparently, the person that was sent to fix the door was also ordered to remove their clothes.

Adon was baffled. After a while, his aimless pacing took him back to the front living room where he took notice to something that he didn't see when he initially walked into the home. It was Charlotte's Burberry scarf that he bought her last Christmas. He slowly picked it up from the hardwood floor and put it to his nose. The presence of her body scent was strong, yet pleasant. Adon immediately jumped the gun.

"She was obviously in such a rush to pack up and leave, she forgot the last thing I gave her while we was together," he was choked up and folded the expensive scarf and put it in his back pocket.

He left the house and made it to his Corvette in time to catch the caller that caused Jim Jones' "Worry About It" to emit from his cell.

"Shamrock?" Adon bellowed through the phone as he thought, *It couldn't be.*

"Try again, killa." the caller said.

"Who dis?!" Adon asked with growing frustration before realizing that his BlackBerry was programmed to Jim Jones' "Love Me No More" whenever Shamrock called, and not "Worry About It."

Man, I'm trippin', " he thought.

"Dis be , Black Magic." The caller said.

"I know. What's it do, gangsta?" Adon shut his eyes. "I can't believe this shit, Charlotte just took my daughter and up and left!"

"What?" Black Magic asked as he was caught off guard.

"Never mind Black, I was thinking out loud," Adon responded. "So wudup?"

"The faculties wanna know what's up with the picnic in August? Is e'vrythang situated? Do you need anythang? What?" Black Magic asked ready to contribute.

"Yeah, yeah." Adon paused thinking that he couldn't have caught him at a worst time. "E'vrthang is set up and under control. I still have to make the necessary arrangements with the Sims Bus Company, but not 'til the actual date gets closer. You still handlin' the security on this, so make sure all points is covered. Plus, be sure that all the females are aware of the different pit-stops for the buses. I got 'em scattered all over the state, so there's no reason why the Forest Preserve shouldn't be crawling with the finest women that Illinois has to offer. You feelin' me, B?"

"Oh hell yeah!" Black Magic responded enthusiastically. "And I heard about the surprise you got goin'. Clue yo' boy in to what's hatnin'."

"Then it won't be much of a surprise now would it."

"You a mafucka, A," Black Magic said with a chuckle.

"I know," Adon continued. "Aiight then, my nigga, I'll meet up with you tomorrow to go over the security provisions, aiight?"

"Aiight, homie."

Adon pushed the end button and called his sis.

"Wassup, bruh?" Natasha asked.

"Have you talked to Charlotte lately?" Adon asked hoping that she did.

"I've been so busy with work that I haven't had the time," she said. "The last time that I talked to Charlotte was when I dropped Joyous off after taking her to Chuck-E-Cheese, and that was three weeks ago. I haven't talk to either of them since. Wassup, is everything okay?" Natasha had great concern in her voice.

"I dunno. I stopped by her house today and they weren't there. The beds wasn't made, nor was the alarm activated. Plus, her whip is in the drive-way but their clothes is gone," Adon said. "I dunno, shit just isn't adding up.

"Well, I'm sure she and Joyous are fine. She probably went out with a friend and forgot to activate the security alarm before she left," Natasha said.

"And took e'vry piece of clothes that she own!" I'm not buying it!"

"I don't know, bruh. You know how she get's sometimes when she's upset with you. Maybe this time she took it a step further and left town to visit someone, just to make you sweat a little. Don't worry, I'm sure they'll turn up real soon."

Adon ended the call and tossed the cell onto the passenger seat. It might've been easy to be as optimistic as Natasha was had Charlotte and Joyous' clothes had still been in their closets.

He dropped his head back on the headrest and started to think back. It was funny that Natasha had mentioned that Charlotte might've left town, because now he remembered how excited she was when she got her passport approved. Charlotte's mother was the only family that she had in this country, and when she died Charlotte's dream was to return to France with her family. Adon was aware of that, but figured such a move would be in the distant future, if at all.

He grabbed his cell and called a few of her closest girlfriends. Neither of them had helpful information. He then tracked down a number for CSU. After connecting with appropriate staff, he was told that Charlotte had cancelled her summer classes.

"Damn!" he bellowed as his body began to jitter. He had forgotten to take his pill today. He took his hands and pressed them up against the sides of his head, as if to squeeze out whatever it was that was inside. Suddenly, he has another flashback of his childhood:

"After all that I've done for your ass! I took you back into my home and this is what you do!?" Macklin Cutti yelled from their bedroom while little Adon hid underneath the blankets with his hands covering his ears.

"I'm sorry, Macklin. Please forgive me! Don't do this to me," Loretta begged. "Don't separate me from my children. I am sorry for what I've done," her tears

streamed like an unforgiving rain, but Macklin had had enough. He was pushed to his limits.

"You damn right you're sorry, and those tears aren't goin' to work for your ass this time," he said, his voice breaking with emotion.

He crotched down where she sat in the corner balled up and said, "Loretta, baby, you did it to yourself. Even if I wanted to accept you back I no longer can." Macklin stood up. "Now I want you out of my house and this time it's for good," he said.

"But, baby," she reached for his crotch, "we can work this out."

"NOW!" he vibrated the walls and yanked her up from the floor.

Little four-year-old Adon was shaking scared and wondered if his sister Ta-Ta was awake in her room. He wanted to go over and see but was too frightened to move. He jerked after hearing loud slaps coming from his parents' bedroom. His mother screamed and more loud slaps followed. Little Adon trembled with fear. He peeked out from under the blanket and stared at the small opening of his door. He anticipated the second when Ta-Ta would dart inside, join him on his bed, and console him as she did every time Mama and Daddy fought. But instead, he saw the blur of his mother run pass with his father heavy on her trail.

"I want you out of here, now! I'll send your shit to you at a later time, but dammit I need you outta here before I catch a homicide!" he yelled and little Adon ran to his bedroom door.

"No, Mama," he screamed. "Don't go! Don't go, Mama! Please, Daddy...noooo!"

CHAPTER 9

Nitty resided in his library located inside of his ten thousand square feet Mediterranean home that he shared with his wife. In complete silence, he laid on his Duraplush lounger, his feet crossed with the tip of his reading glasses between his teeth. The *Chicago Sun Times* sat folded atop his mid section. There wasn't any news in there about the murders that took place at Shamrock's crib. Nitty was more than okay with that.

However, there was a printed article on three undercover FBI agents. Their suspicious disappearance went national nine months ago. According to the article, they were found early this morning floating in Lake Michigan. The news made the front page. But Nitty was okay with that as well, for it had no way of tracing its way back to him. The Convolution made sure of that so it wasn't an issue. Nitty was more engulfed by the matter at hand.

Maybe Adon did follow through with the entire mission, clean-up and all, and just slipped on Shamrock's Mercedes, he hoped.

It was either that or the bodies at Shamrock's crib hadn't been discovered.

Nitty's wife walked up to the library's threshold, unnoticed "Honey," she said, "your guest has arrived."

She snapped Nitty out of his thoughts and waited until he sat up. At her side stood a middle-aged white man clad in a cheap suit. His name was Agent Karpe.

"Thankyou, sweetheart. I will take it from here. Come on in, Karpe, and have a seat." Nitty watched as Odessa shut the mahogany door on her way out.

Agent Karpe was considered an associate of The Convolution, an independent contractor, if you will. He was their mole, there back door to the Government's Special Operations Room. It was because of him, and other lawman like him that made it possible for The Convolution to build an empire worth 2.7 billion dollars from organized crime; with not as much as a parking ticket issued to any of its members, much less trials of murder, conspiracy, racketeering, or any other charges along those lines. The Convolution wasn't quite under the radar, but was untouchable.

"What can I do for you?" Nitty asked as he poured himself a tall glass of rum and limejuice. "Would you like a glass?"

"I don't see why not." Agent Karpe had a seat. "But as for your original question, it's what I can do for you. You see, I have some info' that I'm sure you would find most beneficial to your cause."

"And what would that be?" Nitty asked with an obvious sigh and passed the drink over, hand to hand.

"Now don't be that way," Karpe said after catching notice to Nitty's annoyance. "The evening before Shamrock had *mysteriously* vanished; he received tangible, incriminating evidence that places you directly in the middle of shark-infested waters. The same waters that I'm sure I don't have to remind you of, you've tried so hard to keep under the bridge for nineteen years now."

"How in the hell did that happen!?" Nitty said and sat in his high-back leather chair.

"It was all contrived from another level of the agency. A part that the Bureau has under wraps. It's so tightly strapped down, this investigation, that I have yet to find out the identity of the new operative who's assigned to do what the last agents could not before they were found floating in the lake."

"Well what in the hell am I paying you for? Can you please remind me of that, because I forget!" Nitty said sarcastically.

"If you'll allow me to continue, I'm sure that I can enlighten you. The good news is that although Shamrock had an idea of the package's contents, he didn't even get a chance to review it, thanks to your quick thinking.

"You see, after he spat in the last agents' faces and threatened them with a lawsuit for harassment, they didn't want to take the chance of Shamrock reporting their behavior to the local authorities and screwing up their investigation, so they backed off, but not entirely.

"On the evening before his death he received an anonymous phone call, disclosing the existence of the package, a synopsis of the expected contents, and its location. The funny thing is he never got to it. Now I'm certain that I don't have to tell you that it's vital to your livelihood, as you know it, to get a hold of that evidence before somebody else does."

"And just how would I do that, Karp?"

"It's a funny thing actually, I mean really funny," Agent Karpe chuckled and slapped his thigh. "It's apparent that the verbals they tried to sell to Shamrock he didn't buy. Had he did, I'm willing to bet my retirement pension to your bucket of shit that he would have put Adon on notice. But the tangibles, oh, boy, now that's a whole different school of piranhas. And I don't mean the weak vegetarian kind."

"There isn't any such thing as a piranha that doesn't eat meat," Nitty corrected.

"Well you get my drift."

"Just get to the point right damn now, would you!"

"Okay, okay, don't get all gangster on me" Agent Karpe always did get a kick out of street slang. "Did I mention that this was the most damaging evidence of all?"

"Karp!" Nitty yelled.

"Oh, yes, I guess I did when I gave you the whole bogus piranha analysis. Where's your sense of humor? Gosh, you people are way too serious these days. Back on track now. The good news is I know where this evidence is located."

"WHERE!?"

"First let me assure you that the evidence at best is only circumstantial. Had it not been, you'll be well on your way of celebrating your 19th anniversary of incarceration behind the maximum security walls of Statesville. But I guess you don't need me to tell you that it's definitely sufficient enough to convict you in the streets. Considering how Macklin Cutti is still, 'till this day, viewed by the Gangster Disciples as Barrack Obama is by the African American race. If word gets out that you're the one who killed him, not only is it a guarantee that the Gangster Disciples will go to the ends of the earth to hunt you down, they would pull kamikaze-like stunts to get it done.

"Precisely what the last agents, and now this new operative, are aiming for. Except inducing a street-level war is not their primary task. What they're seeking is someone who is close enough to you, and even closer to Adon; which in turn, would make that person a little touchy toward the dynamics of the evidence that they are presenting. And that is the core reason they targeted Shamrock to begin with.

"As you already know, the Feds believed strongly that Shamrock's camaraderie toward Adon was far more a stronger bond than what you could have ever imposed. And after a full review of the tangible evidence, Shamrock would have had to make a choice: Either solidify his loyalty to you, or uphold the brotherly bond that he has always had with Adon; which would have made or broke their entire investigation.

"If he had done what they were banking on and chose to stand by Adon while throwing his middle finger at you, there's no doubt that he would have given the U.S. District Attorney the power to nail your balls to the wall by *indirectly* cooperating.

"As we both know, any form of cooperation schemefully solicited from Shamrock or not, would have been enough to satisfy the grand jury. That's assuming if what the Feds had speculated, in regards to successfully using Shamrock as a pun, would have panned out smoothly. But of course, a smart man like yourself, you had all of that figured out now didn't you?

"That's why you had him killed. Now what baffles me is how did you get Adon to be in accordance with Shamrock's murder, much less participate in it? Did you lie to him? That's the million dollar question."

Nitty's brows nearly touched in distaste as he sat his drink down on a coaster.

Agent Karpe quickly resumed. "Ahhh," he uttered waving his hand in front of him, "That's fine, you don't have to answer that question. I just want you to be aware that I know all of what's taking place in my jurisdiction.

"But I do and truly ponder this, and I'm just throwing this out there. How could you be so sure that Shamrock wouldn't have stood by you and said 'the fuck with Adon?' I mean he was told by the feds that you were single handedly responsible for Macklin Cutti's murder. At the very least, news of your betrayal should've been enough to bring to Adon's attention, wouldn't you say? I mean, c'mon, they're supposed to be homies, cronies, comrades, the best of buds. He should have felt obligated to, but instead he sat on that information for over forty days."

"And that surprises you?" Nitty raised his feet and planted them on his desk.

"Well, hell yes," Agent Karpe jumped at the question, "and why aren't you?"

"Because Shamrock was far from being a fool. He was intimately in tune with Adon's loyalty to me. And it's like you said, without tangible evidence there's no proof, and without proof there's no way in hell that Adon would have believed him. For Adon to even consider such a story, Shamrock would have had to come correct. To do so, he needed time and that's why *his* was mysteriously cut short."

"You and I, we've been business associates for twenty years now," Agent Karpe cut in, "and I've been in this game for a couple before that. From a beat-cop, to homicide, narcotics, and now a special agent within the DEA division. I've been around a while and I know guts when I see it. I liked Shamrock, he had balls and I admired his heart. Arguably the toughest guy on your team. The entire department knows, from his history alone, he would have never snitched or given the feds what they so desperately seek. Before they would have managed that, he would have provoked a suicide by cop or been a fugitive on the run for killing a cop."

"But they also knew that he was too inquisitive not to embark on his own investigation," Nitty shot back.

"Sure, but you have to admit, they didn't give him much of a choice. The agency is really going outside the box on this one. But if crucifying you is the ultimate reward, they clearly believe it's worth the risk. In regards to Shamrock, maybe you got rid of the wrong guy."

"I guess only time would reveal the authenticity in this lengthy assessment of yours," Nitty said while looking down at his Rolex for the time.

"Well for now I'm sure there's one issue that we could agree on," Agent Karpe said. "If that evidence somehow gets in the wrong hands, particularly Adon, the government may lose some by inciting a street level war, but you…now you would lose everything! Because I doubt very seriously that The Convolution, as great as they are, could prevent the renegades of the Gangster Disciple Nation from tearing up the city just to get to you.

"You know just as well as I, with him being their leader, the Disciples would follow Adon into a forest of fire and be proud to do it. Now there's not one doubt in my mind that you would prevail, but there's also not one doubt that in order to do so you must get your very own hands dirty. And when the massacre subsides and the smoke does clear, that dirt on your hands would be all of what the feds would need to send you straight to Levensworth with an out-date that reads DECEASED on your social face-card."

"Karpe, I'm going to ask you this one more time. Where's the fuckin' evidence?" Nitty's patience was running short.

"Now *this* is why you pay me. And brace yourself because you may find this to be quite ironic. The evidence is in the trunk of Shamrock's Mercedes Benz that I'm sure is right under the roof of your establishment, Magic Hands, as we speak."

"In the trunk!? Are you sure!?"

"Aren't I always?"

"You better be!" Nitty rose from his chair.

"Not so fast. Now before you go happy hunting, where is my money?" Agent Karpe asked as he stood up.

"76th and Cicero Street, in the parking lot of Ford City Mall. There you would find a 1983 Oldsmobile, beige in color with a license plate that reads OGY145. The key would be under the back bumper; two hundred thousand is in the trunk."

"Wait, the deal was for a quarter of a million!"

"Well, sue me."

"I'll be in touch."

"I'm sure you will."

"Calhoun, a bit of free advice," Agent Karpe said as he showed himself to the door. "If you have any loose ends that date back to the 1980's era, I suggest that you rid it because the feds are not done fishing...I assure you."

Nitty's mind's eye instantly flashed an image of Doe.

CHAPTER 10

Malcom sat in his air conditioned office about the size of a prison cell, talking meaninglessly over the business telephone.

"Yeah, baby, it's real like that, so if you truly want to reap the benefits of a millionaire's wife, then I suggest you get on my team now. You feel me?"

"But aren't you just a manager?" Lisa asked.

"I prefer to use the term, overseer. But in a year I'ma own this joint, love."

"So you sayin' that Mr. Calhoun is going to give you Magic Hands before he gives it to Adon? I mean c'mon now, everyone in the city knows that Adon is his number one man."

"But see what you and the city fail to realize, love, I'm Nitty's son."

"Correction, you is his stepson."

"Well I'm the closest thing he has to a son, and a son of his is how he sees me." Malcom was getting riled.

"Okay den big stuff, calm down. You want me to come by yo' apartment, and you want me to bring one of my girls, right?"

"Yeah, bring whats-a-name with you…the one with that traffic jam booty."

"Who Trina?"

"Yeah that's her, but I want you to know that I'm a busy man so we might not get to hook-up as soon as I'd like. But don't feel ignored, because rest assure, we will hook-up," Malcom said.

"First let me get dis straight before I commit to anythang. When we do hook-up or whateva is you sure that Adon fine ass gon' be there?"

"Oh, yeah, love, that's my friend. Hell, I'm more like his big brother. I can make one phone call and he'll jump to my beat."

"And Shamrock gon' be there, too, right?" she asked.

"You know they like eighty-eight and twelve baby. Hell yeah he's going to be there."

Malcom was lying so much that he started to believe his own lies. Let him tell it and the ménage a trios that he envisioned was in the bag, and he was definitely in mack-mode. Just when he was about to proceed further with his shenanigans, the call waiting signal interrupted his train of fabrications.

"Say, Lisa, that's my other end. It's probably my accountant or something," he lied. "But I'll call you soon with the date and time."

"Just make sure Adon and Shamrock gon' be there," she said and hung up.

"Magic Hands manager, Malcom here. How can I help you?"

"Malcom, is Shamrock's Mercedes still there?"

"Oh, hi, pops. I know what you're thinking, but no that wasn't a personal call. I was—"

"Malcom shut up!" Nitty yelled through the phone. "Now listen, this is a very important matter, so I will speak slowly so that you can comprehend what I'm asking you. Is Shamrock's Mercedes in the stall?"

"Yes, sir, it is."

"Okay," Nitty said with a sigh of relief. "Get a hold of the car keys and go to the car. Once you get there, open the trunk, and retrieve whatever papers you see. In fact, just clean out the whole fuckin' trunk and take it all into your office. Do that now."

"I'm on it."

"Malcom!"

"Sir?"

"As soon as you do that, return to this phone. I'll wait."

"I got it."

Malcom pursued his assignment in a hurried fashion, but when he arrived to the car wash's area, his facial expression bared the look of a confused and scared child. Shamrock's Mercedes Benz S600 was gone.

"Who in the hell moved the charcoal grey Mercedes without my permission!?" Malcom questioned every employee, but they all were unaware of the car's whereabouts.

He began to panic. He stood in the central part of the car wash and yelled at the top of his lungs.

"YOU MEAN TO TELL ME THAT NO ONE NOTICED A BIG SHINY ASS MERCEDES LEAVE OUT OF HERE!? I WOULD FIRE ALL OF YOU PEOPLE!"

Malcom rushed back to his office, picked up the telephone's receiver and with reluctance, he spoke.

"The car is gone, pops."

"What!?" Nitty went ballistic.

CHAPTER 11

Adon penetrated the invisible walls of Englewood, speeding through residential streets as if it were a rural area. In his thoughts, Joyous remained in heavy rotation, and he couldn't stop wondering what had to have been on Charlotte's mind when she just up and decided to take his only child away from him. And to France of all places.

Adon placed a Cigarello stuffed with 'dro between his lips. He put fire to it and took an extra long pull and instantly began to cough uncontrollably. His eyes watered quickly. The road was nothing more than a blur. He stomped on the brake pedal, and the tires howled with heat.

"Ooooh weeee, dat there is some fire!" he said, referring to the 'dro.

He used the top of his G-Unit tank top to clear his eyes. He sat back and reclined his head on the words WANT BEEF that was stitched into his head rest when...

"What the fuck!" He couldn't believe what he was seeing. It looked like Shamrock's Benz facing him on the opposite side of the two-way street. Adon stared at the tinted windows as the Benz drove right pass him.

He eased off the brake while cars behind him blew their horns in frustration. He nudged his steering wheel slightly to the right then cut it hard to the left with the pedal to the floor. He made an impressive U-turn, spinning the high-performance Corvette into the Mercedes' direction.

Divine caught notice of the Corvette following her. She remained calm. However, her knuckles were white from gripping the steering wheel hard with both hands.

"Maybe it's nothing," she told herself while constantly darting her eyes to the rearview mirror. "Maybe it's just a regular citizen who realized they were going in the wrong direction and decided to make an illegal U-turn to save some time."

Seven car lengths behind, Adon removed his seatbelt and reached under his seat for the switch that split the back of the passenger seat down the middle. It was an electronic stash spot. Inside was a fully automatic M5.

Divine started to get nervous. After making three random turns, the Corvette, however back, was still on her trail.

"Shit, shit, shit," she rambled and made a left turn on a busy intersection.

Thirty seconds later the Vette made the same turn.

"Who is this person?" Divine was now beyond nervous. She saw a side street ahead and went for it. She kept her eyes on the rearview mirror as she sped forward, anticipating the Corvette's next turn. Instead, she watched as the Corvette drove by the intersection.

"Good, God," she said and just like that her fear was alleviated. She slowed the Benz's speed and reached for her Dior handbag. She moved her .38 Special aside and pulled out her cell, tossing the bag back onto the empty seat. She looked down briefly to dial numbers and put the cell to her ear when she got the surprise of her lifetime.

"Oh Shit!"

The Corvette was idled in the middle of an intersection just ahead. Balanced halfway outside the opened window was Adon with his weapon aimed directly at the Benz.

Divine stomped on the breaks, as the armor-piercing slugs from the M5 tore through the front end and hood of the Benz. Divine ducked and quickly put the gear in reverse and stomped on the gas. The power from the V-12 nearly threw her under the dashboard as she zigzagged backwards, bouncing off parked cars.

Adon wouldn't let up. His rapid fire totaled the windshield, ripped through the seats, and exited the back end of the car. He missed Divine by inches. She managed to get the Benz to the next corner and make a wild 180 degree turn. The Benz came to an awkward stop. But that was the least of Divine's worries. She put the gear in drive and stomped hard on the gas as more shots from the M5 rang out.

Adon got back behind the wheel and tossed the sizzling burna on the passenger seat. He tore ass up the one-way street. He was determined to catch up with the Benz.

Divine drove at high speeds up the side street. The Benz looked like a stunt car in the distance as sparks flew under the frame from jumping uneven portions of the bumpy road. She needed her .38 and glanced down at the passenger seat after feeling for her handbag. It was nowhere in sight.

Adon reached the next corner in a flash and whipped the bend with finesse. "I see you muthafucka!"

The Benz was now in sight. Ahead, an unsuspecting Chrysler was easing out of a driveway. Adon floored it, hitting the Chrysler barely and sending it in a violent spin. The Corvette took the bruise and roared with horsepower for the next half mile while the Benz's V-12 was being pushed to its limits.

A text queen teenager driving a small Neon was oblivious to the Mercedes that sped pass as she approached an empty intersection. With her iPhone in hand, the young girl didn't bother to look both ways before she crossed the intersection and made a left turn. Not exactly a good driving habit. When she finally looked up she pissed her pants. All she saw was something wide, low to the ground with a damaged eye, coming straight at her like a raging bull!

"Oh, no! This can't be happenin!" She shut her frightful eyes. "Please don't let dis be happenin'? I just got my license, and my mother is going to kill me! "

From Adon's perspective what he saw in front of him was a hectic dilemma indeed, but he couldn't stop. Not now! He couldn't bring himself to. Even if it was impossible to squeeze through the parked cars and the Neon, he had to attempt it. By all means he had to catch that Mercedes and whoever was in it.

"Ride or die!" Adon hollered and stomped on the gas.

The young girl opened her eyes and panicked! The Corvette was closing in too fast, faster than she could think. She hurriedly released her seatbelt, and threw herself in the back seat. Adon zoomed between the cars like a lightening bolt, sparks flew from either side, scarring the Vette from front to back.

After Adon found himself on the other end, he discovered the Mercedes was nowhere in sight.

"SHIT!" He continued to eat up the street at one hundred miles per hour while both of his side view mirrors laid spinning in the street.

"Fuck! How could I've forgotten about the Benz!?" he yelled to himself. "I gotta find it and get rid of it before Nitty finds out about it. Fuck! Fuck! Fuck!" He pounded the dashboard.

CHAPTER 12

"Are you sure we can afford to trust, Karp?" Casey asked over his Bluetooth as he drove a Maserati Quattroporte down Lake Shore Drive. "I mean you have to admit, sooner or later he's gonna catch some heat from his own people, and he'll be making all sorts of deals to save his own hind."

"Under these circumstances I cannot afford not to," Nitty responded. "If what Karp says is true then it will put us ahead two steps. And to be honest with you old friend, I'm inclined to believe him. Karpe knows not to fuck with me."

"Just don't forget how he helped to cross Macklin Cutti nineteen years ago," Casey reminded.

"I've dealt with this creep long enough to know what he's thinking before he does. So before it gets to that point he'll be floating be floating in the river, trust me," Nitty assured.

"You know I do," Casey reassured.

"Now the primary task that we have at this point is Shamrock's Mercedes. By any means, find it! And by all means keep Adon in the dark on this whole Doe thing," Nitty said. "So do you have a lead on Doe?"

"I'm all over it, boss."

"Well get it done."

Doe sat on a worn out milk crate inside of his hole-in-the-wall efficiency apartment. It was nothing more than a shit-can that the state provided for ex-cons who had no other place to go upon their release. It wasn't quite what Doe envisioned for himself as a free man. He was living better in the joint. He put his head in his palms. His thoughts raced. There was so much to do with so little time. He needed personal protection, money, a vehicle, and above all he needed to get to Adon and somehow convince him to listen.

He wondered if he made a mistake by showing up at Magic Hands. He only went because after asking a few strangers where he could find Adon, fingers pointed in that direction. They failed to mention that he might encounter Nitty there, let alone that Nitty owned the place. Then again, he didn't ask them neither. Doe signed his own death certificate with his presence alone.

He needed somewhere to think. A place that was open, peaceful, and had fresh air to breathe. His apartment wasn't helping. It reminded him too much of the cell he had left behind. Too closed in with little air circulation. The only upside to this raunchy location was that it was low-key and in the poorest section of the west side.

"No one would ever look for me here," he said, trying to find some solace in his situation. Suddenly, the hairs on the back of his neck stood up. He got on his feet and peeked out of the two-day-old newspaper that covered his filthy window. He noticed something unusual.

"I never seen that type of car around here," Doe said to himself.

He could smell the tension in the air. It was a reliable trait that he learned in the joint and responsible for saving his life more than once. He felt, strongly, that something was out of the ordinary. He eyeballed the fancy car that was parked across the street and sat tight.

Casey, clad in a Georgio Armani three-piece suit, quietly entered the poorly managed building. In his hand was a .9mm Berretta, equipped with a silencer.

His body was positioned sideways, causing the back of his Armani suit jacket to scrape slightly against the wall with every stair that he climbed. He was sure that Doe was in his apartment. His contacts told him so. Furthermore, he knew there was only one way out and he was looking right at apartment 4D.

Casey was only three stairs shy of Doe's front door when he heard clamor coming from above. A drunken man came blundering down the upper flight of stairs, stopping at Casey's ostrich skin shoes. Casey lowered his gun and shielded it from the drunken man's view. He stood to his feet smelling of urine and fresh feces, with a raggedy overcoat draped around his disgusting structure called a body.

81

"Can you borrow an old man some change?" The drunken man asked and approached Casey so close that he could have stolen a kiss. His breath was foul and reeked of lethal fumes of hard whiskey.

Casey grabbed the side of the man's face and pushed him down the remaining flight of stairs.

"Dumb fuck!" Casey mumbled and proceeded up the stairs.

The man went flying face first. His chin caught the brunt of each stair down to the last. He quickly jumped to his feet unshaken and upped an antique rifle at Casey's wide back.

"Dis here is a stick-up and don't make it a ambulance pick-up, you sonvabitch!" The man said and spat out a tooth.

Casey smiled at the apparent setup. The whole drunken man act was classic. And it only pissed him off more.

"Reach fo' da sky, fancy suit!" The man ordered Casey to put his hands above his head.

While keeping his back to the man, Casey slowly began to lift his right arm while simultaneously elevating his left hand, pointing the Beretta's nose against the inside of his Armani suit jacket.

In silence, two dum-dum slugs ripped through the man's chest and heart. He crashed against an occupant's door and fell asleep permanently. Casey didn't bother to look back and confirm a direct hit, he was confident; instead, he kicked Doe's door off of its hinges and stormed in. The small apartment was empty. The newspaper curtain was torn and hung barely from a piece of duck tape along the windowsill. The filthy window was wide opened. Doe had escaped through the fire escape.

"Goddammit!" Casey was pissed.

CHAPTER 13

A don woke up feeling like his old self again. Besides being a bit jittery, upping his dosage was proving to be the answer to his mental troubles. Last night was his first sound sleep in a minute. No dreams, no nightmares. He left his Sybris suite with both his cell and two-way turned on. He was ready to do business.

Still in his bruised-up Vette, Adon pulled at the traffic light on 71st and Ashland Street. A root beer-colored Ford Excursion sitting on twenty-eight inch D'vinci rims pulled in behind him, shaking the entire Corvette with the live concert that was custom built inside of it. Adon was very familiar with the driver. The streets referred to him as Cigar.

Adon let his window down and signaled Cigar to pull up beside him, while he held up traffic.

"Holla at me," Adon said after Cigar drove up and muted his thump.

"Whut goin' on, fam?" Cigar rested his arm on the steering wheel.

"I'm finna pull over across the street at Rainbow's. Follow me over," Adon instructed. Rainbow's was the hood's favorite restaurant and where most of the junkies hung out. Adon pulled into the lot and parked, Cigar followed suit. He climbed out of the Vette and got into the Excursion.

"Talk to me," Adon said rubbing his hands together like they were itching for cash.

"Man, fam, yo' boy need to re-up like yesterday, fam. I been tryin' to contact Shamrock but dat nigga must be face deep in sume pussy, fam. He won't answer his phones or return my messages. Whut? Ya'll ain't fuckin' wit cha boy no mo'?"

"Naw it ain't like dat, cuz. Why didn't you just get up wit' me?" Adon asked.

"Fam, you already know yo number is under the unlisted-hood list act. Plus Shamrock has always been the go to man. Steppin' to you would've felt like violatin', fam. E'vrybody know you deal wit' one man and one man only, Shamrock."

"What cha tryin' to get cuz?" Adon was prepared to do business.

"How much you gon tax me fo' five of dem thangs?" Cigar asked.

"For you, cuz…give me eighty stacks and we can call it even."

"Cool, I got dat wit' me," Cigar said and pointed to the opened gym bag behind him. "Dayuum, fam, whut happened to da sexy Vette!?" he asked after looking over Adon's shoulder. "Look like you tried to squeeze through a gangway or sumthin'."

"Ain't nothin' insurance won't cover, but one thangs fo' sho, my nigga."

"Whut's dat fam?" Cigar asked

"I need to park that bitch, 'cause she hot," Adon said looking around."

"Hot?" Cigar wanted to know details

"On fire, cuz," Adon said cutting it short. He visually scanned the immediate area, and spotted one of the youngens from the hood aspiring to be him.

"Ay, Lil One c'mere!" he shouted out the Excursion's window. Shorty came running to the shiny truck. "Ay, lil homie, you wanna make some money?"

"Fo' sho' Adon, dat's what I'm out here fo'!" Lil One said excitedly.

"You know how to drive right?" Adon asked and reached into his pants pocket.

"Fo' sho," Lil' One looked at him strange as if that was a stupid question.

"Aiight, here." Adon gave the boy a big face hundred-dollar bill and the keys to the Corvette. "Drive that Vette over to 73rd and Woods. Park it and give the keys to a nigga name Black Magic. Aiight?"

"Oh, yeah, I know Black Magic," Lil' One responded.

"Tell him I'll be there in a minute, and Lil' One," Adon pulled the boy closer to the truck by his shirt. "there's some heat in there, so no joy ridin'. Aiight?"

"Aiight," Lil' One answered disappointingly and charged at the opportunity to drive one of Adon's known cars. He got in, started it up, and just before he pulled into traffic, Adon yelled out to him.

"Ay, lil nigga, don't tear my shit up!"

"It's already tore up!" Lil' One yelled back and drove off. Both Adon and Cigar laughed.

"But check it," Adon turned to Cigar on a more serious note. "Until I tell you different just come straight to me. Ain't no need to holla at Shamrock, aiight."

"Is everything cool, Adon?" he asked, being nosy.

"Yeah, he'll be outta town on business for a while, that's all. You know how that fool love to travel," Adon revealed a false smile.

"Oh yeah, he'll be doin' alot of trickin' in da process too!" Cigar said, describing Shamrock's personality.

"You know that's right," Adon continued. "Let's go get dem bricks, my nigga."

After Adon went to another location to fill Cigar's re-up order, the two of them got in route to one of the most poppin' trap spots in the state, and number one in Englewood. A block that he proudly called his own. He supplied this area with kilos of cocaine daily, only to be broken down and sold one-tenth at a time. Due to the Houdini he pulled, he was sure that the spot was dry and his niggas were hungry. 73rd and Wood was the street's name, better known as Murda Park, a place where the Notorious Gangster Disciples dwelled; known to the city as Adon's million dollar spot, and the security was heavy.

"Pull over right here, Cigar," Adon said after spotting his lieutenant, Black Magic.

Black Magic saw Adon in the passenger seat and met them at the curb as the Excursion rolled up. "What it do, stranger," he said referring to Adon being MIA for the past couple of weeks.

"Let's jus' say it's good to be back around," Adon said and the two of them shook hands. "So how we lookin'?"

"Man, A, we dry as a bone." Black Magic paused to put his fingers in his mouth and whistled, as one of the workers caught notice and got in motion. "I wasn't expectin' you to do any pick-ups so I been callin' yo' right hand, Shamrock."

"Don't feel bad, fam," Cigar cut-in from the driver seat. "Shamrock haven't returned nobody's calls."

"Here go dat paper," Black Magic said as the worker that he whistled to earlier approached with a Hefty Glad bag filled with cash.

"How much?" Adon asked sizing up the plastic bag.

"420," Black Magic answered, looking around and checking the surroundings. Black Magic was responsible for the smooth running of Murda Park. Therefore, it was necessary that he stayed on point 24/7.

"That sound 'bout right," Adon commented and took a visual account of how the security members were spread throughout the block. They were posted on the roofs of houses, back and front porches, and just off each corner. And they were all packing serious burnas.

"Oh, yeah," Black Magic started as a thought came to mind. "Lil' One dropped yo' whip off. By the looks of it I figured it was hot so I put it up and stashed the burna."

"That's a good look," Adon voiced his gratitude. "Where's that lil' bastard at anyway?"

"I' on't know, A, I ain't seen him 'round here since then," Black Magic said. "Speakin' of whips, I'ma need one for a minute, and a burna too," Adon informed.

"You can hold one of mine," Black Magic pointed to his '96 Impala SS. It was factory stock and as clean as a spit shined boot.

"That'll work," Adon said and looked over at the worker whose arm was about ready to fall off from the weight of the moneybag. "My bad, homie, you can put that in the trunk of that SS over there, and take this one too," he said. Through the window, Adon passed him the eighty-stack gym bag that he got from Cigar. Adon got out of the truck and turned to Cigar. "Preciate the ride, cuz. Get up wit' me when you ready, aiight?"

"Aiight," Cigar said and took off, poundin' the streets and knockin' people's pictures off the wall in the process.

Adon and Black Magic started toward the SS when Adon took this time to thank him in depth. "Good lookin' on holdin' down the fort while me and Shamrock both been MIA," he said and the worker walked the SS keys to him. "As a token of my appreciation, I'm givin' you the Vette. And don't worry about spendin' yo' hard earned cash gettin' the body repaired, my insurance will handle that. As soon as that's done we can transfer the title."

"Dat's what I'm talkin' 'bout!" Black Magic said blissfully. "Good lookin', my nig." They both gave a thug hug and Black Magic nonchalantly handed him a Glock .40 and two clips. Adon put the 40 in his back waistband and clips in his front pocket before he got into the SS.

"And don't trip, I'ma get that work to you," Adon said. "So tell the clientele not to worry, dis bitch will be flooded in no time. And we still gotta go over the security provisions for the picnic, 'cause it's definitely gon' have to be tight…secret service style." He started the engine and gave Black Magic a handshake when he heard commotion. The both of them darted their eyes in the same direction.

"On dat car! On dat car!" one of the security members yelled from the rooftop and opened fire on a conversion van known for Vice Lord drive-bys. Almost simultaneously, the van's doors slid opened. Three men with bandana-covered faces revealed their gun-filled hands and returned fire. The two who sat up front started squeezing off rounds in Adon and Chief's direction.

"Get down, Adon!" Black Magic bellowed and began to open fire with two .44s.

Adon dove on the seat, reached for the passenger door handle and came out on the other side of the SS letting the .40 go. He joined Black Magic in battle as another threatening vehicle approached from the back. Adon turned on the balls of his feet and got right at them. He gunned the windshield as they shot back aimlessly with Tec .9s. Adon didn't flinch. He quickly released the empty clip with his thumb, slid a full one in and resumed squeezing as he walked toward the vehicle undaunted. The passenger was slumped. And the driver began to regret his decision for picking Murda Park to buck shots at today. Now it was too late. At this point he knew that surrendering quietly wasn't an option. He raised his burna behind the smashed windshield and let off two wild rounds before Adon's deadly *one* split his cranium. It was over for him, he slouched over in his seat as the vehicle slowly rolled on top of the curb before coming to a stop. When the smoke cleared, Adon turned around as the conversion van peeled off into the distance.

"Black, you aiight?"

Black Magic walked out into the middle of the street where Adon was standing with two smoking .44s still visible in his fists. "I'm good, A," he said. He put one of the burnas in his waist and started to whistle and call out nicknames, checking on the rest of the crew.

Adon continued to scan the area for any signs of threats when he saw a body sprawled on the pavement.

"Who is that?" he asked rhetorically and crossed the street to get a better view. He clutched onto the .40 as he approached and was caught off guard with what he saw.

"Lil' One!" Adon shouted and ran to where Lil' One laid. Adon kneeled on his knees, looking at Lil' One's blood drenched shirt. He put his face close to his and felt him breathing, barely.

"Black get the car!" Adon yelled and watched Black sprint to the SS that was left idled. Adon held Lil' One's head in his arms. "It's gon' be aiight lil' man just hold on, be strong," he said as Black Magic pulled to the curb and swung the door opened.

Adon picked Lil' One up with ease and climbed into the back seat with him.

"Drive dis muthafucka, Quick!" Adon exclaimed. The force from the abrupt take-off caused the door to close on its own.

"Is he alive?" Black Magic asked never taking his eyes off the road.

"Yeah, but we gotta get'em to a hospital quick," Adon pulled up Lil' One's shirt. There was so much blood that he couldn't tell where it was coming from.

"Try to stop da bleedin'," Black Magic suggested.

"I can't find the fuckin' wound, there's no way of tellin' where he was hit!" Adon looked into Lil' One's sleepy eyes. "Dat's aiight though, my lil' homie a warrior! It's nothing'! He gon' make it through dis," Adon encouraged and watched Lil' One's eyes get weaker. "Don't you fall asleep on me, lil' nigga," he said looking down at Lil' One who lay on his lap. "You hear me? Don't fall asleep! Keep yo' eyes on me!" he yelled as Lil' One went in and out of consciousness.

"I'm tired, big homie," Lil' One spoke.

"I know, I'm tired too, but we can't go to sleep lil' homie. Not now! We got work to do." Adon said trying to keep him alert. "We got the picnic comin' up-n-shit. I know you wasn't lookin' forward to goin' cause you too young, but don't even trip on the age thang. I'ma pull a string or two and get you in there. You know I can, right? I'ma even let you roll wit' me to the picnic in style, so you can see how da big dawgs do."

"Adon," Lil' One uttered his eyes barely opened, "before school ended for summer break, my teacher asked me what did I wanna be when I grow up. You wanna know what I said?"

"What's that, lil' homie?" Adon asked, happy that he was alert and talking.

"I said I wanna be just like Adon Cutti."

Adon looked away as if Lil' One's words were too hard to bear. "Listen to me Lil' One," Adon said and looked down into Lil' One's half-shut eyes. "You don't wanna be like me, aiight. You wanna be betta than me, betta than the hood, betta than this gang bangin' bullshit! You hear me? I don't ever wanna hear you say that again. When you go back to school in September I want you to tell yo' teacher that you want out da hood."

Black Magic pulled wildly into the hospital's ER parking lot. "Where we gon' drop him?" he asked and brought the SS to a stop.

"Drop him!?" Adon said with a grimace that was as serious as Lil' One's condition.

"I'm just sayin'," Black Magic reasoned. "You know we can't go in."

Black Magic had a point. Adon came to his senses and looked along the entrance of the hospital. He spotted a white man clad in a blue jumpsuit and hairnet. "Drive down on him," he pointed.

Black Magic leaned on the gas and pulled up right along side of him.

"Are you a doctor?" Adon asked the man as he started to get out

89

of the car.

"No sir, I'm just a RN," he said and threw down his cigarette before stomping on it.

"Look, can you help us? My friend was—"

"Oh, boy," the RN blurted after seeing Lil' One as Adon carried him out the whip. "Come, we must hurry!" he said.

"I can't go with you," Adon said in a depressing tone. "Here, you take 'em." He carefully placed Lil' One in the man's arms. He looked the RN square in his eyes and said, "Please, take care of him."

"We'll do the best we can, sir."

Adon reached for the RN's front shirt pocket and filled it with ten crispy one hundred dollar bills. "You never saw me here tonight, aiight?"

The RN nodded his head and ran for the ER's entrance with Lil' One held tightly in his grip.

CHAPTER 14

"Yes hello?" Divine said into the phone.

"Whut it do, Divine?"

"I guess it's doing. Who is this?" Divine asked, not recognizing the voice.

"Dis is Cigar. Let me holla at Shamrock."

He was alive and well. Shakey Shawn never had the chance to pull his trigger. Shamrock owed his life to Divine. It was the sound of her gun that turned the tables on Shakey Shawn. They fled the scene, leaving the four dead bodies behind.

"Just a minute."

Divine, in her birthday suit, followed the fresh rose petals through the living room and up the stairs where she joined Shamrock. He was still nursing his wounds.

Wherever he laid his head it was a must that there was a whirlpool on the premises, and his current refuge held no exception. The two of them were currently inside of his low-key, plush townhouse in Oak Park, Illinois, a Westside suburb. Divine stepped inside of the bubbling waters, crotched down in front of him, and gently grabbed a hand full of his dick. Shamrock displayed a half grin with a stuffed Dutch Master between his teeth and a glass of Hennessy mixed with a little Hpnotiq in his hand. He cradled the remote to a 40-inch LG flat screen in his other.

With seduction, she looked into Shamrock's eyes and with her free finger lightly traced the wound on his chest that she helped remove a bullet from. In a light whisper she mouthed the name, "Cigar," forming both syllables slowly with her vibrating tongue ring exposed for his visual pleasure. She freed his hand of the Hennessy-Hpnotiq mix and passed him the phone. She took a sip and massaged his tool.

"What's hatnin'?" Shamrock asked into the phone.

"Ay, fam, I just left da nigga, Adon," Cigar reported.

"I see the Vice Lords came through Murda Park and got wet da fuck up!" Shamrock said ecstatic, ignoring Cigar's last statement.

"Oh, yeah," Cigar said not knowing. "Dey must've came through afta I left, fam." Cigar paused for a second and asked, "How would you know about dat anyway, fam?"

"You dumb mafucka, it's was on the 12 o'clock news. Don't choo follow da news, nigga?"

"Nope," Cigar said simply.

"See, that's what's wrong wit' da world now. Mafuckas like you don't even know what's goin' on within it. Yo' dumb ass probably don't even vote, do you?" Shamrock asked and took another deep pull from the cush.

"Nope, but I wear Barrack Obama T-shirts-n-shit, fam," Cigar shot back confident that he was doing his part.

"Whateva," Shamrock said. "Did you get those bricks?"

"Yeah, fam, I got five of 'em. And just so you know, fam, dat nigga telling people you outta town on bidness. He carrying on like you not gonna surface, like you really dead, fam," Cigar informed.

"That's 'cause I am dead to him and that bet not change. You understand," Shamrock said sternly.

"Yo' secret is safe wit' me, fam."

"Now make sure you report back to me wit' that fetti once you off dem bricks. And you bet not come short," Shamrock warned as if the kilos were bought with his own money and not Cigar's.

"I got cha," Cigar said fully aware that he was being extorted, but didn't have the balls to challenge Shamrock.

CHAPTER 15

After parking the Lincoln on Lake Street and Central Park, Mick and Mario walked up the block that led to the apartment complex where they were holding both Charlotte and Joy. "Man, I'm not feelin' dis shit," Mario blurted with his head angled down.

"You not feelin' what?" Mick asked in his heavy deep voice and looked over at Mario.

"Being left in da dark on shit," Mario continued. "Like yesterday, Killa Mike sends us all da way downtown to Magic Hands and fo' what!? To see what Nitty is up to? Fuck, he's da mark dat we should've kidnapped."

"Wouldn't that be da ultimate payday," Mick added.

"Dat's what I'm sayin'," Mario said as he looked up for the first time since they left the car.

"I hear what you sayin'-n-all, but you know Killa Mike is takin' orders too," Mick tried to rationalize.

"Yeah, but I don't see him rippin' and runnin' like he got us doin'. All he wanna do is sit under dat bitch Charlotte and smell pussy all day, 'cause he damn sho' ain't takin' it!" Mario argued.

"Of course he's not. Listen to you," Mick said with a frown. "That's not what we're in bidness of doin'."

"Then what is we doin, huh? Tell me dat?" Mario asked and when Mick couldn't come up with a competent answer he continued. "Exactly what I was talkin' 'bout. We in da dark. All I'm sayin' is when dat bitch Mystery calls, barkin' orders at him, he sends us on da goose chase. And speakin' of Mystery, who in da fuck is she anyways!?"

"I dont know," Mick shrugged his huge shoulders. "She's a mystery."

The two of them approached the side entrance of the building when Killa Mike caught notice through a secret window. With his compact Chopper at his side he opened the old heavy wooden door and watched Mick and Mario climb down the descending steps that led to the basement apartment. Once they were in, Killa Mike peeked beyond the threshold one last time to check for any uninvited followers, and secured the door.

"I thought I told ya'll to go to Micky Ds," Killa Mike said after noticing a bag of Burger King in Mario's hand.

"Man, McDonalds is ten miles away. Burger King is much closer," Mario said defiantly.

"Who in da hell do you think you raising your voice to first of all?" Killa Mike clenched his teeth and clutched onto his Chopper.

Mario bit his tongue and said, "Nobody."

"I didn't think so," Killa Mike laid the Chopper on a worn-out recliner. "For the pass two plus weeks the little girl inside that room will not eat anything other than Micky Ds, muthafucka, and you know dat shit," Killa Mike grabbed the bag of Burger King and threw it at Mario's chest. "Now go take yo' ass to Micky Ds like I told you."

Mario held the bag at his chest with both arms, fuming. He brought the bag down to his side and without saying a word he left out the door.

"And hurry up back, nigga!" Killa Mike snarled loudly.

"Whaddup Killa, you seem a lil' tense," Mick said and flopped on the couch.

"Mystery is on her way here to check thangs out. And I can't have that little girl cryin' through the door about how hungry she is, because she's been doin' it all day. And if Mystery hear dat shit she'll think that I'm not feedin' the lil' brat. Like I told you before, she don't want any harm brought to the either of them," Killa Mike explained.

"Well, I wish you would've told me dat before I hit Charlotte," Mick said, referring to day one.

"Jus don't let it happen again," Killa Mike warned.

Charlotte put her ear to the locked door in an attempt to listen to what her kidnappers were discussing. Their words were, for the most part, muffled sounds. But she manage to make out the word "Mystery" and how she doesn't want harmed to come to them.

Why? Charlotte wondered.

How could a person, any person, be so cruel as to kidnap another and be compassionate about them at the same time? She left the door and walked over to Joyous, who sat in a corner. They sat and cuddled.

CHAPTER 16

"This is Celebrities, Vanity speaking, can I help you?" she said into the phone.

"Is Mystery, I mean, is Natasha around?" Killa Mike asked, tripping over his words.

"Come again?" Vanity said.

"Natasha, da owner, is she there?" Killa Mike asked nervously. Nearly slipping up and revealing that it was Adon's sister who arranged Joyous and Charlotte to be kidnapped.

"Please hold," Vanity said and looked around at the loud talkative women that flooded the salon. "Ya'll need to lower it down. I can barely answer the phone," she said in between smacking her chewing gum. She got up from the front desk to look for Natasha and spotted her over by one of the chairs training one of the new girls with a client's perm. The women close by rolled their eyes as she walked along. "Jealous Chicago hos," she said under her breath while swaying her hips as she strutted.

"Tash, you have a phone call." Vanity walked up.

"Who is it?" Natasha asked while tending to the client.

"Oh, you know what? I forgot to ask," Vanity admitted. "I'm sorry, girl, you know I'm new at this. I'll go back and ask," she said pointing to the front desk.

"No that's fine, I'll take it in my office in just a second." she said without looking up.

"Are you sure, 'cause—" Vanity felt guilty.

"No it's fine really," Natasha reassured and looked up. "You good, girl." Vanity turned on her heels and started back for the front desk when Natasha said, "Thank you V." She was very appreciative that Vanity came in to help her out on this busy Saturday afternoon. She managed to take her eyes away from the client's hair long enough to shoot Vanity a smile.

Vanity smiled back, "It's not a problem at all." She figured that helping was the least she could do. Considering she practically fell out of the sky and landed on Natasha's doorstep, and been living in her house every since.

Natasha made it to her office and closed the door behind her. "This is Natasha speaking," she said into the phone and sat behind her desk.

"Wassup, baby."

"Baby? Who in the hell is this?" Natasha asked irritably.

"Dis, Killa."

"Mike!" Natasha started, then abruptly stopped as she realized she was a little loud. She reclaimed her bearing and put the phone back to her ear. "Let's get one thing straight right now," she said, "you're never to call me at my work. What in the fuck are you thinking? You know what, don't answer that question. Apparently this must be urgent. So what is it?"

"Well, I won't necessarily say that it's urgent or nuttin' like that," Killa Mike said. "You said that you was droppin' by to check on thangs so I was wonderin' what da hold up was."

"Are the girls fine?" she asked.

"Yeah."

"Are you feeding them and getting Joyous McDonalds like she likes?"

"Yep."

"Are you allowing them to shower and—"

"They're good, trust me," Killa Mike assured. "How much more longer is dis gonna go on? When are you gonna make yo' move?"

"Have you and your men been keeping up with his daily routes and routines?" Natasha asked.

"Yeah, he has brunch daily at this lil' spot downtown called Damien's with three of the same dudes daily, one of them is a white man. He also stops in Magic Hands every three days at around 12:45 P.M. Plus he visit three different Chase Banks once a week, and he frequents this heavily secure building in Chinatown on Sundays at 5o'clock," Killa Mike reported. "And he keeps security with him at all times."

"Good work. Nitty's days are numbered. Just hang tight," Natasha continued. "Listen and listen very closely. Don't you ever, *ever*, call my place of business again under no circumstances. If you need to contact me then use the number that I gave you. And I'll get there when I get there. Are we clear?"

"Crystal."

"What time did you say he usually goes to the building in Chinatown?" she asked

"5o'clock," Killa Mike repeated.

"Well, don't you think you need to get there to confirm his routine?"

"Yeah, you right."

"For now on, I want you to keep a close eye on Nitty, personally. This means that I want you out there in the field. I've come too far and too close for shit to get fucked up now. I don't know them dudes that you got working with you," Natasha said. "Another thing…don't ever call me *baby*."

Vanity sat at the front desk answering phones, listening to gossip, and scanning through the newest issue of *Essence* magazine while she learned more and more of how Chi-Town women got down. She halted the fanning motion of the pages and focused on a picture of Beyonce and Jay Z.

"They're a cute couple," she acknowledged to herself, and started to fantasize of her and Adon posing for a page or two of their own, as a couple.

Although he was four years younger, Vanity didn't mind at all. Before him she would've never entertained the thought of messing around with a guy her own age, much less a twenty-three year old. No matter how much money he had or how good he looked. She found it to be less dramatic and more stimulating to fuck with a man at least five years her senior.

But there was something to Adon, besides his love-making, that she couldn't shake. Even though weeks had passed since their first encounter, she still couldn't stop thinking about him. He had swagger for days and definitely not your ordinary twenty-three year old. He was rough around the edges, but possessed a caring heart, thoughtful ways, and other such qualities that would most accurately describe his style to be that of a thuggish gentleman. She had an instant attraction to Adon, even in the drunken-state that she first saw him in.

She knew about the situation between him and Charlotte. How after deciding that, together, they had no future, he still gave her the security of owning a home, furniture and all. Vanity was won over. She figured the two of them probably broke up because Charlotte just wasn't enough woman for him. She was young, his age, but he was ahead of his time. She couldn't fathom that a twenty-three year old girl could possibly retain the capabilities of being on his level: Blowing his mind and his dick simultaneously. To the point where his toes spoke sign language while riding him reverse cowgirl style until he tapped out. And still be *all* that he needed at the end of the day.

In her heart she just had to have Adon. Even more so, now that she knew all of these Chicago *hos* were checkin' for him. Looking over her left shoulder, she saw Fatima finishing the last french braid on her male client's head. She casually walked over while dude was getting up from the chair.

He looked Vanity up and down, licked his lips, and proceeded to speak. "What's up sexy?"

Vanity shot him a discouraging glance and kept it moving. He turned and with his eyes he followed her ass until she spun around and stood beside Fatima. He approached her.

"Say, shawty don't be like dat." He reached inside his collar and pulled out a thirty inch platinum chain with a phat ass diamond encrusted medallion that read Vic.

"Dey call me Vic. Can a nigga get just a small fraction of yo' time?"

She rolled her eyes and attempted to walk away when he grabbed her hand.

"Look I don't mean no disrespect or anything, but you don't know me and this ain't that type of party. So please, don't touch me again!" Vanity stressed and yanked her hand back.

"Okay," he said and began to take slow backward steps with his hands up, chest level, as if Vanity was a hot stove and he didn't want to get burnt. "I guess I'll just catch you anotha time shawty." He turned on his heels and bounced.

"Girl is you crazy!?" Fatima asked.

"Why you say that?" Vanity was confused.

"Blowin' dat nigga off like dat."

"Girl, he is *not* my type."

"Yo' type? Bitch you betta chill wit' dat bougie shit. Dat nigga holdin' plenty of cock-suckin' cash," Fatima said rolling her neck.

"And?" Vanity asked not caring how much money he had.

"And he drop money on a pretty face like it's hot!" Fatima dropped her ass to the floor and came back up. "The nigga name is Vic, girl, and believe me it represents more than just his name. You feel me?"

"I'm sure if I don't, you're going to make me," Vanity already picked up on Fatima's character.

"I charged him a hundred dollars to put six braids in his head goin' straight to the back, nothin fancy. And he dropped me three hundred like it was nothin'," Fatima proudly stated.

"Um, okay, whupy-doo," Vanity said sarcastically while thinking, *Bitch, what the fuck is three hundred dollars gon' do?*

"Girl, I tell you one thang. You Seattle hos is slow." Fatima continued to drop game. "Look, you see the shampoo girl over there?"

"Yeah, the one that's always kissing Tasha's ass."

"Oh, snap," Fatima put her closed hand to her mouth. "You noticed dat too huh? Damn and you ain't even been here dat long. I guess you ain't dat slow. Anyway, dat nigga Vic offered dat bitch a brand new Lincoln Navigator just to spend da weekend wit' him."

"And she did it?" Vanity asked with her nose turned up.

"Hell yeah she did, and dat pretty muthafucka is parked right outside. Don't get me wrong, she's a cute girl, but she ain't got nothin' on you and dat's why I know you can make dat nigga yo' 'Vic-tim.' You catch my drift?"

"Are you hitting on me Fatima?" Vanity asked with a smile.

"Bitch, please, I'm strictly dickly don't get it twisted up in here."

"How often does Adon come here? Does he get his hair cut often?" Vanity inquired.

"Adon?" Fatima said adjusting to the swift change in subjects.

"Adon don't come here to get chopped. The place he goes to is called Raekwon's, an exclusive barber not too far from here. But he'll fall through here every other day or so just to check on his sis," Fatima smiled." Dat nigga be lookin' out too. A bitch can't take advantage of his ass though, cause da first sign of you tryin' to get over and—"

"What? He'll beat a bitch down?" Vanity asked, hoping that wasn't what she was going to say.

"Who Adon? Girl, naw. He don't hit women. Dat's not his style, but he'll cut a bitch off quick, assassinate her character, and strip her ass of e'vrythang, you hear me?" She paused and signaled for her next client to come and sit in the chair.

"Since you new to da city I'ma put cha up on thangs. On da really real, regardless of what cha might hear in dem streets. Adon is a smooth young man. He may have plenty of thug in him and it ain't no secret dat he's a true gangsta in dem streets, but he gotta be. I mean he plays da game like it must be played, but overall a person dat knows both him and Natasha know dat they come from da same womb. Cause dat boy is just as sweet as ever if he got love for ya.

"Just like his sister, except Natasha is nice to everybody. She don't have an evil bone in her body. That's why I love dem two so much."

Fatima became quiet while she concentrated on parting her client's hair. She looked up and caught Vanity looking out through the glass window onto the street as if she was expecting someone to appear.

"Girl, you checkin' fo' Adon, ain't cha?" she asked, putting Vanity on blast.

"What?" Vanity was caught off guard. "Bitch no," she said looking around.

"Uh-uh, you can't hide it. It's written all over ya face." Fatima put her rat-tail comb on the counter and put two and two together. "Now it all makes sense. Okay, now I understand why you brushed Vic off. Dat fool ass nigga can't hold a candle to Adon fine ass. You shoulda said sumthin', girl. And wit' yo' sneaky self, comin' over here, all in my space like you came to keep me company. Bitch, you was on a mission da whole time, checkin' for Adon."

"Let me ask you something," Vanity said.

"What is it?" Fatima started back on her client's braids.

"You're a pretty girl, so if Vic is all what you say he is, then why not go after him yourself?" Vanity wanted to know.

"Please, ain't no nigga in his right mind gon' fuck wit' me. Not da type of nigga I want anyway."

"Why is that?"

"'Cause these scary ass niggas too scared of what Shamrock might do to dem."

"Oh, shit, you had me nervous as hell. I thought you was going to tell me you had HIV." Vanity admitted putting her hand to her chest to feel her heart beat.

"I might as well have it. Hell, most of these so-called gangstas is terrified of Shamrock. And da ones dat's not is just playin' it smart by not takin' da chance of tryin' to holla. I'm surprised dat I still have male clients. If it wasn't for Adon, I'd probably be outta bussiness."

"You have a son by Shamrock, right?"

"Hmm-huh, here's my baby boy right here." Fatima removed a wallet size photo from the corner of her mirror and passed it to her.

"Is this, Shamrock?" Vanity asked looking at the man who sat closely to Fatima with the small boy between them.

"Yeah dat's his doggish ass," Fatima confirmed.

Vanity stared at the picture and thought, *I guess Shamrock is okay looking, in a DMX kinda way.*

She passed the photo back to Fatima and with a smile she said, "Your son is so handsome."

CHAPTER 17

After dropping Black Magic off, Adon headed home to Aurora, Illinois, for the first time since Shamrock's murder. For the entire drive all that he could think about was Lil' One. He drove up his driveway and reached into his pocket, and activated the door to his attached three-car garage. The remote was fastened to his personal key chain. He settled the SS next to his Jaguar X-type, outfitted with 23-inch Lionhart rims. He exited the SS with the hefty bag in one hand, while the strap to the gym bag hung from his shoulder, and walked up to the door that provided access to the inside of his home.

Adon had a state-of-the-art security system that required him to place his right thumb upon a digital clearance security window, which was about the size of a standard credit card. This device was situated within the brick aside each door that accessed the interior of his home from the outside.

He stepped through the entry and into his kitchen area.

"Lights," he said and laid his keys on the granite counter top.

He left the kitchen and proceeded through the corridor, relying on the voice activation setup to illuminate the home as he went along. He planted his feet in front of his floor to ceiling, high definition mirror and gave himself a once-over. His Coggi shorts and top, and Gucci sneakers were all soiled with Lil' One's blood, sweat, and tears.

"Damn, Lil' One," he said and placed his hands atop the bridge of his nose in a prayer's position. He shook it off and went into his master suite, sat the gym and hefty bag down, and headed to the master bath.

Fresh out of the shower, Adon busied himself inside the master suite as he got his evening attire together in the nude.

Spreaded neatly across his king size bed was a maroon Prada jumpsuit, white Prada tank top, two-tone maroon Prada silk boxers, and he matched it with a pair of maroon and white Prada gym shoes.

After he was fully dressed, he put on a dab of Farrenheit cologne and ran the palm held brush over his wavy hair. He picked the moneybags up from the floor and took them to the far end of the suite and sat them down in front of a large painting that graced his wall.

The painting was of him and his father. It was the last known photo that Macklin took before his death in 1989. Adon had his taken back in 2006. The artist that he took the photographs to, coupled them both and painted a masterpiece. To top it off, Adon had it framed in rose gold and flawless diamonds. It was undoubtedly the centerpiece of his master suite.

He reached for the side of the painting, tugged on a hidden lever, and it swung open like any door would. Behind it was a titanium steel safe. He counted out four hundred thousand in cash and placed it neatly inside two 310 Motoring travel bags that were already situated aside the painting, and tossed the Hefty and gym bag into the safe and locked it.

On the way toward his rose wood dresser, he noticed a flashing light on the face of his telephone's cradle, indicating that he had unanswered messages. In each ear, he placed a ten-carat diamond earring carved perfectly into six point stars. Activating his voice mail, he wrapped a platinum bracelet with 18.5 carats around his right wrist, and used the ice from his Avianne platinum watch to chill his left wrist. He couldn't leave his fingers naked so he added two matching 10.5 carat diamonds to his pinkies. For the finale, he bowed his head and draped a diamond necklace with a six point star medallion around his neck as his messages continued to speak.

The first three messages were from Nitty, and two from Casey. But it was the very last message that grasped his attention. It said:

"How are you, Adon Cutti? My name is, Doe. Now I know you probably don't remember me, but I was a very good friend of your father, Macklin Cutti. I'm sure you probably a little confused as to what rock did I crawl from under, and what do I want with you, but trust me when I tell you that I will explain everythang if you grant me the opportunity.

"Adon, there's a lot that you don't know, and there's some powerful people who wouldn't stop at anythang to keep it that way…even kill me.

"Look, I can't talk to no machine, and I'm not 100 percent positive that this is even your number, but I'm more than willing to talk to you face-to-face. I will call this number again when things cool down, with a place and time to meet. If this is your number I pray that you'll take me serious and meet with me when I call next…and by the way, the condo that you have downtown…I left sumthin' with the door man." The message concluded.

Adon went over the caller ID, but the line that Doe called from was restricted. He picked up the house phone and returned one of his messages.

"This is Casey."

"Let Nitty know that I'm ready to meet."

"Well you know the drill," Casey reminded.

"I'll meet you at Magic Hands in two hours," Adon confirmed.

"Listen," Casey intervened just before Adon disconnected his end of the line. "has anybody tried to contact you recently? Anybody you may not know; a stranger maybe?" Casey questioned.

Adon hesitated and said, "Naw, old man. Should I be expectin' somebody?"

"In light of Shamrock's betrayal, we've come to the realization that the feds would go to extreme measures to penetrate the Teflon that blankets our organization. So don't take my asking personal, lil' chum," Casey explained and the conversation ended.

Adon's gut was telling him that some fishy shit was going on, and until he was sure, he decided on a whim to keep quiet about Doe. He placed his shoulder-sling holster over his Prada tank top, filled it with the girth of a .44 Magnum automatic, and pushed his brawn arms through the sleeves of his Prada jacket. He jumped in his royal blue Jaguar X type and hit the streets.

Casey removed the Cuban cigar from his mouth and dialed Nitty. "I'll be meetin' wit' Adon shortly," Casey reported over the phone.

"And he'll be sittin' on your cashmere sofa soon after."

"And Doe?" Nitty inquired.

"Well, I'm still workin' on that...but don't worry, he'll be dead long before he gets to Adon." Casey assured.

"That's what I want to hear," Nitty continued. "Another important issue, go back to the scene of Shamrock's home. Check thangs out. Considering that Adon dropped the ball on Shamrock's Mercedes, I have a strong feelin' that maybe things wasn't handled the way it should have. If things were carried out properly there's no way that the bodies should still be there. But if so, I want you to bring Shamrock's head to me and dispose of everything else," Nitty sounded rattled.

"Is everythang okay, boss?" Casey asked.

"It's difficult to tell," Nitty said. "Right now I just don't want to take any chances."

"Consider it done."

Nitty hung up the phone and reached for his two-way. He reread a message that he received anonymously all but thirty minutes ago. It read: YOU CAN REST ASSURE THAT YOUR SKELETONS WON'T GET BURIED ALONG SIDE ME. YOU TRIED TO MURK ME AND YOU FAILED. NOW I WILL SLUMP EVERYONE IN DIRECT CONNECTION WITH YOU, AND THEN I'M COMING FOR YOU!

CHAPTER 18

Mario sat on the worn couch eating corn chips and drinking cheap 211 beer. Killa Mike left him in charge while he and Mick left out to handle affairs that Mystery specifically ordered Killa Mike to cover.

Each time a thought of Charlotte tottered across his mind, he'd replay the serious look that Killa Mike threw at him when he warned him to keep away. So he relied on the television to taper his mind's desire from the likes of her. He noticed some videotapes on the bottom shelf of the television's stand. "Damn," he mumbled after realizing that none of the videotapes had any title labels on them. He picked one and shoved it into the VCR. To his pleasant surprise, Heather Hunter came across the screen in a cowgirl's position, gyrating and pouncing like she was riding an untamed bull. Her pleasure moans gave the impression that she was really feeling it, and Mario really started to get hot under his dirty collar.

He reached his hand into his Levi jeans. He began to massage his dick as Heather Hunter decreased her speed to give the camera man a good shot of her one of a kind technique. Her partner stood up with her in his arms and his dick still inside of her pussy, pounding away. Heather displayed an array of fuck faces for the camera.

By this time, Mario had his Levis and dingy underwear around his thighs with his dick in his hand and beating away. The harder the male porno star gave it to Heather, the faster Mario's right hand gave it to his dick. Before long, Mario slouched down into the worn couch with an exhausted look on his face and a hand full of limp dick, along with the contents that it discharged.

He wiped his nut on the arm of the couch and downed another can of 211. He eyeballed the bedroom door and envisioned Charlotte's lips around him and the blood flow rushed to his manhood. He got up and walked to the bedroom door, and quietly opened it just enough to look in.

Charlotte lied there asleep in a fetal position with one hand between her thighs while the other was propped under the side of her head. Precious Joyous lied beside her.

Mario walked inside the room, closing the door behind him. His dick began to throb as it pre-cummed at the sight of Charlotte's bare thighs. He wanted to fuck her bad!

He reached into his back pocket for his butterfly knife and kicked off his pants and underwear. With the exception of his smelly socks he was completely nude. He stood over her, admiring her natural beauty and cinnamon crumb cake complexion. Even her back calve muscles were sculptured to perfection.

Mario squatted over her face and pressed his throbbing dick head against her partially opened lips. He got overly excited when a thin string of her saliva lingered on the tip of his dick as he pulled away. He took the tip of his knife and reached for the shoulder straps of her satin nightgown.

Charlotte opened her eyes and jumped from terror.

"Shhh," Mario put the knife to his lips and whispered, "If you do what I tell you to do you won't get hurt, but if you don't" He paused and looked over at Joyous. "I will slit her fuckin' neck and make you watch her bleed to death…you got dat?"

Charlotte looked at her sleeping baby girl and nodded in accordance.

Mario leaned in toward her face.

Her body trembled.

He licked her lips and whispered, "I really love da shit outta yo' lips. They so pouting-like ," he t h e n nippled on her earlobe and said, "Turn around."

She shook her head in defiance.

He stood over her and pointed the knife just inches away from her face. Reluctantly, she did what she was told while a waterfall of tears cascaded her face.

The tears didn't faze Mario. Using spit to lubricate her ass, he spread her cheeks apart and roughly pushed his dick inside of her virgin ass hole. She howled! He could hear her skin tearing from his big dick as he tore through her anus.

Mario thrust wildly as if he were the male porn-star in the film that he'd just watched. The pain was excruciating for Charlotte, but all she saw was Joyous' sleeping face. She stuffed her mouth with parts of the sheet to keep from yelping. She didn't want to wake her little angel. This went on for ten minutes, non-stop, before Mario released his fluids inside her.

Charlotte opened her eyes and noticed that Joyous was awake and looking back at her.

"You better not tell Killa Mike about this," he warned, "Or I will kill you both!"

Adon Stretched the Jaguar across the Eisenhower expressway, averaging eighty miles per hour. He knew he had some time to spare before he had to meet with Casey, so he was in route to his 16th floor condominium on 2 East Oak Street, in downtown Chicago. He constantly ran Doe's name across his memory and kept coming up blank. However, there was something familiar about Doe's voice.

What could he have possibly left wit' the door man? he pondered.

Adon arrived on Oak Street and parked the Jag right in front of the high rise. As soon as he stepped out, valet met him.

"I'm not stayin' long at all, two minutes tops," he said and walked into the lobby as the designated doorman for the upscale high rise opened the glass entry. "You don't have to do that, Willard," Adon said to the uniformed clad, elderly man.

"Jus' enjoying my job, Mr. Cutti," Willard said with a bright smile.

"I hear you," Adon said and shook his hand, passing him a hundred dollar bill. "Did somebody drop by and give you sumthin' for me?" Adon asked.

"Oh, yes," Willard said and started for the front desk as Adon followed. "Actually, I wasn't the person who accepted it, but I have it right here."

Willard passed him an envelope over the counter.

"Thanks, Willard, and don't worry, I'll get the door," Adon said, then left the lobby.

Back inside the Jag, he opened the envelope. It was a single photograph and he had no idea of who the people were. He put it in the side compartment and pressed numbers into his BlackBerry.

"Black," he said

"Yo'," Black Magic answered.

"You ready to talk security?"

"Fo' the picnic, I thought you'd never ask."

"Pick me up downtown at the Water Tower."

The second Casey walked into Shamrock's home the smell of rotting dead bodies hit his nose. The stench was unbearable, but for Casey it was just another day at the office. He took the stairs with a machete in his hand and walked into the master suite. He learned quickly that there'd be no use for the machete, because Shamrock's head wasn't there for the taking.

He quickly got out his phone and dialed Nitty.

"This is, Nitty."

"Boss," Casey said calmly. "Shamrock isn't dead. He's alive," Casey reported as he viewed all four bodies: The two girls, Tommy and Shakey Shawn.

"Dispose everythang and bring Adon to me!" Nitty bellowed and slammed the phone.

The anonymous messenger that sent Nitty the threatening text was no longer unknown.

A 1986 Buick Regal drove up behind Shamrock's home. It had a shabby appearance, outfitted with hubcaps and a set of racing tires. The car ran like a NASCAR champion, and it retained all around tinted glass to mask the speed demon behind its wheel.

The driver stepped out and revealed his identity to the setting sun. It was the notorious Shamrock himself.

Shamrock had been mimicking the Maserati's every turn since Casey abandoned the west side in his search for Doe. He held fast from afar and waited patiently for the right time to execute the beginning of his vengeance. He reached the back door of his home and crossed over the threshold. He tied a blue bandana half way over his face, and removed his Air Force Ones and Nike ankle socks. Then he released twin .10mm semi-automatics from the easy-access holsters that were strapped on either side of his bulletproof vest.

Quietly, he moved forward.

Casey walked leisurely to one end of the downstairs to the next, placing small packages of C-4 chargers to the foundation of the house. In between steps he would linger and study some of the framed photographs that adorned the walls and shelf tops inside of Shamrock's media room. In the process he realized two things: One, Shamrock loved to be in front of a camera. Two, it was evident that Shamrock really had a soft spot for Adon in the way one would for a blood brother.

At least 80 percent of the photos that Casey took the time to view were of Shamrock and Adon. Some even dated as far back as when the two of them were just innocent kids.

Casey shook his head as he thought about the *true* dynamics that lead to the neck-high bullshit that they were all standing in. Unlike Nitty, Casey acknowledged that this entire ordeal would leave a nasty taste on anyone's tongue, especially Adon and Shamrock's when, and if, they ever find out the truth.

He placed the last block of C-4 on the inside of a fireplace and headed back for the stairs.

Portraying the eager paw steps of a keen sensed bloodhound, Shamrock prowled inside every room located on the main level. He was on the verge of climbing the stairs that led to the upper deck when an object stuck to his living room's wall caught his eye.

He walked up to it and tilted his head sidewise like a curious dog, staring at the unknown. There was a section of stainless steel resting on top of what reminded him of clay. Small colorful wires connected the two. He was dubious about touching it. Instead, he leaned his face forward and got a good whiff. Now he knew exactly what it was—C-4.

Casey climbed up the stairs with the electronic detonator in his hand. Once he made it to the main level, he started for the homes back exit that led to his Maserati. The plan was to detonate the C-4, and watch his very own Fourth of July show in luxury. Unfortunately for him plans have their way of changing.

"Casey," Shamrock said in an ear piercing whisper.

Casey pulled out his Beretta and turned toward the voice, but he saw nothing.

"Caseeey," Shamrock whispered, dragging out the name in a taunting fashion.

Casey looked to his right and then his left. Still nothing! He clutched on to the electronic detonator and held it high.

Pop! Pop!

Casey took a bullet to his right and left hand. The Beretta went flying in one direction, and the detonator in another.

"Now why would you wanna go and do dat Casey?" Shamrock continued to taunt.

"Show yo' face boy," Casey said in a mild tone, holding his bleeding hands up like a surgeon.

Pop! Pop!

"Ewww!" Casey growled as he took a bullet to each of his thighs, but he refused to fall.

"Casey, I can't even front. You a big ole dude and tough too. And you stay shitty-sharp. Where you get yo' suits at?" Shamrock asked, and oddly enough he really wanted to know.

"Just show your face Shamrock. Man-up, you young punk!" Casey snarled.

Shamrock was surprised when Casey said his name.

"C'mon! Show your face!" Casey yelled.

"Here I am, Casey," Shamrock said and shined a flashlight in his face. He was located at the top of his home's hallway with his head touching the arched 12-foot ceiling, hovering. His bare feet gripped either side of both walls, supporting his weight.

Casey looked up into the bare glow of Shamrock's face. He knew he was defeated.

"Listen, I'm not gon' stand here and try to save myself, but I will tell you…Adon was deceived."

"So you knew all along that Nitty murked Macklin Cutti ninteen years ago, huh? And he was nothin' but good to both of you slimey, shiesty, rat-headed mafuckas," Shamrock said calmly with the threat of the burnas aimed directly at Casey's skull.

"Awwww!" Casey uttered in both pain and anger, and charged for the detonator.

Pop! Pop!

Shamrock cut Casey's pursuit abruptly short with a couple of slugs to the back of his dome. His forehead was nothing more than open house for an anatomical study, caused by the exit wounds. His body went limp instantly, and all of its 310 pounds went crashing into the floor. A puddle of blood formed instantly around his swelling head.

Black magic was behind the wheel of his moving Audi A4 while Adon sat next to him.

"So that's how the shit hit the fan," Adon said to his loyal lieutenant, Black Magic. "Now you know e'vrythang."

Adon explained the surveillance tape of Shamrock snitching to the feds, and how he was murked because of it.

"Okay," Black Magic said, trying to process everything. "So why is we goin' back to the scene, A?"

"Because I just wanna check shit out," Adon said.

Shamrock strolled passed Casey's Maserati to get to his Regal. He had parked it against the Maserati's back bumper, in case Casey would have managed to escape the house before he got to him. He would've found his vehicle blocked in and going nowhere fast. With the detonator in his left hand, Shamrock turned the ignition and put the Regal in reverse.

Black Magic pulled his whip close to the curb.

"Wait here, I'll be right back," Adon said and jogged lightly to the front of Shamrock's security gate. He noticed that the locked entrance was broken. He went through and resumed his jog until he met with the home's front door.

Black Magic wasn't feelin' the vibe at all. Shamrock snitchin' was just something he couldn't see. And returning to the scene where the murders went down was even more mind boggling. Nevertheless, he wasn't about to sit back on the sideline while the game was in full swing. He wasn't no sideline type nigga.

"Fuck dis!" He reached for a secret switch and flipped it, and what happened next was some straight 007 shit at its finest! The leather flaps where the standard air bag used to be parted down the middle, and a mechanical holster brought a .380 Glock forward. He grabbed a hold of it as Adon cracked the door open with his .44 Mag. automatic secured in his fist.

Black Magic hopped out the whip and noticed something moving behind Shamrock's crib. It was a Buick Regal taking off fast, leaving behind a thick cloud of dirt.

"Adon!" Black Magic yelled just as Adon walked over the carved stone below the door.

He turned to Black Magic in haste and noticed him jumping up and down and waving his arms, signaling for him to come back.

"Get outta there! Now! RUN NOW!" Black Magic yelled at the top of his lungs.

Adon took heed and like a track star in the Olympics, he ran for the gold. As soon as he cleared the security gate there was a big explosion that threw him fifteen feet into the air. There was nothing left of Shamrock's lavish home but debris and rubble.

CHAPTER 19

"You have contacted the Central Government District," a federal agent informed over the phone.

"Yes, this is Agent Berry speaking. Please patch me through to Special Agent Cunningham," Divine said keeping a close watch outside the townhouse window.

"Of course, Agent Berry, I'm patching you through now."

During the short interlude, Divine paced the floor with her personal cell phone to her ear while waiting impatiently for her superior to announce himself on the other end of the line. She continued to peek out the window blinds, checking for any signs of his unexpected arrival.

"This is Special Agent Cunningham, are you all right, Agent Berry?"

"Yes, sir, I'm fine. I'm just checking in and also have a crime to report," Divine said.

"And I'm assuming that you're in a secure setting?" Agent Cunningham asked.

"You'd be assuming correctly, sir." Divine lied.

"Okay, lay it on me."

"There was a quadruple murder that took place over two weeks ago at Shamrock's home in Country Club Hills," Divine reported.

"For crying out loud, did Shamrock kill again!?" Special Agent Cunningham asked.

"Actually, he had the only clean pair of hands on the premises, sir," Divine said.

"Brief me on it," Special Agent Cunningham ordered and Divine's body jumped at a disturbing sound coming from the outside.

With speedy mobility she sprinted for the window and peeked through the blinds. She was relieved to see the neighbor and not Shamrock removing groceries from the trunk of their car.

"Berry, are you there!?"

"I'm here, sir."

"Berry are you sure you're in a secure setting?"

"Yes, sir, I'm fine."

"Very well, carry on then," Special Agent Cunningham ordered. She took one last look beyond the window blinds and began to summarize her line of events.

"Okay, there were two other of Shamrock's girls at his home along with myself and him. Apparently Adon Cutti set up a hit for Shamrock to be executed, and one of the girls, a cross country stripper that goes by the name of Miss Boo, was also involved in the setup.

"Are you referring to the Adon whose supposedly the closest thing on this earth to Shamrock, his counterpart for Petes sake!?" Special Agent Cunningham asked as he peered through The Convolution Crime Organization file.

"That would be correct, sir."

"Well that doesn't make any sense…okay, carry on."

"Two hitmen, one who claimed to be acting under the strict orders of Adon, came into the residence. My belief is that Miss Boo let them in. Anyhow, the two hitmen killed both girls. Perhaps simultaneously or otherwise, I'm not sure.

What I do know is that they dragged both dead women into the master suite, where I was concealed inside of a walk-in closet. The entire time Shamrock was soaking his wild oaks, literally, inside of his Jacuzzi and totally unaware of what was occurring. When either of the girls and myself failed to return to his location he decided to come to his master suite to find us and that's when all hell broke loose!"

Divine paused to peek outside of the window blinds.

"Exactly what hell broke loose?"

"Well after a bunch of hoopla, Shamrock managed to get a hold of one of the hitmen, while the other shot them both. Killing his own partner and wounding Shamrock in the process. That's when I stepped in."

"Stepped in? What do you mean *'stepped in'*?"

"I shot the standing hitman and disabled him."

"With your service weapon?"

"Um, no, sir. I was unable to get to mine, so I had to use a gun that Miss Boo had secretly hid inside a jacket's pocket that I took notice of."

"Was the subject facing you?"

"No, sir. I was positioned behind him, but he had his gun to Shamrock's head with the intent to kill."

"How many rounds did you fire?" Special Agent Cunningham asked, while he used her information to check specific boxes on an evaluation sheet. This tactic was commonly done when an agent appeared to be under distress while working undercover. It was used to determine rather or not said undercover agent is fit to proceed or should be pulled from their current undertaking.

"One initially, sir," Divine answered.

"Initially?" Agent Cunningham was confused.

"Well, yes…let me explain, sir. Once the subject fell to the ground with a non-fatal wound to his buttocks, Shamrock picked up the hitman's gun and turned it on him, by the way, the henchman goes by the street name of Shaky Shawn."

"Oh, yes, Shaky, aka Shaky Shawn, aka dip shit. He has a heap of dead bodies under his belt. I just sent some Agents out to apprehend him for a couple of murders that he committed in Detroit just a month ago. Well I'm guessing with the way this story is going I shall remove his name from the indictment list. Carry on Berry."

"Yes, sir. Well Shamrock began to pistol-whip him, while he interrogated him. That is when Shaky implicated Adon, and that only Adon, as being the hit-caller."

"But even we know that's a crock of shit."

"Yes, sir, but for some reason Shamrock hasn't figured that out yet. Right now he's being fueled by his rage and mangled emotions. More so because he couldn't fathom Adon's betrayal.

"After Shaky Shawn implicated Adon, Shamrock gave him an ultimatum. And since he was desperately looking to negotiate a new lease on life with a gun to his head, Shaky agreed to call Adon and inform him that the hit was a success. The brief call was on speaker for us all to hear. Adon pretty much confirmed his own involvement.

116

Shamrock was crushed by Adon's betrayal."

"But you and I both know what this has stemmed from, and this is not what we wanted. I don't need another war on the streets, the city of Chicago doesn't! I refuse to go another year with this city being the murder capitol. Not on my watch," Agent Cunningham said. "Now continue, Berry."

"Yes, sir. Minutes after I revealed myself, I'm not sure how or where he may have seen me before, but Shaky began to conjure up memories of me, and my true occupation with the Bureau"

"And?" Special Agent Cunningham persisted.

"And in order to prevent from being made, and preserve the investigation. I had to kill him," Divine confessed.

"Look Berry, I think you've gotten in too far and too deep on this. I'm afraid that I may have to pull you out. I've already lost three Agents on this particular case, and I do not want to lose a fourth—"

"No, no you don't have to do that! You can't! I've worked my ass off on this, and I am so close to getting the evidence we need against Nitty and The Convolution! Just give me some more time, and I assure you that I will get the job done," Divine pleaded.

"Is there even a slight suggestion that Shamrock may have captured a leery eye toward you when you killed the subject?"

"No, sir, absolutely not. In fact, he trusts me even more so now that I've committed a murder for him. He's comfortable with me. He finally left me alone in his plush town home in Oak Park. Sir, no one has ever been here before, not even Adon knows about this place," Divine said. "So to be frank, sir, I am going to bring this piece of scum down! All I need is for you to keep me in."

"Well, why did it take you so long to check in, and to report this hideous crime?" Agent Cunningham asked still not convinced.

"This is the very first time that he has left me alone long enough to make this call. The only other time was when he had me sneak into Magic Hands and drive his Mercedes out of there. Even then I was on the clock, but would have had time to give you a heads up if Adon wouldn't have spotted the car and opened fire."

"Whhaaat!?" Agent Cunningham yelled.

"Sir, I can do this."

"I don't know about this, Agent Berry."

"Sir, with all due respect, my track record speaks for itself," Divine said with confidence.

"Proceed in accordance Agent Berry and keep me posted. Berry, make some progress and soon. I mean it. Now give me the address to the Oak Park location."

CHAPTER 20

Shamrock arrived at his townhouse and his front door was slightly ajar. *What the fuck?* In a blink of an eye his palms was filled with the plastic grips of his twin burnas.

He pushed the door with the barrel and entered the place while the twins led the way. One of his senses became aware of the soft fragrance that passed through the air, and another recognized "Miss Independent Remix" by Ne-yo crooning mildly from his Bose stereo.

He followed his trained instinct to the bedroom and to his pleasant surprise Divine laid there on her stomach, facing him with her back arched like a feline in heat. Her glass stilettos were tall and her naked body was saturated with baby oil. With her come-fuck-me eyes, she lured him over

Shamrock's dick was about ready to bust out of his Blac Label jeans. He placed the burnas atop the dresser and freed himself, as the jeans fell to his ankles.

Divine had a body like Buffy the Body, and the oils maximized her gluteus-maximus far beyond his imagination. He was ready to dive in as he stepped to the edge of the bed, but she halted his action when she began to crawl slowly into his direction. Scented candles were scattered about, producing just the right amount of sensual aroma.

Divine ran her hand over his six-pack and before he knew it she had all of him in her mouth. Slowly her head bobbed back and forth. Her plump lips were wrapped around him like a tight condom and her throat swallowed him continuously without gagging.

Oh, hell yeah. Suck that dick," Shamrock encouraged.

Divine caressed his balls and sucked away at his shaft as if she was toothless.

Shamrock grabbed her head with both hands and slightly turned it to the side, meeting her jaw with each thrust. Divine handled it like an oral champion.

"Take it. Take it!" Shamrock demanded as he thrust faster and harder against the inside of her jaw. "Here it come," he calmly informed her.

He ejaculated in her mouth and she welcomed every bit of it, sucking him dry. He didn't even have to wipe his dick off. After ingesting the last of him, she removed herself from the bed and sat him down on the corner of it. She began to whine her body slowly like a belly dancer. He was becoming intoxicated with her sex appeal. Divine leaned over and kissed him with her creative tongue.

Shamrock had a stripper's pole custom built in his bedroom. The mirrors complimented its surroundings and gave it that real-live strip club vibe. Ne-yo had to have been on repeat because "Miss Independent Remix" started again, and Divine took center stage. Shamrock peeled off his shirt, reclined on his elbows, and watched the erotic show.

She placed her left hand around the pole and spun around it with her left leg enclosed around the lower part of it. She went on to do many tricks while the pole acted as her reliable dancing companion, revealing her skills to her lover. She even offered to show him just how much Grade A beef she was working with by spreading her ass cheeks and placing the warm pole between the two, allowing them to touch on the other side. The pole sat snug between her butt-cleavage.

The song persisted as Shamrock's dick started to rise again. Divine took notice and left the stage.

Shamrock watched all that ass fluctuate as she swayed her hips to the other end of the room, where she retrieved a chair. She turned to him and maintained her art of seduction with a slow Stacy Dash style of walk, and dragged the chair along behind her.

She stopped short and placed the chair directly in front of him. He highly anticipated her next move and watched as she threw her leg over the chair and turned on the ball of her other foot. She was facing away from him. Her legs were parted with the chair beneath her. She crotched down and began to grind lightly against the seat of the chair. Shamrock's dick grew to a new height.

Smack! Smack!

He slapped her ass and watched it jiggle. Divine was completely aware of his infatuation with her ass and she used it to her advantage.

On cue, she made each cheek bounce individually and then together at once with the bass line. At this point, Shamrock was at the edge of a cliff and about to jump. He grabbed a hold of her small waist and guided her voluptuous ass right over his massive dick.

Divine bent forward and put her legs behind her and around either side of him like the letter U. She gripped the sides of the chair and slowly came down on his swollen heat until he met with her cervix. "Awww," she groaned in both pain and pleasure. Her pussy was wet and her walls were tight as Shamrock stretched her out. He laid flat while she clenched her muscles on the upstroke, relaxing on the downstroke, riding him to oblivion.

Divine accomplished what she had set out to do. She drained the very consciousness from Shamrock's body. He was spread out across the king size bed, and produced a snore that had the sound resemblance of a lawn mower. The only thing that was on her mind was Magic Hands.

"Cunningham said he wants results, right?" she stated to herself as she got dressed. "Well, call it a hunch. I just may get lucky."

CHAPTER 21

Black Magic and Adon drove inside of Magic Hands and parked in a stall. Besides the heavy rotation of a 'dro filled Garcia Vega cigar, there was no interaction between the two as they sat in complete silence. Adon was stunned to say the least, and Black Magic couldn't even begin to process recent events.

Adon looked down at his Avianne timepiece and then out into the car wash area. He wondered where Casey was. They were suppose to meet there twenty minutes ago, but he was nowhere in sight. Adon slouched in the passenger seat and rubbed the top of his head, clearly in deep thought.

Black Magic passed the 'dro and broke the silence.

"What da fuck is goin' on, A?"

"At this point, yo', your guess is as good as mine."

Agent Karpe was sitting patiently inside a Grand Cherokee across the street when the Audi A4 drove inside Magic Hands. Courtesy of the wire-tap that he had on Casey's cell phone, Agent Karpe knew that Adon would be meeting him there tonight. His main mission was to find the new operative that was assigned to the cold investigation, and do to that agent what he'd done to the last three. His gut told him that laying surveillance on Adon would bring him closer to that goal.

"Hmmm what do we have here?" he asked himself after observing a female on the opposite side of his location. He turned the Cherokee's ignition and put the view of Magic Hands in his back windshield as he drove away.

Divine was set and ready to do what she does best; decipher what was hidden and spot the obvious, and pile more incriminating evidence along the way. Her main objective was to gather enough evidence that'll bring Nitty and The convolution to its knees; Shamrock was just a stepping stone. With her trusty camera in tow, she was currently peering through her Federal issued binoculars with her sights aimed steadily on the entrances and exits of Magic Hands.

"Good old fashion detective work, just how I like it."

While her point of attraction sat in one direction, Agent Karpe parked his Cherokee approximately thirty yards behind her Ford Mustang.

He studied her suspicious behavior through his very own Federal issued binoculars. Elevating his cell phone, he pressed down on one button and speed dialed Nitty.

"This is Nitty."

"Do you recall our small conversation about the unknown operative that the Bureau has designed to be responsible for your calculated demise?" Agent Karpe said in his usual cocky demeanor. "Well I have good news for you Mr. Calhoun. That Agent's identity is no longer in question, and the matter would be handled accordingly. In the mean time, work on getting me my money," Agent Karpe didn't wait on a response.

He closed his cell shut and went into action.

"Look, ain't no secret," Adon said. "Murda Park is goin' to be outta commission for a while until shit cool down. That's the main reason why I fought for a peace treaty, and founded the statewide picnic, because of shit like this"

Adon hit his palm with his fist. "Can't nobody make money and war at the same time. It's impossible," he said and Black Magic nodded in agreement. "But a nigga still gotta eat, right?"

"Fo' sho, A," Black Magic said.

"We'll be aiight, trust me," Adon said with conviction. "As for the picnic, you know how it go."

Black Magic nodded.

"Secure the perimeter, make sure all entrances and exits are covered, and above all, keep yo' eyes open for Vice Lords. I can't stress that enough," he continued and looked Black Magic square in the eye. "I know having Shamrock wit' us on this woulda helped out tremendously, but rest assure that before I'm anythang, I'ma soldier so I'm wit' you. Like I said before, I have a very important guest comin', so security gotta be tight, secret service style."

"I got cha," Black Magic assured.

"Aiight, my nigga," Adon said and they both knocked fists. "Pop yo' trunk."

Adon got out the Audi for the first time since they drove into Magic Hands, and went around to the trunk area. He took his two 310 Motoring travel bags by the leather straps and removed them from the trunk. Suddenly, he looked up and found himself surrounded by three men in suites.

"You're comin' with us," a man with an African accent said.

Adon dropped his moneybags and went for his gun, but was beaten to the draw as he looked down the barrel of one. One of the men reached into Adon's Prada jacket and removed his burna. Adon looked over and saw that Black Magic was held at gunpoint. His burna was taken as well.

"Pick up your bags and come quietly," the African man said calmly and led the way while the other two, plus the one that had Black Magic hemmed up, followed.

A small ring tone abruptly interrupted Divine's close kept surveillance. She wanted to pass on the call and remain glued to her visual task, but she knew it could only be one person calling her federal issued cell phone, and she couldn't afford to piss him off.

"Yes, sir?" she spoke into the phone.

"Agent Berry, are you in a secure setting!?" Special Agent Cunningham asked vehemently.

"Yes, sir," Divine confirmed.

"Intelligence just informed us of the identity of our mole," he reported.

"Well, sir, who is it?" Divine asked never taking her eyes off the Magic Hands' exits.

"His name is Special Agent David Karpe."

Adon, along with the four men, walked out of the exit. They all poured into a black colored Ford Expedition. Divine took notice. She started her Mustang and wrapped her hand around the stick shift.

"Sir, can we pick this up at a later time?" she asked.

"Listen to me, Berry, and you listen close," Special Agent Cunningham said sternly. "This, this traitor is single-handedly responsible for the savage murders of three undercover agents that worked this investigation before you."

"I understand, sir but—" Divine said as she watched the Expedition dart into traffic.

She shifted her gear into first when she felt an odd jerk, and found it difficult to accelerate. With the phone close to her ear she stepped outside of her Mustang and discovered that both of her hind wheels were flattened.

"Agent Berry your life *is* in immediate danger!" Special Agent Cunningham shouted through the phone. "There's a good chance that Karpe has made you. In fact, he may have you smack-dab in the middle of his headlights at this very second! Berry, it's vital to your life that you pack up and get out *now* before it's too late!"

At that very intense second, Divine turned to the revving sounds of an engine, only to see the high beam lights from a SUV charging straight for her.

CHAPTER 22

The closer they got to their apparent destination, the more Adon became convinced as to who sent the four men: Nitty.

The African driver drove up the main strip where the 50-Yard Line was located. The 50-Yard Line was a popular nightclub and Nitty was the owner. The place stayed crackin', and the host of people that stood behind the velvet rope only confirmed that tonight wasn't going to be an exception.

The African driver had to navigate the SUV at a snail's pace, because there was so much action on the streets. The parking lot resembled was a live block party.

They finally made it to the end of the strip and parked in the back of the club. Adon was pulled roughly out of the backseat and escorted through the side entrance of the club. The African grabbed a hold of the moneybags and followed them in.

They walked down a narrow hallway that led to a stair casing. Lil' Wayne's "A Milli" filled the club as Adon was taken to the basement.

"Have a seat," the African said and pointed to the only chair at the center of the floor. At this point, all the men had their guns drawn.

Adon didn't make a fuss. He sat down calmly as Nitty walked in from a secret door.

Nitty walked before Adon and snapped his fingers. One of his men hurried to a far corner and retrieved a chair. He brought it over and positioned it behind Nitty. He sat down directly in front of Adon with only a few feet between them. For sixty seconds he didn't say one word, instead, from under his tilted brim he stared into Adon's eyes. Adon didn't waver.

"What's this about?" Adon tried to speak, but Nitty quieted him with a single index finger to his mouth. Adon looked around at his gun-toting goons and remained calm.

Nitty removed his Fedora and placed it over his pricey Valentino covered knee. "First, you fall off the face of the earth," Nitty said. "Then Shakey Shawn follows suit; Shamrock's Mercedes is stolen from my establishment, and all of a sudden my right hand is missing."

With a confused frown Adon said, "Casey is missin'?"

"Yes," Nitty responded. "You care to explain what the fuck is goin' on?"

"Look, all I know is that I was suppose to meet Casey tonight at Magic Hands, and what I got was these muthafuckas," he said pointing a thumb at the goons. "The Benz I take full responsibility for. I slept on that and will accept what I got comin'. As for me being MIA for a minute, well I was goin' through some serious mental shit and I needed to take a break from it."

"A break!" Nitty said raising his voice. "There's no breaks in this business. You don't take a break unless I tell you that you can take a break. You understand?" Nitty seethed.

Adon barely nodded.

"And what about Shakey Shawn?" Nitty asked, knowing the answer.

"Shakey Shawn," Adon repeated the name for clarity. "He's in Miami. You know that."

"Nope, guess again," Nitty said.

"What do you mean, guess again?" Adon was confused.

"The last phone call that I got from Casey, he said that he was looking down in Shakey Shawn's dead face. And I believe that it wasn't long before Casey joined him.

"How the fuck is that possible!" Adon wasn't buying it.

"I want you to read something and *you* tell me what it means to you," Nitty pulled his two-way from his belt and passed it to Adon. Adon began to read in silence until he was interrupted.

"No," Nitty continued, "read it out loud for all to hear."

Adon looked up at Nitty and again to the goons who stood at attention, and then he began: "Your skeletons will not get buried along side me. You tried to murk me and you failed. Now I will slump everyone in direct connection with you, and then I'm coming for you."

Adon finished reading and passed Nitty the two-way.

"Now what does that mean to you?" Nitty asked with a scrutinizing stare.

"Shit, it sounds like a muthafucka is out to murk yo' ass," Adon stated bluntly.

"No, let me tell you what it really means," Nitty said matter-of-factly. "It means that both Shakey Shawn and Casey are dead, which in turn means that Shamrock is alive."

"Hell, naw," Adon said raising his pitch. "It's impossible."

"Possible it is, and let me shed some light, Mr. I-Need-A-Break. Shamrock will get to you way before he could ever dream of getting to me, which means you have a major problem on your hands. And until you rectify the problem your water is completely shut down," Nitty said.

"Hmm-huh, that big pretty house in Aurora and your condo downtown, your toys, it will all be taken away from you and your membership within The Convolution will be revoked! You get that."

"Yeah, I got'cha," Adon said still taken aback by the news of Shamrock being alive.

Nitty looked down on the floor at the 310 Motoring travel bags and said, "How much?"

"Four hundred," Adon answered.

"Well, I'll fill your order when this matter is resolved. In the meantime, I'll hold it for safe keeping," Nitty said and snapped his fingers. On cue, the African walked up and handed Adon his burna. "Now you can leave my club."

"I would be glad to, but I didn't drive."

"Take the silver car out back," Nitty said and stood to his feet as the African tossed him a set of car keys.

"Black Magic said that he saw a primed-up Buick Regal leaving the scene just as Shamrock's house was blown to pieces," Adon said as he slid the burna inside his holster.

"Oh yeah, we know about the Regal," Nitty continued, "Now you need to find him before he finds you."

Adon arrived outside at the rear of the club and noticed that there were *six* vehicles parked inside the private parking lot, and they were all silver.

"What the hell," he mumbled and ran his eyes across two H2 Hummers, a BMW 760i, Cadillac STS and CTS, and a Ferrari F36 Modena. He pointed the remote start in the vehicles' direction. The lights to the Ferrari shone and the calm revving of the engine purred like a kitten.

He got in and sped off.

CHAPTER 23

Shamrock awoke from his deep sleep and saw that Divine wasn't laying next to him.

"Where da fuck is this bitch?" he asked, and almost shouted out her name until he caught a flashback of the last time he yelled a woman's name throughout the house. He damn near didn't make it out. Still in the nude, he jumped to his feet and filled both hands with his twin .10 mms.

As usual he allowed the two of them to lead the way, while one was pointed sidewise at chest level and the other fully extended in front of him. The townhouse didn't pose a great size, so he didn't have much area to cover.

His first destination was the living room and it was empty. He checked the front door and confirmed that all six locks were secured. He made it to the bathroom. It turned up nothing. That left the upper level.

He climbed the stairs at a snail's pace, and ended up at the start of what he referred to as the "boom boom room."

"Hey, daddy," Divine said with soapsuds up to her chin. "Are you ready for round two?" she asked from the whirlpool.

"Do a bear shit in da woods? You damn straight." Shamrock said and placed the burnas on top of his outdated *Black Men Magazines*.

"Baby, before you jump in and get some of this tight lovin' can you do me a favor?" she asked nervously.

"Name it, baby," he said and walked around the whirlpool to kiss her luscious lips.

"I'm thirsty. Can you get us something to drink?"

He looked at her and scrunched his face.

"Look here, shawty, now don't get beside yo' self up in here. Pimpin' Shamrock don't wait on *no* bitch, bitches serve Pimpin' Shamrock!" he declared.

"Now, baby, you know no one knows that better than I do, but I'm afraid that I may not be any good doing what I do best if my mouth is dry daddy," she said and touched the tip of her nose with her pierced tongue.

Shamrock thought about it, then thought again.

"Don't make dis shit no habit," he said and left for downstairs where his mini-bar was located.

Divine sighed heavily and jumped to her feet in a hurry, fully clothed and covered in soapsuds and drenching water. She had just made it back to the house in a nick of time to say the least.

She managed to dive between two parked cars, barely escaping a near death experience with minor scrapes and bruises. By the time she got off the ground the SUV was already turning the corner. All Divine was able to gather was the back of what appeared to be a man's head and a partial plate. She had no idea that it was infact, the mole, Agent Karpe.

She raced to undress while minimum time permitted. First it was off with her light jacket, blouse, bras then on to her Donna Karan low-rise jeans and sequence thongs and footies, and she hid the dripping wet attire behind the whirlpool.

She reclined in the lukewarm water and inhaled deeply to calm her nerves when she heard Shamrock returning up the stairs. He walked in with two champagne glasses, a bottle of Belvedere and one serious hard-on.

CHAPTER 24

Black Magic had just got off the phone with Adon as he pulled in front of Celebrities. His hair resembled Simba in "The Lion King" having taken down his braids. If the heavy shit Adon threw at him didn't already take him aback, hearing that Shamrock escaped the hit and was now out for revenge definitely had him on edge.

Before he got out of his whip he peered into the large glass window. It was 10:11 P.M. and the number of patrons was at a low.

"Girl I am hungry. Do ya'll want something before I go up the street to Harold's Chicken and buy the whole damn restaurant?" Vanity joked.

"Yes, girl, please," Natasha said while she sat in one of the booth's chairs massaging her feet.

"Count me in too. As hungry as I am I can eat a baby," Fatima said.

"A baby?" Natasha asked with an unusual look on her face.

"Yeah, girl, a baby chicken, pig, or some shit!" Fatima quipped and the three of them busted out laughing.

"I am so thankful this place is nearly empty," Natasha said with a stretch and reclined.

"Are you coming with me?" Vanity asked, looking at Fatima.

"Uh-uh girl, I got one more head to braid and I'm done. The way my fingers and lower back feel right now, if Black Magic decided not to show up, I won't be mad at all," Fatima spoke her truth as Black Magic walked in, barely fitting his afro threw the door. "And speakin' of the devil," Fatima said and popped her chair with a chair cloth to rid any loose hair.

Black Magic's dark brown eyes were captivated by Vanity's breathtaking figure. Fatima caught notice and zeroed in.

"And where you goin', lookin' all debonair-like?" Fatima asked, bringing him out of his trance.

Black Magic hunched his shoulders and struck a pose in his Giorgio Brutini suit while the ladies looked on. "I'm steppin' out tonight," he said and sat down in Fatima's chair.

"Here, V," Fatima handed Vanity a piece of paper and a twenty dollar bill. "I wrote down what I want."

"Damn, you eatin' that much that you had to write it down?" Vanity asked. "Hell, you know the girl could eat a whole cow," Natasha jested.

"Fuck both you bitches! And since you talkin', you already know what Natasha want so you gon' have to stop by Fat Albert's Restaurant too, now," Fatima said teasingly.

"And what is that?" Vanity asked and placed her hand on her hip.

"An Italian Beef," Fatima took the liberty of answering that one for Natasha.

"Yes please! I can taste it right now," Natasha said licking her lips.

Vanity aimed her open-toe sandals toward the exit.

"And don't forget to tell them to dip it in hot peppers with four slices of cheese, thank you sweety!" Natasha yelled as Vanity waved her hand on her way out the door. "Fatima I'll be in my office if I'm needed," Natasha gently stepped to her feet. With her Nike Air Max in her hand she walked barefooted to her destination.

About twenty minutes later Vanity sang along to the lyrics of "I Wanna Luv U" by Donell Jones while she visualized Adon singing it to her. She smiled her pretty smile and turned on the street where Celebrities was located. The aroma from the food filled the car, causing her stomach to growl.

"Damn," she said after seeing that her parking space was taken. It wouldn't have been as bad if the nighttime atmosphere didn't make it that much harder to find a vacant spot.

"Shoo, they just will have to be upset with me 'cause I'll bust these bad boys down in this car if this takes any longer," she said referring to the mild sauce covered wings that were calling out her name. "There goes one."

She saw an empty spot ahead and parallel parked about ten car lengths away from Celebrities. She stepped out of the car and bent over to grab that good smelling food.

Walking up from the rear was Vic, and he enjoyed the view. Courtesy of light winds, Vanity's cheerleader-style skirt swayed to-and-fro, exposing her bright red thong.

"I told you we'll meet again, you uptight bitch!" Vic said and snatched the thin string to her thong and shoved her forward.

The force from the push landed her face in the passenger seat and her mid-section crashed into the armrest. She was trying hard to catch her breath when a cool breeze slipped by her vaginal area. She knew then that her precious parts were bare and what was bound to come next if she didn't do something quick.

She spun around to her backside smashing the bags of food and lunged a kick at his testicles, but her aim was way off. He caught her heel in his hand and threw her leg over the steering wheel, and her other leg over the headrest.

"Hmmm," he uttered and laid his body between her thighs.

"Don't fight what you deserve bitch!" he said and ripped the front of her blouse open.

She continued to struggle.

"What!? You think 'cause you from Seattle a Chi-Town nigga ain't good enough for yo' conceited ass? Bitch I could've gave you everything. I'm havin' money!" he croaked and threw a stack of twenty-dollar bills in her face.

She screamed as loud as her vocal cords would allow. She fought her hardest but she couldn't break free. He forcefully placed his platinum rings over her mouth to muffle her screams for help.

"Owww! You TRAMP!" Vic bellowed after feeling the sharpness of her teeth bite into his finger. He raised his hand to the car's ceiling and came down with mighty force, but before he could strike the priceless jewel that only God could bless a woman's face with, he felt the collar of his Polo shirt cut off the air to his windpipe. Like a golf ball caught in the hose of a suction pump, he was yanked out of the car like a rag doll.

Adon pulled him from the ground.

"Vic!?" he blurted, realizing who he was, and punched him in the face.

Vic fell to the pavement while the women came out of Celebrities to watch the show. Black Magic, freshly braided, copped a seat on the hood of someone's car and grabbed a handful of cheese popcorn from the big bag he had in his hand and shoved it into his mouth.

"I love it when dis nigga put hands on a mafucka!" Black Magic said in excitement. "That nigga A is a beast!"

Holding Vic by the collar, Adon turned to Vanity and asked, "Is you aiight?" She couldn't say a word. She was choked up and stunned senseless.

Adon was heated! He pulled Vic from the ground and met his rib cage twice with four sharp knuckles.

Vic coughed up blood.

"What the fuck you think dis is nigga!? You think shit sweet!?" Adon snarled and stole on him again. "Do you know who she is? Do you have the slightest idea who you FUCKIN' WIT'!?" Adon yelled.

Vic shook his head pitifully, while a golf ball size knot began to develop on his forehead.

"That's family right there, fool!" Adon said and pointed to Vanity who was standing near Natasha's car.

"I swear Adon I didn't know!" Vic pleaded.

"Okay, bruh, that's enough. He got the picture," Natasha said from the sideline, causing Adon to take his eyes away from Vic.

Vic jumped at the opportunity, landed a sucker punch on Adon's jaw, and turned to run.

Adon was quick on his toes. He pulled out an old childhood trick and used the front of his foot to trip Vic up from behind. Vic took a dive, breaking one of his platinum teeth on the pavement.

Black Magic burst into laughter. "Oh, you don' fucked up now tree jumper!" Black Magic said, barely keeping the popcorn in his mouth. "Now dis shit here is hilarious."

Adon casually walked over to Vic and kneeled down to grasp a hold of his platinum chain. He wrapped it around his clinched fist and continued in that motion until the tip of his knuckles touched his chin.

Like curling a dumbbell, he elevated Vic's weary body to its feet.

Vic was shaking in his drawers when he was forced to watch while Adon pulled back his right fist and unleashed more power than he ever had before. Four bones in Vic's face broke under his fist. Adon snatched the platinum piece from around Vic's neck as he collapsed in the middle of the street.

Vanity was frightened. Her body shook from the sound of Vic's body plummeting to the pavement.

Adon tossed the platinum necklace to Black Magic. He allowed the empty bag of popcorn to be taken by the wind and caught the chain with both hands. He hopped off the car's hood and walked over Vic. He was laid out. Adon made it over to Vanity who was being comforted by Natasha and Fatima, and gently wrapped his brawn arms around her.

"Is you aiight?" he asked.

"Now that you're here, yes," she answered and buried her tear-soaked face into his chest and tightened her grip around him. His alluring Fahrenheit cologne instantly intoxicated her.

"Did he hit you?" Adon asked and looked down at her face.

"He didn't get a chance to," she said. "Adon, I don't know what I would've done or what would've happened if you didn't show when you did."

"You don't have to worry about that now," Adon said and looked down into her light brown eyes. As the tears streamed down her attractive features he noticed a lot of nothing. No running mascara and not even the slightest trace of make-up. She was 100 percent natural, and beautiful.

"Would you please hold me?" she asked and watched Adon's fingers approach her face. Her reflexes caused her eyelids to lower. Unaware of what would follow, she felt him wipe her tears away and a gentle tug of her waist brought her closer to him. A warm kiss caressed her forehead just before he rested his cheek on the side of her temple. She likely would have passed out from an emotional over-load, but she couldn't take the chance of missing out on something she'd regret.

She was calm, safe, and no longer hungry for Harold's Chicken. Their embrace lasted for mere seconds but felt like hours to her. She fell under his Fahrenheit hypnosis and could've remained there until infinity. Then suddenly, her intuition prompted her to open her eyes.

"Oh, my God, what is he doing!?" she shouted hysterically.

Adon turned on his heels with the quickness and observed Black Magic standing over Vic with his twin Glock .380s. Adon reverted his vision back to Vanity and clearly saw that she wouldn't be able to stomach murder right before her eyes.

"Ay, Black!" Adon hollered out. "Freeze that, cuz, you know we ain't tryin' to kill nobody."

Black Magic got the drift and slid the Glocks into their holsters.

"C'mere, lemme see if I can get somethin for you," Adon walked over to the Ferrari and opened the front hood. Coincidently, inside were a few of Nitty's shirts fresh from the dry cleaners.

"Your shirt is all torn up, take this," Adon said and passed Vanity a Gucci button down after removing it from the plastic. She put it over her torn shirt and allowed the flap to drape over her ass.

"Are you okay, baby girl?" Natasha asked as she walked up.

"I'm fine, Tash," Vanity said.

"Well, let's go inside so I can lock up," Natasha said and they started that way.

"Black," Adon called out just before he walked in the front entrance. "I'll be inside, wake that chump up and send him on his way," he said, and winked his left eyelid before Vanity tugged on his arm for him to come inside.

Black Magic knew all too well what the left wink meant. "Oh yeah, I got plans to send you on yo' way all right." He dragged Vic two blocks down where he initially saw Vic's Lincoln Navigator when he was in route to Celebrities an hour ago.

Adon walked into Celebrities behind Vanity as she whispered something in his ear, and then left his side. He scanned the area in search of Natasha, but all he saw was one female hairstylist finishing a female client's hair while another girl in the waiting area appeared to be waiting for her friend.

"Where's my sis?" Adon asked.

"Um, she's in her office, Fatima said and walked over from the sink. "Listen," she said quietly as she walked up to Adon. "I saw Murda Park on the news earlier and it's a shame what happened to that lil' boy. But is you okay?"

"Yeah, I'm good," Adon responded with the same tone. "And I'm sure Lil' One gonna pull through," he began to step off. "Well, lemme go holla at sis before I bounce."

"Okay," Fatima said. "And now that I'm thinkin' about it, where's my chicken?" she asked and looked around for Vanity who was nowhere in sight. "Where did that heifer go that quick?"

Adon was well off into his stride.

"Heeey, Adon?" the hairstylist spoke in a flirtatious matter.

"How you ladies doin'?" Adon spoke to both women as he passed. As he got closer to Natasha's office he could hear Kenny G's saxophone coming from within. He slowed his pace. He knew that whenever she'd listen to jazz something was weighing heavily on her mind.

He knocked on her door and waited for her permission before he entered.

"You straight, sis?" Adon asked as he walked in and shut the door behind him.

"C'mere," she said and walked from around her desk to hug him. "You know that was a really good thing you did for Vanity."

"Yeah, I'm just grateful that I came in time," he said. "But what about you? How are you?"

"I'm fine bruh," she said pulling her arms from his neck. "I'm just stressin' over this hair show that's coming up in Atlanta."

"Oh, don't worry 'bout that. You got mama's blood runnin' through your veins, and you know the type of diva she was. You'll be good. Betta than good. You gonna win that bitch!" Adon said enthusiastically. "And I'ma be right there in the ATL cheering you along."

"I hope you're right," she said and sat behind her desk.

"I wanna ask you sumthin'," Adon said in a serious tone.

"Anything," Natasha said catching on to the instant change in the atmosphere.

"Did Charlotte say anythang to you about goin' anywhere, maybe outta the country," Adon asked, purposely leaving out the name of the country he was referring to.

"You know, it's funny you've mention that because she sure did. She said that she was planning to visit her family in France. You know, connect with her Creole heritage. Why, you still haven't heard from her?"

"Naw," Adon said depressingly.

"Well you know what, I'm sure that's where she went to for her summer break and took Joyous along with her. As I said before...You know how she gets when she's mad at you for whatever reason. And that's probably the reason she didn't tell you. But don't worry her life is here. She got two more years in school. She'll be back before fall semester starts."

"Yeah," Adon said faintly as he became convinced that was the case. Although he wasn't happy about it he felt a relief. At least she wasn't *kidnapped* or anything else along those lines. He reached into his pocket and laid a worn photo on her desk. The photo was of a man in his early twenties holding an infant.

"Do this mean anythang to you?"

Natasha viewed the photo and shook her head, "Why, should it?"

"Do the name Doe ring a bell?" Adon asked looking at her attentively.

"Nope," she said casually.

"Well, apparently he knows pops. He contacted me and left this photo behind with my doorman," Adon explained.

"Never heard of him. Besides, who doesn't know or knew our father. Or at least claims that they did?" Natasha said.

"You right. Ay sis, you wouldn't mind if Vanity didn't come home tonight, would you?"

"Why, where's she going?" Natasha quizzed.

"I'ma take her wit' me."

"You sure that's what you want?" Natasha asked, shifting in her seat.

"She just needs to get away for a minute and feel safe, that's all."

"Okay," Natasha said and the two of them hugged, and said there goodbyes before Adon left her office.

Natasha sat back down and put her backhand under her chin. She knew exactly who the person was in the photo. She even knew the infant. But in order to stay the course, it was imperative that she deny having knowledge. Furthermore, as far as she was concerned, Doe was completely justified for committing murder nineteen years ago. It was just a shame that he had to go to jail for it.

Unexpectedly, Natasha heard screaming coming from the front of her salon.

"What is it, now," she said, racing out of her office and into the work area.

Adon was holding on to Fatima who was bawling uncontrollably, while Vanity stood closely beside her stroking Fatima's hair.

"What's wrong with her," Natasha asked as she approached.

"Her mother just called and told her that somebody set off a bomb in Shamrock's house and they found five bodies that they can't identify," Vanity reported.

"What I'm gon' do? What is my son gon' do without his daddy!" Fatima wept. "I don't want my son to grow up wit'out a father.

"It's gon' be aiight," Adon consoled. "Junior ain't gonna hurt for nothin', word is bond. I got ya'll," Adon said and held her tight as Fatima cried in his arms.

CHAPTER 25

Black magic was enjoying the Navigator's wheel suspension while he bobbed his head to Young Jeesy's "I Put On." He reached over and used his fingers to check Vic's vital signs. Besides being unconscious, he was still very much alive.

"Yeah, tree jumper, I got sumthin' extra special planned out for you," Black Magic said and stopped the truck in front of a ran-down neighborhood garage where the local's frequent to get small jobs done to their cars.

"Say, old school…yeah, you," Black Magic called out to an elderly black man who was sitting on a stoop in front of the garage.

The elderly man stretched his legs and pointed to himself, as if he wasn't sure who Black Magic was referring to.

"Don't make me get outta dis truck you old muthafucka," Black Magic said and the elderly man began to walk toward the Navigator.

"How can I help you, young man?" he asked chewing on tobacco.

"I need a real thick rope, you know, the kind that dem pink ear crackers use to lynch you black folk wit' back-n-da-day."

"I'm not sure, young man, lemme check for you," the elderly man said and disappeared into the garage.

He returned a minute later with a thick ten-foot rope.

"Yeah, that's perfect, old school. How much you want for dat?"

"Uhh, I think twenty dollars would be a generous offer."

"What about a pocket knife. Do you got one of dem too?"

"Well…" the elderly man pulled out a timeworn pocketknife that was probably older than he was. "I never had any intentions on parting with this."

"How does fiddy dollars sound?" Black Magic asked.

"Well—"

"Okay, one hunnit."

"You see, I don't think you understand, young man. This knife survived the Vietnam War wit' me and—"

"Okay, old school, you don't have to work me wit' that history lesson you tryin' to tell," Black Magic said and handed the elderly man five hundred dollars. "Just take dis and shut da fuck up."

"Thank you, young man. You just bought yourself a fine knife there."

"Yeah, yeah," Black Magic said and peeled off.

Fifteen minutes later, Black Magic stopped the truck and hopped out. With the rope around his neck and knife in his pocket, he walked around and yanked Vic out the passenger door. He dragged Vic some twenty odd feet through shrubs and sharp rocks until he made it to a set of railroad tracks. He sprawled Vic's body across it and took the rope from his neck.

"You wanna go 'round rappin' bitches-n-shit, huh? Well, dis what we do to muthafuckas like you," Black Magic said and cut the thick rope in four parts.

He tied Vic's hands and feet tight to the steel rail, and pulled hard on each knot to ensure that Vic could never escape. Before he walked away from the scene, Black Magic stood over him and popped the collar to his Giorgio Brutini suit.

CHAPTER 26

Lisa turned on the street where Malcom's top floor apartment stood high in a ten story high rise in South Holland, Illinois. She immediately scoured the parking areas for any "flashy whips" that would confirm Adon's and Shamrock's presence inside.

They gotta be there! she thought.

Malcom had promised her that Adon and Shamrock would be there and this was one time where she was counting on that weasel to come through. He didn't have a clue of what Lisa was *really* up to.

"Shit! I don't see any whips out here that Adon or Shamrock would usually drive," Lisa said and parked her 1999 Dodge Intrepid behind a primed-up Buick Regal.

"Are you even sure that Malcom is even here?" Trina asked. She was the chick with the traffic jam booty that Malcom inquired about before.

"You betta believe it!" Lisa bragged with confidence. "All that juicy-kinky shit I put in his ear over the phone that nigga think he gon' get some pussy. Boo-yow! There goes the nigga's Durango truck parked right over there." Lisa said matter-of-factly.

"To be honest wit' you, boo," Trina started, "I think the nigga is lying to you. Adon and Shamrock is not up there. In fact, I doubt very seriously that Adon even fuck wit' him like that. Malcom ain't on dem niggas level."

"He still a part of their circle, though," Lisa said in support of the groundwork that she's laid up to this point.

"Only by marriage, though." Trina brought her back down to size, rolling her neck. "His mama has only been married to Nitty for a little while now. He ain't cut like dem, come from where they come from, or any place like it. Considering how well-off his mama is I wouldn't be surprised if that fool was raised in the burbs as naive as he is."

"I know dis, that's why I was able to trick his ass into helping me set-up this lick. And for some reason I just have this feeling that he's gonna come through for me."

"Well, all I can say is I hope you on point wit' your feelins 'cause the Vice Lords just rolled up," Trina pointed to a light green '84 Grand National that parked up the street.

Lisa quickly scanned the area again hoping to spot a flashy vehicle that would confirm that Adon and Shamrock was a least in the vicinity.

Maybe they rolled in a plain Jane, incognito-like, Lisa reasoned with herself and jumped when her cell chimed.

"You know that's him," Trina said and nodded toward the Grand National and the phone rung again. "Bitch, you betta answer it!"

Lisa picked up the cell. "Hello," she said reluctantly.

"What's da hold up?"

"Who dis?" she asked, acting like she didn't know.

"Look Lady-Lord, don't play wit' me!"

"Oh, this T-Bone, my bad. I was just tellin' Trina how I was wondering what was taking ya'll so long to get here," She lied and looked over at Trina who just shook her head. T-Bone was talking so loud that Trina could hear his every word.

"We here now, so what's da fuckin' hold up? Get yo ass up there!"

"Okay," Lisa said with a frown. "I'm going up there now."

"Remember, make sure you take yo' cell and call down here to us as soon as you see Shamrock and Adon; and at least one of dem betta be up there. I'm givin' yo' ass twenty minutes to find a way to call, and I advise you to leave the apartment as soon as you do. You got dat!?"

"Yeah, I got it."

"Tell Trina to stay her ass in the car. Don't fuck dis up!" he hung up his cell.

Lisa and Trina stared at one another, speechless.

"Did you just see that!?" Lisa blurted, looking out the corner of her eye.

"See what!? What are you talking about?" Trina asked as she too became a bit jumpy.

"Dis car in front of us with the deep black tint."

"This jacked up Regal right here?" Trina asked, confused.

"Yes, I saw it move like somebody's inside."

"Bitch you trippin' and now you got me trippin'. Ain't nobody in that damn car. Lisa, you probably hallucinating because of anxiety and you scared right now, which is totally understandable."

"That ain't got shit to do with shit. I know what I saw," Lisa said and made a move to get out of the car.

Trina touched the back of her hand and said, "Just keep in mind that no matter what happens tonight, we're doing this for Chief Flukie Lord and his daughter. Somebody gotta answer for what happened to them. May they rest in peace and good luck to you…Almighty."

"Thankyou, I needed that. And Mighty, Mighty to you too," Lisa said, expressing her gratitude through their Vice Lord/Lady-Lord lingo.

T-Bone, and three from his crew, sat back and watched as Lisa walked under the apartment complex's bright canopy and to the front door of the building.

"We finally gon' make these niggas pay for what they did to Chief Flukie. Ole bitch ass niggas!"one of the back seat passengers fumed.

"Glazed donuts is the type of niggas they is and we gon' eat'em up," the other back seat passenger said, bitting down on his bottom lip.

"That's right, Lords," T-Bone rose over the voices of his comrades. "With the death of Shamrock and Adon, Flukie will finally rest in peace…Almighty."

"Mighty, Mighty," the three men responded in unison, and filled their hands with heart-stopping weaponry.

Lisa pressed her fancy fingernail against the button that read '1011' beside it.

"This would be Malcom Calhoun's residence. Who may this be?" Malcom said through the intercom.

Lisa hesitated before answering and shook her head at how pathetic this dude was. His last name was Connors, not Calhoun.

"Heeey, baby. Now unless you're expecting some other chick just as fine as me do you need to ask who I be?" she freestyled a rhyme.

145

"Lisa!?" Malcom tried to hide his excitement and failed miserably.

"In the flesh, baby. Now buzz me in," Lisa said and looked in T-bone's direction.

"The elevator will be on your right," Malcom informed.

"Okay baby," she said and opened the door to the annoying buzzing sound.

Trina held her breath and watched Lisa turn to look back at her one last time before she walked in.

"I hope she hasn't gotten herself in some shit that she can't make it out of." Trina knew how T-Bone-n-nem were. They were trigger-happy gunslingers, who shoot first and ask questions later.

Trina closed her eyes and began to pray for Lisa when the sound of an engine turning abruptly cut her prayer short. She opened her eyes and watched as the primed-up Regal casually pulled away from the curb and drove away.

"I'll be damned," she said. "I guess Lisa wasn't hallucinating; there *was* somebody in that car."

"Say, Mighty?" the front passenger spoke up.

"What's up, Lord?" T-Bone acknowledged.

"Did you just see dat?"

"Dat Regal? Yeah, I saw it…and?" T-Bone asked for his point.

"And dat didn't look strange to you?"

"Don't let any distractions get you riled up for nothin'. Stay focused on the mission at hand, and that goes for all ya'll!" T-Bone said sternly to his three-man crew.

Malcom hurried throughout his suite, picking up underwear, dirty socks, and other unsightly things and began to light sweet smelling candles. He rushed to put on a dab of Eternity cologne and looked in the mirror.

Lisa stepped out of the elevator on the tenth floor and was immediately impressed with the high rise's upperclass atmosphere. The expensive light fixtures, wall to wall carpet, even the elevator was plush. Very different from the Rockwell housing projects that she was accustom to.

She made it to apartment 1011 and knocked on the door.

Malcom smiled at the pleasant sound and hit the play button on his stereo. "Slowly Pleased Tonight" by Dave Hollister emitted through the surround sound speakers.

"You may enter," he said just loud enough for her to hear.

She looked down at her wrist. The time read 12:51 A.M.

I got eighteen minutes to make this happen," she thought and obliged Malcom's request.

"Nice," she said upon entering. "Wow, I can get use to this."

She looked around at the pricey décor and how spacious the apartment was. It reminded her of Eddie Murphy's place in the movie *Boomerang* when Robin Givens first arrived, except she didn't smell any homemade dinner being prepared for *her*.

"I love what you did with the place."

"Me too, but not as much as I like what you did with yourself tonight," Malcom said from the love seat. He had on a short Terry Cloth house jacket with a cigar sticking out of his mouth.

"You like?" she asked and gave him a full enticing view of her body that filled out a Coggi skirt outfit fabulously.

"Oh, yeah, daddy like." he affirmed and made his move toward her. "Allow me to take this for you, and please, make yourself at home," he said and reached for the strap of her purse where her hair met her shoulder. He sat it down on his sofa and she watched him closely. Without saying a word, he left the room.

She sat down on the loveseat and said, "Trina couldn't come, her *man* wouldn't allow it." She secretly cased the place for any signs of Adon and Shamrock. "Um, where's Shamrock?" she asked and crossed her legs to keep her pantyless area her little secret.

"Oh, they'll be here shortly. He just called. They running a bit late." He lied. "Can I get you something to drink, beautiful?" he asked as he walked back into the kitchen. From there, he had a clear view overlooking the living room.

"Yes, you can," she said and looked at her wrist. It was 12:54 A.M.

"Anything special you like?" he asked and snorted a gram of cocaine.

147

"Anythang is fine, just as long as it's not strong."

Malcom placed two small glasses on the countertop and poured Tequila in both.

"Yes, it is on tonight. She won't know what hit her," he mumbled and reached under the counter to retrieve a bottle of Rohypnol; a powerful date-rape drug that was tasteless, scentless, and difficult to detect and guaranteed to effect the brain almost instantaneously.

Malcom knew what the drug was capable of, this wasn't the first time he added it to his game. He told his last victim flat out, "I spit venom."

What she didn't know is he meant every word, literally. But she figured it out the hard way when the very next morning she shockingly found herself in his bed, fully clothed with a sore pussy. She walked inside the living room and she saw him asleep on the couch, where he'd claimed to have been the entire morning after she had passed out from having "too much" to drink. The poor girl stormed out of his apartment and never reported the incident or told a soul.

He added the powdery substance just as before, except this time he was going to try something new. He doubled the dose.

"This shall double the length of play time. As fine as she is I must have at least ten straight hours of suckin' and fuckin' her," he mumbled with a smirk.

"What are you smiling about?" Lisa asked as he approached.

"I was smiling at the idea of how happy I would make you as my wife," he said.

"Is that right?" She blushed and placed a few more pretzels in her mouth that was held inside of a glass-serving bowl atop a glass table.

"Sure it is," he responded.

"So are you gonna call Shamrock and Adon and see wassup?"

"Baby, they'll be here shortly. Besides, your girl didn't come so it's just me and you, anyway. What we need with them?" he asked and Lisa balled up her face.

"Well, I'm 'bout to leave 'cause that wasn't the agreement," she said and stood to her feet.

"Baby, baby, relax," he said. "I told you they'll be here soon. They just called about a minute before you showed up. Here, have yourself a drink," he said and handed her the secret venom.

After snacking on those pretzels her mouth was a bit dry and in need of something wet.

"Thank you," Lisa said and swallowed a gulp without any regards to the drink's potency. She fell right on her ass upon the loveseat, and began to choke and speak at the same time. "I thought I asked for something not strong!?"

"Slow down some, love…it's not a strong drink. You're just drinking it too fast," he said and patted her back.

"Boy, you a lie! This is Tequila and this shit *is* strong! Usually I'll be upset, but it just so happens to be my favorite drink. So I'ma let you slide this time," she said with a faint smile and looked down at her wrist again. 12:56.

"What? You got somewhere you need to be?"

"Um…um…" Lisa didn't realize she actually glanced at her watch while he was looking. She was at a loss for words and desperately needed an intervening period so that her mind could catch up with her tongue. Not knowing what else to do, she downed the rest of her Tequila to buy some time.

"Oooh shit!" The Tequila made its presence felt. "Um…no…not at all. I was just wondering what was taking Shamrock-n-nem sooo long." Her speech was starting to slur. She began to feel sluggish and before she knew it she was helpless.

He watched maliciously as the powerful drug transformed her.

Straight venom baby, he thought.

"So, love, whatever happened to big booty Trina? Wasn't she supposed to tag along?" he asked only to further confirm that the drug was doing its job.

"I dunno," she shrugged her shoulders and slowly drifted off until her face met with the seat.

He was overly excited like a male homosexual with a bag filled with dicks! He peeked under her Coggi skirt and marveled at her 'camel's foot'. He reached into his cloth pocket and came out with a vial. He twisted the top and poured a line of cocaine from her kneecap to her crouch, and snorted it all before coming up.

"Yes! Yes! Yes!" he chanted and left the room.

Lisa came to. Her vision was a blur and her head was too heavy to lift.

"Trin...Trin...Trina...help...mmeee," she murmured and reached out for her purse that lay on the sofa across the room. "I...I...mussst... call."

Malcom entered the room with a tube of KY Lubricant and four packs of Magnum condoms in his hand.

"Hey, love, what do you think you're doing?" He grabbed her hand and threw it back. Her body went limp again; eyes shut. He smirked, removed her outfit, and was over-the-top delighted with what he saw. With the exception of her red pumps, she was now very naked.

He pushed his tongue in and out of her pussy and shoved three fingers inside. He was really having one buffet-of-a-time when she opened her eyes and gazed over his shoulder. "Shaaamroock," she moaned and passed out again.

Malcom was insulted. He rose up in anger and said, "Bitch do I look like Shamrock's black ass to you!?"

"Absolutely not. There's only one Shamrock," said a voice from behind, "And you don't fit the mode."

Malcom turned and received a stiff blow to his head from the butt of Shamrock's .10mm. Malcom staggered before tripping to the floor.

"I see you up to yo' old tricks, date-rape, sucka," Shamrock said.

"What are you talking about, man!?" Malcom asked and reached for the top of his head and felt a bloody gash.

"If you don't know, then I won't tell," Shamrock said and walked over to view Lisa's face. "Oh, you fuckin' wit' da enemy. She cute though, I'll give you that," he said recognizing Lisa as a Lady Lord. He looked down at Malcom and asked, "Now why do you think I'm here?"

"I don't even know how you got in, much less why you're here," Malcom cried.

"C'mon, take a guess," Shamrock said and ran the burna over his baldhead.

"Shamrock, I don't know, man," Malcom was nearly in tears.

"How 'bout dis," Shamrock continued. "Yo' loving *"father"* tried to have me murked."

"Who, Nitty? I swear I didn't know anything about that. I just wanted your car out of the washing stall because it was holding up business, and you know I just got the manager position and I didn't know he was going to kill you over it, and—" Malcom rambled.

"Enough," Shamrock said calmly, but Malcom was fear-drunk.

"And, and Nitty isn't my real father anyhow—"

"ENOUGH!" Shamrock bellowed but Malcom wouldn't quit.

"What that got to do with me anyway? I'm saying—"

Shamrock upped his burna to his dome and Malcom sobered up and stop talking with the quickness. He gazed up from the floor with a sheepish look.

"My intention was to come here and slump yo' pathetic ass," Shamrock hesitated and looked over at Lisa. He'd realized why she was there. "Tell you what I'm gonna do, though," Shamrock reached into the pocket of his black Louis Vuitton trench coat and pulled out a .32 revolver. "You wanna live?"

Malcom nodded.

He tossed Malcom the .32 and said, "Well, good luck 'cause you gon' need it."

"Why would I need this?" Malcom asked dumbfounded.

"You wanna live, right?" Shamrock asked, lowering his gun.

"Yeah," Malcom responded.

"Well, stand to your feet and prove it. If I was you I'd concentrate on yo' front door," Shamrock said and made a mad dash to the rear of the apartment at exactly the same time the front door was kicked off its hinges.

Shamrock grabbed a hold of a rope and placed one leg outside the window that he used to get inside. Then he sat on the windowsill to watch Malcom in action.

Malcom was stunned to say the least, but his reflexes were on point.

T-Bone was the first one through the door and Malcom had the ups on him. He aimed the .32 at T-Bone's chest and pulled the trigger twice. Click. Click.

Malcom looked at the burna, then in Shamrock's direction when he realized the cross. "YOU DIRTY MUTHA—"

T-Bone raised his Tec-9 and sprayed Malcom full of led.

With his usual half grin, Shamrock extended his leather covered hand and released six .38 revolver bullets that he took out the burna before tossing it to Malcom. They fell silently onto a bearskin rug. He rose off the windowsill and lowered himself down to ground level unseen.

"Ay, Lord, ya'll search over that way. And you come wit' me!" T-Bone directed his men.

They swept the entire apartment before they concluded that neither Adon nor Shamrock was there.

"Shit!" T-Bone yelled. "Let's go, Lords!" T-Bone barked and his crew bailed out the door. On his way out, he caught sight of Lisa, naked and laying on her back.

"Lisa! Lisa!" he yelled but she didn't move.

"Let's go, Mighty!" one of the Lords hollered from the doorway, and T-Bone ran to catch up with his crew.

The atmosphere of the living room was polluted with gun smoke.

Malcom was DOA and slouched over at Lisa's feet. She was alive but her pulse was weak. She started to shake violently. Her body muscles contracted involuntarily as she underwent a convulsion. She foamed at the mouth and her eyes went into her forehead.

Suddenly she became still, and her heart rate went flat. Lisa couldn't fight it any longer. She died of an apparent overdose from the deadly date-rape drug, Rohypnol.

Trina watched as T-Bone and his crew bolted out of the apartment complex and ran to their Buick Grand National. The abrupt action caused her to sink low in her seat. Then she saw something else. She squinted her eyes to get a better view through the darkness. It was like a scene from a movie as a man with a trench coat lowered himself from a tree and appeared at the back bumper of the Grand National. All she saw was fire breathing from his hands while the loud bangs echoed through her ears. And just like that, the man in the trench coat was gone just as quick as he came.

Trina looked up to the top of the high rise where she figured Malcom's apartment to be as she came to terms with Lisa not going to be walking out with a story to tell.

She dialed Lisa's cell number hoping she'd answer. She didn't.

Trina was scared as all hell, wondering wear the stranger in the trench coat had gone, and whether or not he was coming back.

She scooted over to the driver's side of Lisa's Intrepid and turned the ignition, and slowly pulled away from the curb. The horn from the Grand National was non-stop. The closer she approached the louder it got, and the more terrified she became of what she might see. She drove up beside it and forced herself to look inside.

All four bodies were slump. Brain matter and blood tinted the windows a dark red, and what was left of T-Bone's head rested on the horn of the steering wheel.

Shamrock made it around the street corner in long strides while he replaced the empty clips with full ones, and kept the burnas exposed at his sides. He arrived at the beginning of an alleyway where his Regal was parked.

He hesitated.

Sumthin' ain't right, he mused and scanned the area.

"Well, well, well," he whispered after observing two silver H2 Hummers parked on a side street.

He threw himself against the side panel of a garage and held his breath in an effort to hear even the smallest of sounds. His instincts were right, he could hear them. However, low-pitched, he was able to make out a man's voice that seemed to be of African decent. Shamrock exhaled and held his breath again. Through the darkness he spotted eleven infra-red beams coming from patios, balconies, and pathways, and they were all trained on his Regal.

Very impressive Nitty, but If you wanna be a worthy competitor then you gotta be mo' creative than that, he thought and secretly ducked away in the opposite direction, quietly rapping the lyrics to "Many

Men" by Curtis "50Cent" Jackson.

"Honey…Honey, wake up," Nitty's wife half-asleep, reached on the nightstand to pick up her husband's two-way.

"What is it?" Nitty asked irritably and turned over to see what she wanted.

"Your damn bug-a-boo machine has been vibrating. Here," she said with attitude and passed him the two-way. She pulled her sleep eye mask down from her forehead, covered her eyes, and laid her head on the pillow.

Nitty rolled over and turned on a small lamp that was on his side of their bed. He removed his reading glasses from the nightstand and held them close to his eyes without actually putting them on. After a couple of hard blinks he read his latest message: TWO DOWN AND SO MANY TO GO…I'M COMING!

Nitty looked over at his wife. She appeared to be sound asleep, but he knew if he moved one muscle outside of their bed she'd be up just that quick. He placed his glasses and two-way on the nightstand, shut down the light, and went back to sleep.

Vic gradually woke up to the pain that inflamed his face. He squeezed his eyelids shut a few times to regulate his vision to the stark darkness that completely caught him off guard.

Where am I? he asked the scattered stars throughout the sky.

He attempted to move his arms and legs.

What da fuck!

He struggled but there was no use. Just like Vanity he couldn't break free.

Suddenly he heard a horn in the distance. A horn that as it got closer, sounded less and less like any common vehicle. He looked around him, then at the ropes and what they were tied to.

"Railroad tracks!" he mumbled and strained to lift his head off the rail. About a mile down he saw a big bright light penetrate the darkness. It was a freight train and it was closing in fast.

"Ummmm!" He tried to scream for help but the crushed bones in his face would not allow his lips to part much. Instead, he watched as he jaws expand from the air in his body. He began to move about violently, but the double-knots would not budge.

The train was closing in at a rapid pace as it now appeared to be just a block away, and slowly he gave up on the fight and began to silently pray.

Lord, I'm not gon' ho up now 'cause my back is against the wall. But all I ask is that you make dat nigga Adon pay...Amen.

"UMMMMM!" The train's steel wheels tore through him like a razor blade to cheese.

CHAPTER 27

Vanity sat comfortably in the family room reading Wahida Clark's *Thugs, And The Women Who Love Them,* identifying with the female characters to the highest degree.

It had been over three weeks since Vanity's brush with Vic. During that time she's been a little standoffish toward Adon. It wasn't that she didn't want to get next to him, I mean *really* get next to him, but each of the two times that she tried she couldn't help but to visualize Vic's ugly face, the way that he looked at her, his hands, and the way he handled her.

The bruise on her stomach had just healed. She really couldn't understand it herself when she really thought about it. The sex her and Adon had in Natasha's guestroom was amazing. Easily the best she'd ever had. Niggas in Seattle couldn't compare. Adon was her savior. He was whom she wanted. Being in his house for a day, let alone weeks was something she would've did anything to see happen any time before she was violated.

Surprisingly to her, Adon seemed to be cool with her failure to please. He didn't cop an attitude or act funny about it at all. He didn't pressure her to do anything that she wasn't ready to do. It was as if there were other things more important than just sexing her, one being her comfort level and she dug that.

He offered his bed while he slept in one of his guest rooms. He was exceptionally supportive and even brought her breakfast in bed every morning. She returned the favor each night with a candle lit dinner. It was evident that he had once shared this home with a female because other than visiting Bath & Body Works to pick up a few femininity items for Vanity, he didn't have to leave the house for anything. He was pretty well balanced. But there was something else going on. Something that he was going through that she couldn't tap into.

Although she'd really gotten to know him during her time at his home, he built a brick wall around what was troubling him; even when it was clear that he'd rather rid it, he protected it from harm.

Adon was in his security room situated on the main level of his home. He stared forward while "The Game" by Common played in the background. In front of him were twelve monitors that allowed him to see everything on the inside and outside of his home.

Nitty called him with the latest killing and made it clear that he wasn't happy about it. It was now comprehendible that Shamrock was out there somewhere, and he was playing the game for keeps.

Adon knew it was only a matter of time before shit came to a head and that time was near. The thought of losing everything he'd worked hard for hung in the balance, and Shamrock was the last nigga he wanted to battle in order to keep it. To prepare for that, Adon put in an order for sixty keys with another connect that he kept contact with out of Miami, and the shipment was scheduled to arrive tomorrow. He wasn't about to let Nitty, The Convolution, or anyone else stop his cash flow.

Charlotte and Joyous had been on his mind since he'd discovered that she'd just up and left. And since then, thoughts of her had only intensified. Granted, he noticed a change within her during the months after their separation, but leaving without telling him was an act he never considered. True, he hadn't been the best father to his child but would Charlotte punish him to that degree?

He still couldn't wrap his mind around it. His gut was telling him that there was more to the story. But he didn't know where to look, where to start, or who to ask.

Then there was Doe. He made sure to keep his phone line open awaiting his call, but Doe hadn't contacted him as he said he would. He couldn't explain it, but he felt that somehow this stranger, Doe, could bring some clarity to his life; there was something familiar about his voice. Adon's mind was like a piece of chewed bubble gum, being pulled in all kinds of directions.

"We Fly High" by Jim Jones chimed from Adon's BlackBerry, bringing him out of his daze. He knew immediately who it was.

"Wudup, Black," he said.

"Just out here keepin my eyes peeled, A," Black Magic said. "I called the hospital like you ask me to."

"And?" Adon asked and sat straight up in his chair.

"Is you sittin' down?" Black Magic knew that what he was about to report would be a hard pill for Adon to swallow.

"Talk to me, Black."

"Lil' One didn't make it, man," Black Magic broke the news.

"Aww, damn. Fuck! Fuck!" Adon yelled in Black Magic's ear and let his cell fall to the carpet as he interlocked his fingers atop his head.

Black Magic heard the impact of the cell meeting the floor, but by Adon's inaudible he knew he was in earshot so he continued to talk.

"The lil' homie was a soldier though. Lil' nigga took four to his upper body and was still alert long enough to hold a conversation wit' you. Doctors said his vital organs were ripped to shit, it was a miracle that he lived through the first night, let alone a few weeks.

"A, I heard what you said to him on the way to the hospital. That was good shit and I have no doubt in my mind he fought that hard and lived that long because of you, A, and the encouraging words that you told him."

Black Magic sighed heavily.

"A, it wasn't yo' fault, fam. He came outta nowhere and got caught up in da crossfire...A! A!" he called out while Adon listened to his every word.

Adon picked up his phone.

"The picnic is tomorrow, make sure you on top of yo' shit," he said and tossed the cell on the console.

Adon slouched in his high-back chair. He ran his hands from his forehead to the bottom of his face, and glanced at monitor number three that overlooked the entire family room. Vanity no longer graced the screen.

He quickly sat up in his chair and darted his eyes from monitor to monitor, Vanity was nowhere in sight.

Suddenly Adon felt the softest touch caress his shoulder. He didn't have to look back. He knew whom she was and was instantly put at ease by her touch.

"Ahhh," he moaned as he felt her massaging hands work out the knots around his shoulder blades.

Vanity tugged on his shoulder and spun the chair on its swivel.

Adon ran his eyes up and down her body. She had on a camouflage bra and boy short set with Petit Peton heels. He stood to his feet and grabbed her by the waist, bringing her close.

"I wanna be your soldier girl," she whispered and met his lips with hers.

He gently pulled back and said, "V, you don't have to do this if you not ready."

She looked deep into his medium brown eyes and whispered, "A, stop talkin'."

"I got'cha," he said and met her lips halfway while another one of Common joints entitled "I Want You" ignited their moods.

Adon picked her up and she wrapped her legs around him. They both were in another dimension as they kissed all the way to the "off-limits" living room. He sat her down on a raised, stone hearth that had a blanket on top from last night when Vanity talked him into melting marshmallows over the fire inside the fireplace. Although it was the summer season and out of the norm to be sitting by a fire, Adon had never partaken in something so simple and Vanity eased his reluctance. They talked and laughed all night long.

"Baby strike up the fire again," she said holding the back of his neck.

"What is it with you and fire?" he asked. "Is there a connection?"

"It's romantic, A," she mouthed.

"But it's summer time."

"Puh-leeze?" she begged. "I never made love by a fire before."

"I got cha," Adon released her hips and set a flame to the walnut wood. He stood and watched as the fire brewed. He half jogged back to where the stereo resided and put on "The Greatest Sex" by R. Kelly and cranked up the volume.

When he returned, Vanity stood on her heels atop the stone hearth and did what she do best to attract the male species. She cycloned her flawless body slowly to the platinum rated ballad, giving Adon a riveting performance while the flame from the five foot tall fireplace acted as a daring backdrop.

Adon took his time removing his silk lounging robe and pants, keeping his undivided attention on Vanity. Once he was free of his silk, he walked up to her and rested his hands on either side of her revolving hips. He looked up to her. He was mesmerized. In his eyes, she was a Goddess treading in midair. He licked his lips and started planting damp kisses around her pierced navel.

Damn, she smell good, he mused.

She easily brought her hands down from above her head and rubbed his hair against the grain, pulling his waves up as she massaged his scalp. He was craving her. Adon looped the band to her boy shorts around his thumbs and walked his hands down her thick, toned thighs, bringing the boy shorts down to her ankles.

She dropped her bubble ass low and sat on the blanket. She extended her legs in front of her and Adon pulled the boyshorts over her heels one at a time, while she undid her matching bra and tossed it away from the fire. They kissed fully and Adon cupped her bubble in his hands.

She laid flat on her back and he transferred his kisses to her neck before he worked his way down to her D-cup sized breast. He licked around her areola and watched her nipples harden.

"Ahhh," she moaned.

He gently sucked on her nipples, dividing equal time between the two. Her chest heaved. She wanted more of him. Adon went from the inside of her thighs to the prized jewel. He grazed her pussy lips with his tongue. She sat up on her elbows and, slowly, Adon licked the length of her wetness. Vanity moaned with pleasure and palmed her own breast. He focused on her pearl.

"Oh, yes, A...yesss!" she hissed and threw her head back.

Adon squeezed her bubble and lifted her up. He began to lick every angle of her pussy before he moved down and tasted the sweet nectar between her moist ass cheeks. She was really beginning to lose herself as she threw her legs around his neck. Adon used his broad shoulders to lift and balance her body as he used his tongue to quench his thirst.

Vanity flailed in ecstasy.

"Ohhhh, baby, what are you doin' to me?" she cried as he lowered her bottom to the hearth, jolts of pleasure shot through her body.

Adon licked her unique taste from his lips and said, "Damn you taste good, V."

He looked between her open legs and her pussy swelled tremendously. He grabbed a hold of her and she threw her hands around his neck. He picked her up from the hearth and began to walk her over to the dinning room.

"A, I want to feel you from behind baby," Vanity whispered in his ear.

Adon sat Vanity down on his Birchwood dining table at the same time "Sex In The Kitchen" started to play. The pricey table was sturdy and quickly she saw there was no need to worry. She turned on all fours and parted her knees further out, allowing Adon easy access. She felt Adon's dick push against her soaked pussy.

Vanity thrust back, four inches of his dick slid into her. She continued to push back and more and more of Adon's stiffness disappeared inside her warmth.

Soon Vanity felt her ass cheeks pushing against Adon's lower abdomen. She began to rotate her hips slowly just to settle him in. Adon ran his hands over her small back before he grabbed her hips tightly. He pulled out several inches and thrust hard. The neighbors could hear the sounds of his balls and legs slapping against Vanity's ass and thighs as they both howled like a couple of wild animals.

He picked up his speed and intensity while Vanity met each forward thrust with a back thrust of her own. She started to buck and flail.

"Ohhh, you killin' me! Ahhhh, you killin' me softly!" she screamed, her legs danced in bliss. "Baby, please, baby, baby, please...don't stop!"

Adon picked one of his legs up from the floor and rested his foot on a chair. This maneuver allowed for deeper penetration as he obliged Vanity's demand. He went to work, long stroking as he watched Vanity's body twitch with pleasure.

"Ohhh! Ohhh!" Vanity got buck wild and Adon was loving every second of it, as he smacked her ass on both sides.

Before long he suspended all movement, and allowed Vanity to ride him cyclone-style from behind.

"Owww, baby, yo' ass is immaculate!" Adon praised her as she thrust her hips back and forth and around, all the while keeping his dick inside.

"Yes! Yes, A!" Vanity exhaled and dipped her back low, throwing her ass further into the air. Adon grabbed a hold of her waist just to hold on, and he joined back in.

"I'ma let it loose, V! It's about to blow!" Adon hollered.

"Me too, daddy! Me TOOOOO!" Vanity spoke in tongues. Her head shook violently from side to side as if she was undergoing an exorcism.

Adon contracted his thigh muscles, his body stiffened.

"AHHH, it's here!" he announced and let loose.

He coated her pussy with a flood of his fluids and her sex cream flowed over his shaft. They were left exhausted and panting.

CHAPTER 28

The time was 11:37 A.M. and the temperature was already reaching upwards of ninety degrees for the 2nd Annual Statewide Picnic, held at the Forrest Preserve. Black Magic supervised and coordinated the placements of a hundred-man security unit who were heavily armed, alert, and ready to clap if he even *thought* about giving the order. The bulk of the soldiers were Murda Park survivors, itching for signs of drama.

Black Magic was posted in front of the only passable entrance that led to a broad, fifty square acre of green land. He was currently directing the Sims bus company to their designated parking areas.

There were ten buses in total and all were filled to capacity with young females eager to party. Once he gave each driver the green light to release their doors, the girls poured out by the dozens. Black Magic used the effectiveness of two bright orange batons to direct traffic, which included a parade of vehicles that fell into succession.

This was the ballers time to shine as they made their grand entrance in some of the flyest whips this city has ever seen. And the ladies wasn't left out. The many that met the "status" criteria also partook in this line of "hood royalty," as they fell in with their Compressors, BMW's, and SUV's.

There's two sides to every coin and this here was the "glory side" at its finest! Truly the benefits of what being an above average nigga who played the game well was all about. Plenty was rockin' HI HATERS T-shirts, but on this day they were hollering, "Bye haters" and hi to the niggas who knew how to turn crums into solid bricks.

This was what every reputable breed of man around these parts looked forward to every year. No matter the organization or occupation. If you were "plugged" then this was the place to be. Undisputed crowns were handed down and honored with the utmost praise. And it was here where the up-and-comers could showcase just how good their hustle has been to them.

For this special event the heavy hitters would go as far as to drop six figures on vehicle's price-tags, just to show the people from the land who the "Boss Hogs" were in their city. Then what was initially a mere car show would turn into a widespread platinum and diamonds exhibit the minute they stepped out of their fly whips.

If the people still wasn't clear of who's ego should be stroked the most, it was off to the crap game where the dice determined who's money was the longest and it was all done in good fun. Every one displayed great energy and were truly having a good time together.

This event was something they all have come to cherish. It represented their city streets rather well, and that alone made them a proud people. And the social atmosphere added immensely to the positives of effective networking.

Great minds had come together on these neutral grounds in the past and benefited immensely simply by exchanging valuables in the form of input. In a short time after each event, the heavy hitters would get heavier in the game, while the up-and-comers always seem to get in where they fit in. Just last year this was the place where Black Magic approached Adon for a position, and since then Black Magic hasn't wanted for anything.

This extravaganza really served its purpose. With the exception of the Vice Lords, in attendance were six Chiefs from six different organizations that ran the everyday operations on the streets and things were peaceful. Quite the contrary to the many baths they were taking in each other's blood just three years ago; before a time when Adon formulated a plan that brought each Chief to the table. In a result, they found a middle ground while they, the street-share holders, were able to focus on what was important—their money.

The Forest Preserve was a replica of the Freaknic back when it was hosted in Hotlanta in the early '90s. The Disc Jockey from the most popular radio station, here in Chicago, WGCI, was in attendance and he brought his entire booth along with him as "Good Life" by Kanye West earth quaked the land from the concert speakers that surrounded the area like an electric fence around a prison camp.

The aroma from good smelling barbecue and different types of "herb" filled the air. Several photograph sites were scattered throughout with a variety of background settings to choose from, and there were twenty well-trained horses on site that were accompanied by a guide who gave out brief horseback rides. Plus there were horse shoe games and card tables were put up for spades and dominoes. For the crowd's viewing pleasure, the ladies put use to the custom built stage and participated in a "drop it like it's hot" contests while a twenty by twenty foot wide screen displayed the video footage to the song.

Compliments of Adon, everything here was free. From the gallons of top shelf drinks to the high grade marijuana along with many souvenirs that made this day all the more memorable for anyone who attended.

Any weapons outside of the security unit and any mind-altering drugs other than killer weed, beer, and alcohol was forbidden, and strictly enforced. The spot was hot with entertainment. And anybody who was somebody was there, except for Mr. Highly Expected himself, the host.

"Where da hell is Adon at anyway?" Black Magic said into his headgear walkie-talkie and dialed Adon's cell number.

Adon was in the process of burning up the expressway at 130mph, as he became one with his Suzuki Hayabusa 1300R like a jockey racing a prize winning horse. Vanity, getting a high from the rush, tightened her thighs around him and held on to his waist with her ass hiked in the air. Due to the loud revving and vibration of the 1300R, he was oblivious to Black Magic's attempt to reach him. He guided the crotch rocket onto the exit ramp and executed several illegal turns and short cuts that placed him at a shopping center just off the corner of 87th and Cottage Grove.

Adon had the grey utility van that held his sixty kilos in view. He used the front of his sock-covered, pink and white, Air Force One tennies to place the Suzuki's gear into neutral.

He looked down at his watch and said, "Right on time. Their shippin' and handlin' services is sweet. You ready baby?"

"As ready as I'll ever be," Vanity said with confidence.

"That's my girl. Now you don't have to worry about a thang just follow me, aiight?"

"Aiight," she said sounding just like him.

"Go do yo' thang." He smacked her ass and she got straight to it.

Vanity casually crossed the busy intersection and walked toward the utility van when two guys rode up in a '72 Donk sitting tall on 28-inch rims. "Wassup, Ma. Where we headed?" the driver asked after muting his bump.

"Excuse me?" Vanity said trying not to make eye contact.

"You heard. I said where we headed, ma?" he repeated and displayed his platinum teeth.

Why do these Chicago niggas think somebody owe them something? she mused and said, "I don't know where you goin', but I'm goin' to my car," Vanity said.

"Well lemme tell you where I'm headed, good hooker, I mean, good looker," he said and his passenger chuckled.

Vanity rolled her eyes and stopped walking.

"Me and my mans here, we headed to Adon's 2nd Annual Statewide Picnic baby. And I know da nigga so even though you might not be invited I can get cha in. Just show up wit' me. I'm considered a heavy hitta around these parts, if you know what I mean," he said and rubbed his goatee.

Vanity put her hand on her hip and glanced over at Adon who was across the street and sitting on his bike.

Adon removed his helmet from the side clamp that locked it in place. He put it over his head, brought down the deeply tinted shield and tugged on his burna.

"Damn, why this girl gotta be so fine? So bad she stoppin traffic. Get rid of those niggas, V," he said quietly as he continued to watch just how Vanity would handle herself.

"Hooker, huh?" Vanity said and rolled her neck. "Well let me put you up on a lil' sumthin' sumthin', Mr. Heavy Hitter. I got a pretty lil' friend that lives in my pocket. She's thirty-two with a cute snub-nose. I call her pearl, 'cause when I handle her that's what I'm holdin'.

"Now for your sake you'll be smart and drive this country ass car down the road 'cause I swear if she pops up on the scene, she's comin' with a *bang!*"

"Fiesty! I like 'em like dat," he said slapping palms with his buddy. "Okay den, shawty. I ain't into chasin' no bitches that don't wanna be caught anyhow. I'll see you again."

They then drove off.

"Whatever," Vanity said and watched the Donk until it made it to a corner and turned off the street. She walked to the van and reached under the back passenger side wheelwell and got the van's keys like Adon instructed. She got inside, took a deep breath, and started the engine.

Vanity's cell chimed.

"Hello," she answered.

"Good job," Adon said.

"Thank you."

"Now follow me." Adon pulled into the busy intersection and Vanity got right behind him, poised and in control.

Twenty minutes later, Adon pulled in front of Chicago Self Storage on Fullerton Avenue. He hopped off the bike and directed Vanity on where to park the van. A big solid 330 pound man standing at six-six climbed out of a Suburban and walked up to Adon.

"Wut it do, A," he said and extended his hand.

"Gorilla G," Adon greeted him and gave a thug hug as Vanity walked up.

"Dayuum!" Gorilla G said after laying his eyes on Vanity. "She wit' choo, dawg?"

"Calm down big homie," Adon said and patted him on the shoulder. "Yeah, she's wit' me."

He stepped aside and introduced the two.

"Vanity, this is Gorilla G; Gorilla G, this is the lovely Vanity."

Vanity couldn't help but to blush from Adon's charming words.

"Hi," she said and shook Gorilla G's hand.

"Hi to you, too," he returned, not wanting to let go.

"Aiight," Adon said, breaking Vanity free. "Baby, I'll meet you at the bike?"

"Okay, A," she said and walked toward the Suzuki while Gorilla G became spellbound by her strut.

"Now stay focus big homie," Adon suggested.

"I got choo, shawty jus' fine dats all," Gorilla G explained and took his eyes off her and focused on the task.

"Now the storage unit is reserved," Adon continued. "The number is W1977, here's the key and the keys to the van also. Park it somewhere close, but safe."

He placed the keys inside of Gorilla G's obese hand.

"The van is there. You did bring help didn't you?"

"Yup, I got two of my lil' nephews wit' me," Gorilla G said.

"Aiight, you know what to do," Adon said as he was walking off.

"But Black Magic said that I was s'pose to be yo' personal security today."

"What?" Adon was hearing it for the first time.

"Yup," Gorilla G reconfirmed.

"Well, don't worry 'bout that I'll holla at Black."

"But I'm tryin' to get to dat picnic, dawg," Gorilla G said seriously.

"Be easy, you'll get there soon enough. Them barbecue ribs and chicken wings will be there when you get there. Just take care of this first, aiight."

"Okedoke," Gorilla G said and went to work.

Adon made it to the Suzuki where Vanity awaited.

"Don't worry about him he cool people, and harmless to women," Adon stated to Vanity.

He hopped on the bike and they were in the wind. Vanity wanted to freshen up before she went to the picnic so he dropped her off in front of Natasha's house. Before she walked away Adon shared his thoughts with her.

"I'm gonna do somthin' special for my sis today just to show her how much I appreciate her, you know. I don't know what it is I'm gonna do yet, but when it takes place you'll know it and I want you to make sure she goes along."

"You so sweet, A. That's why I love you...oops," Vanity blurted and held her hand in front of her mouth. She hated herself for slipping at the tongue, and her embarrassment showed through her flushed face.

"It's aiight," Adon said and grabbed a hold of her waist. "C'mere." She gradually came closer and united their tongues. "See you soon," he said and watched her go inside. Before he wheelie down the block, he called his home and checked his voice mail, but Charlotte still hadn't called.

Gorilla G was already running late when Adon called him with a change of plans. Per Adon's request, he rushed to Natasha's home and began to knock on her front door like he was the police.

"Who is it?" Natasha asked as she approached the door.

"Gorilla G."

"Who?"

"Gorilla G. Adon sent me over."

Natasha wasn't trying to hear that garbage. Adon had never sent a nigga to her house, and he didn't mentioned anything about a "Gorilla" coming to her home. She looked through the peephole and her eye widened in an effort to fit his huge build within her frame of sight. She was not feeling this shit in the slightest bit and eased a .25 automatic from the pocket of her housecoat.

"Tash," Vanity said and startled her with the sudden call of her name, and Gorilla G started his pounding again, causing her nerves to jump for a second time.

"Look, I'm going to ask you one more time. Who are you and why are you here knocking on my door like you're nuts!?" Natasha yelled through the door.

"Oh, my fault. I guess I didn't realize it. I'm kinda heavy handed," he said. "But like I said, they call me Gorilla G and Adon sent me here to take you somewhere that you recently told him you wanted to go."

"Take me somewhere?" Natasha said. "Now I know you on some BS!" Natasha was just about to up her burna when Vanity spoke up.

"That's Gorilla G," she said recognizing his voice.

And this must be her surprise that A was talking about, she mused with a smile.

"You know him?" Natasha asked and slipped the burna back into her pocket without Vanity ever taking notice.

"Well I don't know him, but I met him earlier today."

"And how did you meet him?" Natasha asked with a scrutinizing stare.

"What? Your brother introduced us," Vanity said.

"Well you open the door, since you know him," Natasha walked away and Vanity opened it.

"What's poppin' ladies..?" Gorilla G said and entered the home like it was his. He stopped and looked Vanity up and down in her new outfit.

"Umm-huh, I know who you is. And you're off-limits," he said and looked over at Natasha. "So you must be Tasha?"

"Yeah, that's her," Vanity offered.

"Thank you, Vanity," Natasha said sarcastically.

"Heeey, sis." Gorilla G ran over and hugged Natasha and picked her up like they were long lost friends. He released her and looked into her face. "Man, ya'll look jus' alike. You know, me and yo' bruh go way back. I've been overseas fo' da last three years playin' pro ball, but I got injured and, so, now I'm back home."

"I'm sorry to here that," Natasha said, still a little rattled by his upbeat energy.

"I ain't. It is wut it is," he said. "But can't we go now, 'cause I need to get to da picnic."

"What did you say your name was again?" Natasha asked.

"You can call me G, sweetheart," he said and kissed the back of her hand.

"Well, G, there's your girl right there." she said and pointed to Vanity who was obviously ready to go.

"Tash, wait," Vanity said. "Aren't you going with us?"

"I'll pass," she said and walked out of the living room.

Vanity turned to Gorilla G and threw up the "one."

"Wait a minute," she mouthed and caught up with Natasha in her bedroom. "Girl, you have to go. I don't know this man and did you see how big he was?"

"How could I not?"

"Well, don't make me go by myself."

"If Adon sent him then you don't have anything to worry about, V. Besides, you met him earlier."

"He still a stranger and I don't want to go alone, sis."

"I'm not even dressed," she said and looked down at her nightgown.

"Pleeease?"

"Girl, I tell you, you are just as bad as Adon with that please mess."

"So does that mean you're going?"

"You really make me sick, you know that?"

"Yes, but you still love me."

"Unfortunately," Natasha said with a playful smile. "Let me throw some clothes on, but I'm warning you, we have to make this quick because I have to be somewhere soon."

Every other minute Black Magic conversed with his security team over their walkie-talkies. He kept a close ear, eye, and in some cases finger, on everything and everyone that moved and did not move. He wasn't taking any chances on overlooking even the smallest sign of trouble. He was responsible for every life on the grounds and he took the burden very seriously. He directed each man on his team to refrain from using the safety device on his weapon and to keep one in the chamber.

It was the event of the year. The father of all events hosted in Chicago and yet he and his security team were the only individuals there that weren't mingling in the festivity. However, they weren't stressing it, in fact, each of them had high hopes to partake in a party of a different kind. The type that provided that raw, rapid fire, "heart-stopping" action!

Adon had finally arrived just as his surprised guest touched down. Twista and his entourage sat at the intersection in front of the Forest Preserve.

The traffic was heavy and Adon yielded to Twista's parade of vehicles. They began to drive each whip, one after the other, into the entrance while Black Magic and several men from his team held up all opposing traffic and directed them in.

"Ooooh, weeee! Them niggas stuntin' fo' real!" Adon said.

Adon enjoyed the sight as each vehicle rolled their "grown man" rims slowly over the speed bump. They were all different models of modern Cadillacs, ranging from coupes, sedans, to SUVs with the exception of one Rolls Royce Phantom. They even added some flava to their personal motorcade display with blue and grey color-coordination.

The whip that seized all eyes was the two-toned, grey and blue, Rolls Royce Phantom that harbored Twista and it fell directly in the middle of their seven-vehicle formation.

As the vehicles drove pass Adon, each driver blew his horn to acknowledge him and Adon threw his index finger above his head, indicating "One Love". After the last vehicle rolled over the speed bump Adon gradually let up on the Suzuki's clutch and pulled in behind them.

Practically all those in attendance erupted with excitement when they saw the seven car celebratory procession as Adon began doing short wheelies and making plenty of noise from the revving of his engine. All the women went insane when the Phantom's rear window declined and Twista revealed his face from the luxurious depths of the backseat. They followed the stretch of concrete that led behind the stage and Adon detoured the Suzuki onto the grass and over to where Black Magic stood.

"How you feelin', gangsta?" Adon asked and extended his hand.

"Much better now that you've made it here in one piece," Black Magic responded and took a hold of his hand and they performed their customary handshake and thug hug.

"Where Gorilla G at? I appointed him as yo' personal security."

"Ohhhhh," Adon taunted in a playful manner. "Don't tell me you was worried for the kid," he said and reached for his dazzling medallion that spelled out his name in diamonds.

"Man, A, you know we at war and you should have security wit' you at all times," Black Magic stressed.

"I am security," Adon responded seriously. "And don't ever forget that."

Black Magic considered that for a moment before realizing Adon had more training and skill than his entire security team, including himself. "Well, where's Gorilla G at anyway?"

"I ran into him, but I got him handlin' some business for me," Adon said. "Man, it's beautiful out here. Look at this," Adon said, referring to the sunny weather and the fiesta that has grown since last year.

"Everythang is runnin' smooth so far," Black Magic said cutting straight to business. "The Black Stones, Four Corner Hustlas, Black Disciples, Black Ganagstas, Mickey Cobras, and of course the Gangsta Disciples is here. And now that you here, all of the Chiefs are accounted for. As you can see, the ladies out number the men by five to one."

"Yeah, I see that," Adon said with a smile and waved at a crew of women who were eyeing both him and Black Magic. "That's just how I planned it."

"And of course, the Vice Lords ain't show up," Black Magic said. "Then again we wasn't expectin' them too; not peacefully, anyway."

"Speakin' of them, do you have this entire area sealed tight?" Adon asked.

"Tighter than a virgin's pussy, A. Believe me, if they come through here on that monkey-ball-shit we gon' stand on them. Word is bond," Black Magic assured.

"If that does happen you just make sure that whatever you do, Twista and his crew is priority. Get them up outta here safely if somethin' does jump off."

"I got that and I gotta say, last year you surprised everybody when you got Scarface to roll up in dis bitch, but dis year you killed them wit' Twista, my nigga," Black Magic said and they gave each other pound.

"Have you heard about Malcom?" Adon asked.

"Yep, and T-Bone-n-nem too. I got my own theory about that one. What about Charlotte and Baby Joy, did you find out anything?"

Adon pushed the start button and revved the Suzuki's engine.

"We'll talk about that later, right now lemme get backstage and get this party started," Adon drove off slowly through the crowd as the DJ blasted "What Them Girls Like" by Ludacris.

CHAPTER 29

Gorilla G guided the Suburban close to a curb at the outset of Siheed Dealer Group, a car dealership.

"What is going on?" Natasha asked, confused.

"Girl, just c'mon," Vanity said and opened her door.

The three of them climbed out the truck and walked up to the glass doors. The owner, Siheed, made his approach as the doors retracted on their own.

"Good afternoon, ladies...and you too, sir," Siheed said as he quickly sized-up Gorilla G. "So which one of you is, Natasha?"

"That would be me," Natasha said skeptically.

How this fool know my name?

"So that would make you Adon's sister, Natasha, yes?" Siheed asked.

"Yes," Natasha responded.

"And you must be her close friend from Seattle, Vanity yes?"

"Yes," Vanity confirmed.

"Well nice to meet you, two. Such beautiful girls," Siheed said and slightly bowed in their direction.

"Thank you," the two of them said in unison and then looked at each other.

"Siheed," Gorilla G said and glanced around, "where's yo' staff?"

"Staff? I dismissed for entire day," he said. "Today is a special occasion for my culture."

"I hear dat. Today is a special occasion fo' my people as well. Speakin' of which, I need to be gettin' my step on at the picnic I'm missin'," Gorilla G said and started doing the Chi-Town step on top of Siheed's carpet. To be a big fella he was light on his feet.

"Aren't you the owner here?" Vanity asked.

"That would be accurate...yes," Siheed answered.

"Wow, Adon must have a lot of pull to have convinced you to go through all this trouble," Vanity said.

"No trouble," Siheed assured.

"She ain't knowin', huh?" Gorilla G commented. "You ever heard of da Bird Man? Well, Adon is the Juice Man fo' real."

"He is a very good man, yes" Siheed agreed. "Well, if you ladies would follow me," Siheed said and led the way between vehicles and through an opened door of a carpeted room that had three brand new supercharged Range Rovers on display.

"What you see here are three of the same vehicles that are identical except only in color. Ms. Natasha Cutti, per Adon's instructions you can have whichever one you choose," Siheed said with enjoyment.

"Wh…What!?" Natasha couldn't believe it. "Are you kidding me!?

"I'm afraid not," Siheed said and Vanity started clapping.

Natasha turned to Vanity. "You knew about this all along?"

"Well, sort of," Vanity said and hugged her friend. "Happy pre-birthday, pre-Christmas and all of that!"

Without saying a word, Vanity picked the Java Black as she got behind the wheel and saw that the keys were all ready in the ignition. "Oh my, God, I must be dreaming."

"Nope, this you girl," Vanity said as she leaned on the window ledge.

"The paper work is in the glove compartment," Siheed said.

"Oh thank you!" Natasha got out of the truck and hugged Siheed.

"It was my pleasure, but be sure to thank Adon. Because of him, this is all possible," Siheed said and released her.

"I will," Natasha said wiping tears from her eyes.

"Now can we please get up outta here, fo' real," Gorilla G asked impatiently. All that he could think about was the hot-to-def ladies and good tasting barbecue that he was missing back at the picnic.

"Yes we can go, G," Vanity said, settling him down. She joined Natasha inside the Range.

"Okay, now if you can follow me out this exit, then you can be on your way," Siheed said and started to lead the way.

Natasha turned the ignition and placed the gear in drive, and slowly followed Siheed to the side exit. She pulled up to the exit and saw that an Acura TL blocked it with a huge red bow wrapped around it.

"It looks like somebody else reserved this day to surprise somebody, too," Vanity said unsuspectingly.

"Yes, Vanity," Siheed said as he walked up to the opened window. "That somebody is you. Courtesy of Adon, say hello to your brand new platinum colored vehicle."

"Ahhh!" Vanity screamed with excitement.

The number of people attending the statewide picnic had made it to the thousands. It started five feet from the stage and ended at the boundaries of the land. All eyes were focused on the stage as they jammed to a local rap artist named Iroc G. His setup was good. His background dancers were some fine sistahs and their moves were on point. At the end he gave a few shout outs, the crowd showed him love and he wrapped up his set and left the stage.

"Bring out Twista! Bring out Twista! Bring out Twista!" the crowd chanted.

"Man, cuz, you hear that crowd!" Adon yelled as he stood behind the curtains that concealed the backstage area.

"Bring out Twista! Bring out Twista!" the crowd was persistent and the noise increased.

"Now that's what I'm talkin' bout!" Adon said and passed the lit Garcia Vega to Twista as he took center stage. An uproar ensued as Twista came from behind the curtain rapping "Overnight Celebrity." Adon climbed down the stairs where Black Magic was waiting.

"I gotta couple of people who wanna see you," Black Magic said.

"Who dat?" Adon asked.

"Let 'em through!" Black Magic yelled to his men on the far end.

"Oh, damn." Adon's bottom mouth dropped after he laid eyes on Vanity. Fatima was along side of her, but as far as he was concerned, Vanity was all that his eyes could see. She had on an extra short liquid metal skirt that revealed sneak peeks of her flawless skin underneath. A beaded harness concealed the front of her breast, exposing her shoulders, most of her back, and her entire flat stomach where she displayed her navel ring. Nitty had told him once that a woman's shoulders are the frontline of her mystique. It wasn't until now that he fully understood what he meant.

A Chanel choker sat snugged around Vanity's neck and a pair of Chanel open-toe sandals added inches to her five feet, six inches of curvy framework. Her slightly bowlegs and enticing sway of the hips complimented her sashay. The closer she approached the more he wanted to eat her up.

Without uttering a word, Vanity stepped to Adon and placed her lips softly to his, tongue flirting. She released his lips and said, "Thank you so much for the car. Nobody has ever done something even remotely close to what you have done for me," she gazed into his eyes and displayed her deep dimples with a sexy smile.

Adon was oblivious to everything around him.

"I'm glad you liked it," he responded and licked his lips."

"Let da man breathe, V," Fatima said and slyly nudged her, then stole enough body room to give Adon a hug. "Hey, boo," she said and kissed his cheek. She pulled his head close and whispered, "You know that girl is crazy-checkin' for you."

"You're so late wit' that memo," he said.

"Well, excuse me," Fatima threw her hands on her hips.

"So how you been?" Adon asked attentively.

"Well, since the dental results came back and determined that Shamrock wasn't one out of the five bodies found. I feel a whole lot better. Even though we ain't together and he hardly does anything fo' his son, I take comfort in knowing that my baby's daddy is still breathing," Fatima said. "But I gotta question for you," she said narrowing her eyes. "Why was it that you were unbothered and all calm-like when all dis shit went down?"

"When all what shit went down?" Adon queried.

"When Shamrock's house got blown up, you were all blasé about it," Fatima clarified.

"I wouldn't go as far as to say blasé, but confident I was," he said.

"Confident? About what?"

"About Shamrock not laying down so easy. I had no doubt that he wasn't one of the five."

"I hear dat, now I just wanna see his black ass," Fatima said with sexual thoughts. "He gon' be here, right?"

"I guess we'll see," Adon said and redirected his attention to Vanity.

Black Magic couldn't seem to unglue his eyes from the sight of Fatima's well-rounded ass. Her royal blue cat suit that Serena Williams made famous accentuated that bubble effect so well. He immediately recognized the distraction and broke away from it as he walked away and got on his walkie-talkie.

"I see you got Twista in da building," Fatima said butting in again.

"Yes, and he's bringin' the house down," Vanity said as her eyes got round. "And we got Tash good, too."

"Did she like it?" Adon asked, hoping that she did.

"Like it!? Boy, you made the girl cry! She was so shocked and happy it's a wonder she didn't pass out. She loves that truck soooo much!" Vanity said.

"Well I'm glad, And you?"

"Oh, you know I'm in love with my Acura. She's just as sexy as me," she said and shot Adon a seductive look.

"That's for doin' such a good job today."

"That's it?" She asked disappointingly. "I mean it wasn't done because of who I am as a person, you know, me being me and perhaps your feelings for me?"

"It has e'vrythang to do wit' you being you," Adon said.

"A!" Black Magic called out as he approached from the far end.

"Give me a minute," Adon said to Vanity and turned to Black Magic. "Wudup, cuz?"

"Lemme holla at cha," Black Magic said and tapped Adon on the elbow.

Adon left the ladies and went off to the side with Black Magic.

"Look, the other Chiefs requested to talk to you about the Vice Lord situation. Now I don't know wassup, but I ain't feelin' da vibe, A."

"Relax. Where they at?"

"Jus' 'round da corner by da side of da stage," Black Magic said.

"Then let 'em through."

"Lemme round up security first," Black Magic grabbed the mouthpiece of his headgear when Adon grabbed his forearm.

"Just let 'em through," Adon said sternly.

"Let 'em through!" Black Magic yelled and all five Chiefs came from around the corner and began to make their way toward Adon.

Fatima observed what was going down and spoke up. "Adon, is e'vrythang, e'vrythang?"

"Fo' sho, you two just go out front and enjoy the rest of Twista's show. I'll join ya'll in a minute," he said.

Fatima and Vanity began to leave the backstage area.

"Damn you look good, shawty," a high yellow nigga by the name of White Cloud said to Vanity as they passed by. He slowed his walking pace for a response and she kept it movin' without bothering to look back.

"Stuck up bitch!" White Cloud said as he and the other four Chiefs arrived at Adon and Black Magic's standing location.

"Do you wanna know what I did to the last muthafucka who disrespected her?" Adon asked.

White Cloud looked around and then back to Adon. "What cha tryna say?"

"Watch your mouth," Adon said calmly.

"Nigga!" White Cloud bellowed and attempted to get violent until Pablo latched on to him.

"Man, you don't need to hold that nigga. I'll dress his face up and in two months he'll still have the mask on for Halloween," Adon said without raising his voice. Black Magic stood at his side ready for whatever.

"Look, we ain't here for that!" Pablo said, looking at the both of them. "Now unless you two wanna be the reason that a three year peace treaty has gon' to shit then I suggest ya'll chill."

"Adon," J-Stone cut in and walked in the middle of the circle. "You and me, we've always had a good line of communication, right?"

He paused and Adon nodded in accordance.

"And though we haven't always seen eye to eye, you and me, we always have managed to find a fair medium for the past three years now. Wouldn't you agree?" J-Stone asked.

Without any regard, Adon blatantly looked down at his icey Swiss Timepiece watch and said, "If we continue at this pace we'll be here all day, so say whatever it is you tryna say."

Adon's I-don't-give-a-fuck demeanor took J-Stone by surprise, but he brushed it off and came straight out with it.

"Did you kill Chief Flukie?"

"What do you think?" Adon said.

"Say, joe," Levi spoke up, "we don't need that type of stagnation right now."

"No I did not kill Chief Flukie," Adon said.

"Well the Vice Lords sure seem to believe so," Mo-Dawg commented.

"Well quite frankly, right about now I don't give no fuck what they think," Adon said adamantly.

"What cha sayin'? That you're willing to break a peace treaty?" White Cloud asked.

"What peace treaty? Nigga haven't you seen the news!? Them fools declared war the day they decided to come through my spot blazin'. As far as I'm concerned, wit' Vice Lords, the peace treaty is broken!" Adon announced.

"I talked to their newly appointed chief, and all he's tryna do is get to the truth," J-Stone said.

"The truth!?" Adon looked in disbelief. "Muthafuck their chief 'cause if he was really concerned about the truth he would've came to me man-to-man, and not send his goons to kill young kids on my block. Muthafuck their Chief!" Adon fumed.

"So you won't be against takin' a lie detector test to prove your innocence in Chief Flukie's murder, right?" Pablo asked.

"What!? Are you niggas the police or some shit!?" Adon asked.

"Hold on, hold on now!" White Cloud said.

"Hold on to my dick, nigga." Adon snarled.

Black Magic said one word over his walkie-talkie and stepped in the middle of the men before the situation got out of hand. "Dig, this discussion is over!'"

"What!? Nigga what authority do you got to even open your mouth!" White Cloud yelled. At that second Gorilla G and five armed men charged in from the right end while another five armed men approached from the left, sealing off both exit routes.

"So is this how it's gon' be?" White Cloud asked as Gorilla G and the men surrounded them.

"Not unless you make it," Adon replied.

"Let's disperse gentlemen," Black Magic said and the chiefs began to turn toward the only exit that Gorilla G allowed.

"Can I have a word with you, comrade?" J-Stone asked.

Adon winked his right eyelid at Black Magic, allowing him to stay behind.

"Adon," J-Stone began, "we've broke through alotta walls and jumped over several hurdles to get our operations to run as smooth as they are today. And we got you to thank for that.

"You've worked the hardest of us all. You're the one who pulled our coat to it being a betta way for us to co-exist and still eat well enough to get full on these streets. You're the one who started this statewide annual picnic and the rejoicing that came wit' it, and we supported it, we supported you. So I'm sure you could understand when I say that I'm disappointed by your sudden ride-or-die mentality that you've adopted. It's the same attitude that you had, we all had, three years ago when we were killin' up each other and going bankrupt all at the same time.

"Hear what I'm sayin', Adon. We, you included, have a damn good thang going. Myself, along wit' the brothas that came back here to talk to you, we're only tryna alleviate the problem. That means assisting you and the Vice Lords in any way that we can to get to the bottom of this and usually you would be favorable in handlin' a situation such as this accordingly, if not heading it yourself. Or at least that's what your past disposition has displayed up till now.

"But now it's like since you became one wit' The Convolution you've become cocky, like you don't give a damn and you and I both know that attitude and the actions behind it will put a lotta lives in danger, including me and you. And wit' all due respect, I would expect that sort of behavior from Shamrock but not you, you're too wise for that.

"Adon, I'm thirty-eight years old. I have seven beautiful children, two grand babies, and a loving wife; everythang a man could want and I've been around the world twice. I've lived two lifetimes within my half of one, and though I'm not ready to leave my family, but if shit cracked that way I'm perfectly content wit' sayin' I lived a full life.

"Now I ask you Adon, are you capable of truly sayin' the same?" J-Stone asked and just before he turned toward the exit he added:

"And for the record, I know that you didn't kill Chief Flukie, but you know who did."

CHAPTER 30

In full uniform, Natasha drove a rented work van to a black iron security gate. She pulled down on her cap and reached for a button that resembled a doorbell. She was aware of the security camera just above her, and made sure not to look into it. The retractable gate began to pull back. She slowly accelerated forward and the iron gate shut behind her. She was now on Nitty's property.

According to Killa Mike he was home. She'd waited nineteen years for this moment, and the time had come. Her mission was clear-cut; Nitty killed her father, now she must kill Nitty. The sooner she does that the sooner she could let Charlotte and Joyous go free, but not until then. For they were her insurance in case things didn't go as planned. She hated to take such drastic measures, but she knew all too well of Adon's loyalty to Nitty and she couldn't take the chance of Adon interfering. At least this way the burden of Adon possibly siding with Nitty over her didn't sit square on her shoulders. She was certain Adon wouldn't choose sparing Nitty's life over his own daughter. And she had a damn good feeling that it would come down to that.

In steady route, she passed by an ornamental water feature that resembled the Buckingham Fountain in downtown Chicago, and pulled behind a couple of foreign vehicles. She didn't realize just how big this place was until she made it on the other side of the security gate. She saw armed security men in place, but wasn't fazed.

She made it up the short flight of stairs with her tool belt around her waist, and to her surprise an elderly black woman greeted her at a fancy oval glass door as if she was waiting on her arrival.

"May I help you, dear?" The maid asked.

"Sure, there's been a major sewage problem in the area. I'm going to need your permission to check your septic tank for any accumulated undigested solids," Natasha said.

"You're a plumber I assume," the maid said.

"I sure am, ma'am," Natasha responded and gestured toward her van that had the words HAMMON'S PLUMBING along the side of it.

"Well, welcome and come on in," the maid said and shut the door behind Natasha. "I never would imagine such a pretty girl like yourself being a plumber. Not in my day, oh no. But that's good," she said. "Good that we colored women are entering the trades. That makes me a proud woman."

"Thanks, ma'am," Natasha said and tilted the front of her hard hat out of respect.

"Well, lemme inform the owners—"

"No, that won't be necessary," Natasha interrupted. "I don't want to be a bother on this nice Saturday evening. All I need to do is check the septic tank and I'll be on my way."

"And you're right, because the woman of the house is mourning her son's recent murder, she don't need to be bothered. I'm in the process of cooking her supper now. And the man of the house, well," she said throwing her hands in the air, "jus' do what you have to do. But, baby, I must admit, I don't even know what a septic tank is let alone where it's located."

"Oh, it's almost always located in the basement," Natasha said. "I'm sure I can find it."

"Okay," the maid said thinking about her pot roast in the oven. "Walk down this arched gallery here," she said pointing. "Take a left, then a right, and walk down another arched gallery. That'll lead you pass the conference room then you take another right, and left, and the door to the cellar would be straight ahead."

"Okay, thank you ma'am."

"No, thank you," she returned and started walking toward the gourmet kitchen. "And don't leave without having yourself a plate of my award winning cooking," she said with a smile.

"I won't," Natasha responded and watched the little old woman disappear into the kitchen.

Natasha didn't waste anymore time. She began to walk down the arched gallery while she squeezed her hands into a pair of latex gloves. She reached in her tool belt and filled her fist with a .45 ACP, and made a right instead of the left that the maid suggested.

Natasha could care less about a septic tank. She observed what she could along the way as she walked through the rotunda. This part of the home reminded her of an art museum. She was an enthusiast when it came to precious paintings and was very intrigued by the pieces that hung from the high walls.

Natasha approached a pair of bridal stairs and climbed the flight until she made it on the second floor. She walked to another gallery and noticed the connecting rooms. She was stealth in her pursuit. She quietly opened doors and peered inside rooms.

There were no signs of Nitty or any human presence until she suddenly heard the speaking of her brother's name. The voices were coming from the den. She crept to the slightly opened door and eaves-dropped:

"History is repeating itself once again, is what I'm saying," Sundown, one of the The Convolution's forty-three members, said. "It's identical to where we were at this time nineteen years ago, except this time we will win."

"So what are you implying? That nearly two decades ago we didn't win?" Nitty asked.

"What I'm implying is simple. Adon is a mere replica of Macklin Cutti and the present times are a reflection of the olden days. But you see this time we're getting what we need to take over the distribution of Opium from Afghanistan and that is complete control over the Gangster Disciples. And since the only man that had the power and resources to upset that merger in the past is no longer here, that person being Macklin Cutti, The Convolution's conquering of full and complete distribution on Chicago's streets will finally run its course and it would do so with the essential assistance of his son, Adon Cutti," Sundown explained.

"I would not be so sure as to assume that," Nitty said.

"Sure I would, and there's no good reason that you shouldn't. Granted, Adon is just as bullheaded as his father once was but the difference there is evident. Unlike Macklin, you've managed to earn Adon's undying trust and he would follow any directive that you lay upon him, And to add to it all, he is enthused about having become 'one' with us, The Great Convolution, as he should be."

"Yes, but under false pretenses," Nitty stated.

"Who is to say that they are? You?" Sundown poked at Nitty's chest. "I mean let's be rational here. The opportunity that's well within Adon's reach will undoubtedly make him a very rich man. Not only would he be set for life, but it would open doors much greater than the doors he has already walked and would ever walked through in his lifetime, had he not been chosen by us."

"But at what cost," Nitty responded and got up from his chair.

"One could never prosper without sacrifice, and I'm sure that this is *a* sacrifice he's willing to take," Sundown stated and followed Nitty over to a glass window that overlooked his aquarium of exotic fish.

"Apparently you do not know Adon like you think you do. He is very loyal to his organization," Nitty said while he kept his eye on the colorful fish.

"We are his organization now. The Convolution!" Sundown challenged.

"But the GDs are his family! He would never abandon, betray, and above all, dishonor them. No matter the reward!" Nitty bellowed. "If he sensed even for a minute that he was being taking for granted, he'd react and it wouldn't be pleasant."

"I'm not so sure. I mean after all, he did participate in his comrade's *attempted* murder that you orchestrated and I don't see you experiencing any unpleasantries," Sundown stated.

"How dare you! You know damn well he only agreed to that because of the alterations done to that bogus surveillance tape," Nitty replied.

"My point exactly," Sundown said and spread his arms.

"Well in spite of your obvious disfavor—"

A voice sounded from an area that Natasha couldn't see from her location. Suddenly a white man in a pricey suit appeared from the den's corner.

"Adon is now 'one' with The Convolution. And you damn well better make certain that you do what you have to do to ensure that it stays that way."

He paused and made his distance shorter as he walked leisurely toward Nitty.

"Otherwise, I would make damn sure that history does not repeat itself in its entirety. Because unlike two decades ago, when you failed miserably at convincing Macklin Cutti to comply with the merger, because you were too busy playing footsie with his wife, this time there would be no redemption for you. You won't have to worry about the feds, or Doe, or Shamrock for that matter, because I will damn well see to it that Adon knows Macklin Cutti's killer, and ultimately how you were responsible for his mother's slaying as well.

"So if nothing else, be mindful of this. If you in fact repeat that part of your history I can guarantee that Adon would not be the only one dying a brutal death, but you will suffer an even greater one," he said and ended his footsteps right in front of him.

"Do I make myself clear, Nitty?"

"Yes, Nefarious."

Nefarious was the man behind the scenes whom dictated the dictators. He was ultimately the Chairman of The Convolution, and his name was fitting.

Well, I'm going to get justice on all three of you motherfuckas! Natasha mused and raised her burna when she heard the maid walking up from behind.

Shit, I don't want to have to kill this sweet old lady.

Natasha quickly darted around the corner and waited. Her heavy breathing was audible.

"Well, Agent Karpe," the maid said as they approached, "I'm sure Mr. Calhoun is inside the den with the rest of 'em," she said and stepped aside the den's door, granting him access. Agent Karpe stopped shy of the den's threshold and turned his head, looking around the arched gallery. His facial expression bared a distasteful look deriving from his gut as he heard irregular panting.

"Is everything okay, Agent—"

The maid attempted to speak, but Agent Karpe shushed her and quietly walked to the other end of the gallery. He pulled his service weapon from his snap-holster and inched closer. He jumped out and around the corner. But no one was there.

Natasha didn't stick around. As soon as she heard the word "Agent" she got the fuck out of dodge! She found a back stairwell that led to the main floor. She had no idea where she was within the mansion. She walked ahead trying to find her way to the front door when a woman appeared out of nowhere. Natasha quickly darted inside the nearest room and peeked out.

"What are you doing out of bed, Mrs. Calhoun," the maid said and reached out for her hand. "Come here once, lemme take you back up to your room. I'll bring supper to you."

That's Nitty's wife? Natasha couldn't believe the appearance of Nitty's wife. She looked a hot mess and not the jewel in the crown that she saw in photographs.

She must really be taking her son's death hard, Natasha thought and looked over her shoulder.

It was clear that she walked in some type of videoroom. There were all kinds of equipment setups and several brands of recording devices, cameras, monitors, computers, and whatnots along the shelves. It reminded her of an advanced, bootleg downloading and editing room, especially with how the VCRs and DVD players were situated. There were also several disks scattered across a table.

Out of curiosity she walked to the cluttered table and began to read labels attached to each disk. There were a heap of them and after she ran her eyes over the ones on top, she carefully started to dig into the pile of those that were buried underneath.

Suddenly one dropped to the wooden floor and sent out a disturbing noise! She darted her eyes to the room's entrance and upped her burna. Her heart was racing!

After making sure the coast was clear, she continued to search through the pile and there it was…In her hands were two DVDs. One of which had the scribbled words SHAMROCK, THE EDITED COPY; and the other read SHAMROCK, THE UNEDITED COPY.

Natasha stuck both DVDs inside of her jumpsuit and left the room.

The front door was finally in view and she was nearly there when, "Are you done checking the septic tank, dear?" The maid asked, coming down from the upstairs.

"Oh, yes, ma'am," Natasha said and stopped at the front door. "Everything seems to be working just fine, so I'm going to be leaving now."

"Well, at least lemme make you a plate of some good home cooking for your trouble," she said and started for the gourmet kitchen.

"There was no trouble at all. I was just doing my job and now I have to get back," Natasha said uneasy.

"Okay then, I don't want to get you into trouble, so you can go and I'll open the security gate for you. Bye, dear," the maid said.

"Bye," Natasha returned and walked out of the house, and shut the door behind her.

As the curvy road straightened and allowed Natasha to balance the van's steering, it appeared to come straight through Shamrock's side view mirror as she sped passed a parked Toyota Camry without bothering to pay it any mind.

Shamrock knew exactly who was behind the wheel of the mock Hammon's Plumbing van. He was there at that precise parked location when Natasha initially pulled up onto the property.

Shamrock became alert when the iron security gate began to retract again. He remained crouched down in his seat and peeped just above the window seal. The front end of Sundown's McLaren was the first to drive out, followed by Nefarious' Bugatti, and Nitty's Bentley GT. Then Agent Karpe followed suite in his Grand Cherokee. The four vehicles sped past the parked Camry in a hurry, as their preoccupied minds were clueless to the killer that lurked right under their noses.

Shamrock covered his face with a ski mask. He stepped out and quickly bolted to the other side of the road, and with a running start, he jumped and managed to grab the top of a twelve-foot concrete wall. He hoisted himself upward, over, and landed feet first on Nitty's green space. Dressed in an all black oversized "Wu Tang" jumpsuit, he immediately ran to the only vulnerable spot on the grounds and kneeled behind a bush as he observed what was expected.

There were three men stationed on the inside of three individual guard towers.

Shamrock removed a strap from his shoulder. He placed the narrow case that was attached to it flat on the lawn, opened it, and began to assemble a high-powered rifle.

It took him all but two minutes to study two of the men who were seriously lacking in their observation duties. One was seated with an assault rifle resting in his lap and a bag of corn chips between his hands, stuffing his mouth. The second one, several yards apart, buried his face inside a magazine with his feet propped on the console. It was apparent that when Nitty leaves the premises his watchdogs get lax.

Shamrock decided to make those two idiots his last targets and focused on the third man who was clearly on point. It was evident that he took much pride in his job. With his body fully erect, and an assault rifle in his hands, he paced the small platform back-n-forth like a real soldier guarding his master's castle.

"Nitty would be so proud," Shamrock jested with a half grin.

Upon twisting a silencer on the start of the barrel, he pinned his knee into the surface and braced the butt of the rifle against his shoulder. With one eye peering through the scope, he pulled the trigger and picked the first man off. Two more bullets sliced through the air and, like dominoes, the last two idiots fell in rapid succession.

Shamrock quickly disassembled his rifle, placed it back into its narrow case and swung the strap over his shoulder. He made his way to one of the side doors and attempted to turn the knob. It was locked. He wrapped a blue bandana around his fist and quietly smashed it through a small square framed glass. He unlocked the door from the inside and let himself in.

He made it up the staircase and to the grand master suite that Nitty shared with his wife. Upon entering, he saw that she was lying down, facing the opposite of him, so he intentionally produced a sound of entry.

"Honey, would you mind making the necessary arrangements of getting Malcom's things moved out of his apartment? I do not have the emotional nor physical strength to do it," she said to who she thought to be her husband.

"Now why would I care to do that, honey?" Shamrock asked in his best Nitty impersonation, and she turned to him in total s h o c k.

"Who are you!? Where is my husband!?" she demanded.

Shamrock rushed her, put a pillow over her face, and pulled the trigger twice. He twisted the silencers off his .10mms and slid them in either of his side leg pockets. He reached over the deceased and grabbed another pillow. He removed the pillowcase and headed for the dresser where he bagged all of their priceless jewels. He exited the bedroom as the maid was entering.

She looked up at the black mask and trembled in fear.

"Don't you scream," he said quietly and walked around her, leaving her unharmed.

The maid ran over to where Nitty's wife laid.

"Mrs. Calhoun," she said and removed the bloody pillow. "Bloody Jesus!" she blurted.

Mrs. Calhoun's eyes were opened with two quarter-sized holes in her face. The maid reached for the pain inside her chest, and fell to the floor. She squirmed but she couldn't overcome. She died right there after suffering a massive heart attack.

CHAPTER 31

Twista started spittin' some of his classic joints off the *Adrenaline Rush* album and the audience got crunk! They joined in word for word with his lyrics, and reminisced on the things they were into when the song first dropped. They were die-hard fans that related not only to Twista's flow, but to his journey. This made his songs theirs just as much as it was his.

"Should we be worried about those fools?" Gorilla G asked and bit into a barbecue rib as he, Adon, Black Magic, and a few security personnel members sat around a picnic table right in the center of everything.

"I got the utmost respect for them niggas," Adon started. "Well a lil' less for White Cloud, but for the most part the respect is there. I also understand their concerns, but if they bite off the wrong end of this Vice Lord beef then there's gonna be problems, and I don't mean for us. Just let me worry about that. For now ya'll have a good time! This is for ya'll!" Adon proclaimed and patted Gorilla G and Black Magic on their backs.

"Oh, yeah," he continued, "there's finna be some changes in regards to the revenue and you two are gonna play key parts in it. Since Murda Park is outta commission for a minute, I intend to expand my operations in anotha direction, which means mo' chedda for e'vrybody. I'm talkin' real live scholarship money."

Adon paused and turned his attention to Black Magic.

"My nigga, I've known you since we were shawties and you've been a part of my money clique for a year now. You've proved yourself over and over again, and I'm proud to give you this opportunity 'cause you deserve it. Straight up and down," he said and Black Magic initiated a token of his appreciation by extending his hand.

The two of them performed their customary handshake.

"And you Gorilla G," Adon continued, "well let's just say that you in the right place at the right time, and yo' rep don't hurt neither. So rest assure, I'ma put you in big homie."

Adon rose up from the picnic table and stood over Gorilla G.

"Whatever you do, G, just don't fuck me."

"If anythang, I'ma fuck wit' choo, dawg. You don't have to worry about me, A," Gorilla G assured. "I would shake your hand too, but as you can see, they a lil' messy," he said referring to the barbecue sauce that saturated his hands.

"Ain't no thang, cuz," Adon said and sat back down.

"A," Black Magic spoke up after he received communication over his head-gear, "that nigga Cigar just made an appearance and s'posely he got one bad ass bitch wit' him too."

"Well, is she hotter than that fine lil' mama over there?" Adon gestured in Vanity's direction. She and Fatima were over at the photo site posing for flicks.

"Shawty there *is* tight to def," Black Magic said, taking a long look at Vanity.

"I'ma put it to ya like this." Adon stood up and put Cigar's date into view, and his eyes widened. "If Twista was auditioning only the *loveliest* breed of ladies to be in his next video, and at the end of the day there was only one slot left and those two showed up, trust me, he gon' free up a spot 'cause he ain't turnin' neither one of them around.

"Is that a fact?" Adon asked not taking his eyes off Vanity's sexy poses.

How 'bout you just judge for yo'self," Black Magic suggested. "The nigga Cigar claims he need to holla at cha anyway."

"Aiight, send them over," Adon said and peered down at his timepiece. It read 6:33 P.M.

I wonder if Charlotte called? he mused and reached for his BlackBerry.

He dialed his home number, and entered his security code. There was one new message:

"Hey there Adon, this is Doe. Listen, I would've gotten with you much sooner than this but since I've been home, particularly since I first attempted to make contact wit' you, I've cheated death countless

*of times. I haven't slept in over five days. I can't make a move without somebody either shooting a camera lens in my direction or bullets. To put it in a nutshell, I'm afraid that I won't live another day if I don't meet with you soon. Meet me at the Evergreen Plaza today at 7*P.M. *... Adon, please come."*

"That'll definitely work," Adon thought aloud as he put his cell away.

It just so happens that Evergreen Plaza was only a mile up the road.

"Gorilla G," Adon called out. "I should have some gear and a motorcycle helmet in the trunk of Black's Audi. Do yo boy a favor and go grab that," he said and before Gorilla G ran off he added, "Grab the vest, too."

Adon had no real way of knowing what was to come at 7o'clock, so he figured he might as well get ready for whatever.

"Here he is, A," Black Magic walked up with Cigar.

"Wuts good, famo?" Cigar said and extended his hand.

Adon latched on to it and used it as leverage to rise up from his seat. Unexpectedly, he caught a glimpse over Cigar's shoulder of a female worth subscribing to. He tightened his grip around Cigar's hand, nearly breaking it and moved him aside like the peon he was. Black Magic laughed quietly at the blatant gesture.

I told ya shawty was hot! Black Magic thought.

The view was spectacular and Adon didn't attempt to disguise his interest in the slightest bit. Shawty was all what Black Magic said she was, and then some. She was clad in a tight-fitting Norman Norell dress that appeared to be a second layer of skin. The material was lace with opened cleavage that had every man in the vicinity gaping. The end of her dress lasted just below her knee, and her Manolo shoes would trap any man who had a foot fetish.

"And you are?" Adon asked, walking into her space.

"Divine," she answered willingly.

"My name is—"

"Adon," she said, cutting him off.

"Have we met?" he asked.

195

"No, but words have its way of getting around," she responded.

"Well for my sake, I hope those words were good," he said and she smiled.

"Say family, can I holla at cha—" Cigar tried to intervene but Black Magic snatched his coattail.

"Be easy," Black Magic said. "He'll get to ya."

"So is this yours?" Divine asked Adon in reference to the festivity.

"Naw, this ain't me alone. This belongs to e'vrybody you see here...including Twista. So what brings you here?"

"Well, this fiesta is only the talk of the city and since Cigar offered to bring me, I had no thoughts of refusing."

"So, you wit' him?"

"We came here in the same car if that's what you're asking."

"You know what I mean."

"No, I just met him. What about you, are you with anyone?" she asked and Adon glanced over at Vanity who was still by the photo site, peering back at him.

Vanity had her eye on him ever since she'd noticed that his eyes were no longer on her. Divine was an attractive woman and there wasn't any doubt that she felt threatened, but she didn't want to make that evident. She certainly didn't want to overstep her boundaries, neither; especially since her and Adon have yet to discussed being exclusive.

"Here you go, A," Gorilla G walked up and handed Adon the bike helmet, gear, and vest.

"Good lookin', big homie," he said and turned to Divine. "Can you excuse me?" Adon asked politely and walked off with Gorilla G.

On their way to their original picnic table, Adon noticed that Black Magic and ten of his men were dragging some unconscious man who bled from the head.

"What's that all about?" Adon asked and placed everything on the table while Gorilla G shielded him from any possible onlookers.

"They caught that fool snortin' heroine behind the trees over there," Gorilla G said and bit into some barbecue wings. "You know they gon' pumpkin his head."

Adon removed his platinum chain and pink and white Iceberg shirt and sat it on the table, baring his chiseled biceps and muscular chest that bulged under his wife beater. He kicked off his tennies, nearby women took notice and began making advances. He shot them a smile and slid a pair of Next Unlimited leather pants over his white Iceberg shorts. He stepped into his shoes and put on the Teflon vest. His shoulder-sling was next, equipped with the .44 automatic. Next, he pushed his brawn arms through the sleeves of a matching Next Unlimited leather jacket.

"A," Black Magic jogged up. "The five Chiefs just left together and they took their faculties wit' 'em. Now that's some real fishy shit, especially since it's way too early to be blowin' da spot; especially when the spot is as hot with entertainment as this one."

"I feel you on that, cuz," Adon said. "Look, don't cause no panic. Just get everybody up outta here in a calm and timely fashion. Foremost, escort Twista and his crew and DJ Barbecue Bobby up outta here. Those that rode the buses, get them all boarded, and those that drove in their own whips get them in their cars and safely on the road."

"Man, Adon, I know we ain't gon' punk out and end this because of them," Gorilla G said. "Otherwise, why wouldn't you have canceled it to begin wit'?"

"Because, Big Homie, I knew that wit' those individual heads in attendance, the Vice Lords wouldn't come through here sprayin' bullets at e'vrythang movin'. Remember, their peace treaties are still intact and the only beef the Vice Lords have is wit' me. Now since they're no longer here, this entire place is open season for them. Even wit' our security team itchin' and ready to clap, there's still a good damn chance that bodies will fall. So if I could prevent innocent people from catchin' slugs on my account, I'ma do just that."

"But—"

"It ain't nothin' else to discuss, G, aiight! I'm shuting this piece down," Adon said and turned to his Chief of Security. "Black, stand on that."

"Fo' sho," Black Magic said and moved into action and Gorilla G followed.

"Fatima!" Adon called out and she approached him. "Look, I want you and Vanity to get up outta here now."

"But for what? I'm tryna get my party on. Twista just started rappin' 'Get It Wet'!" Fatima said and started rolling her hips.

"Listen to me," Adon said sternly and grabbed her roughly by the forearm. "Don't ask no fuckin' questions, aiight. Just get Vanity and get the fuck up outta here! And make sure that she gets to Tasha's crib safely. You know she don't really know her way around the Chi."

"Okay, I will," she said sensing the urgency and ran to get Vanity.

Adon looked at his timepiece. He had ten minutes before his meeting with Doe. With the extra helmet in his hand, he started running for his bike when he heard his name called.

Adon stopped and turned to the voice. It was Divine walking toward him. He had forgotten all about her. They met halfway and without saying a word she politely unzipped his breast pocket and slid a piece of paper inside, and politely zipped it back.

"That's my number, use it at your own risk," she said and made it a point to turn and walk away before he did, solely just to leave him with a memorable impression of her ass .

"Ay!" he called out and Divine turned to him.

"You sure we haven't met before?"

"Trust me, if you and I had ever met before today, I'd remember," she said.

"Aiight," he left it at that and spun on his feet, in route to his bike. Divine watched as he sped off on his Suzuki.

It was true. Adon was very different than any of the other street gangstas that she had studied or been assigned to in the past. He possessed this certain aura that made him pleasant to remember. Even her colleagues back at headquarters spoke of him differently.

Although they all plotted ways to bring Adon and The Convolution down, her fellow agents had this unsaid respect for him. A respect that she never once saw attached to any other street perpetrator that managed to get so notorious as to make their list of investigations. Through what she has gathered from her extensive studies, he was definitely his father's son.

And incredibly attractive, Divine thought.

CHAPTER 32

Doe looked up at the huge clock that hung from the skylight at the midpoint of Evergreen Plaza mall. He was mad nervous about meeting Adon for the first time as a grown man, and more worried about not meeting him at all, shall Adon choose not to show.

He walked leisurely around the plaza and the atmosphere amused him. It's been nineteen years since he'd visited anything remotely close to this. Everything seemed to have been simplified to some form of technology. Computers for public use were posted throughout the place. Some people even strolled about with what appeared to be hand held mini-computers no bigger than their palms. For a while he thought there was a field trip of some kind being held here for the mentally ill, as countless people walked passed him talking to themselves.

On a few occasions he even acknowledged them with a "What was that," "Come again," or "Excuse me," because he was convinced that they had to be talking to him. Then he noticed the small devices attached to their ears and figured that as far-fetched as it was, they were using that device to communicate with other people. Imagine that.

He continued to window shop and observe diverse crowds interact with one another: blacks, whites, Hispanics, you name it, and inter-racial couples holding hands. Just when he thought he saw it all he noticed many white girls with hips and asses like sistahs, and they even possessed the strut to match.

Wow! he thought. A far change from his days.

He glanced at a Starbucks. He figured that would be a good place for him to sit for a while. All that walking had his feet hurting, and his lack of sleep had him drained. He reached into his pocket and fiddled with small change, when he looked up he was already at the front counter.

"May I help you, sir?" a young female employee asked.

"Goddamn," he said calmly after looking at the overhead menu.

"I'm sorry, Miss, I didn't realize how expensive your beverages were. Can I have a small glass of water?"

"Sure," she said and came back with a small paper cup that was filled to the rim.

"You wouldn't mind if I sat on that stool over there now would you? I'm waiting on my ride to come and pick me up," he said.

"Well usually you would have to purchase something, but if you're sure that it won't be long then help yourself, sir."

Adon sat low inside a booth that was only twelve feet away from where Doe was standing. In one hand was the old photo that Doe left with his doorman. He studied it while sipping on a cappuccino. The man in the picture bore a striking resemblance to the man he was currently observing. By the condition of the photo and style of clothing, Adon guessed the photo to be about twenty years old. And if this was the man that stood before him then he hadn't aged at all.

Doe sat on the stool with his knees pointed toward the opened area of the mall and continued to people watch, swallowing his fresh water a little at a time. He peered up at the huge clock, it was now 7o'clock.

"Sir," a male employee walked up from behind. "Here's your cappuccino."

"But I didn't order this," Doe said with the quickness trying to avoid any discrepancies.

"I don't ask questions, Mister. I just deliver. Maybe you should take it up with the gentleman sitting at the booth," he said and pointed in Adon's direction.

Doe followed the kid's gesture and saw a young man in a royal blue leather jacket, sitting low behind a table. Besides him and the person that he was now looking at, the sitting area was completely empty.

"Adon?" he said in a low tone and squinted his eyes in an effort to get a better look. He left the stool and started that way.

"Stop right there," Adon said when he came within three feet of his table. "Are you holdin'?"

"Holding what?" Doe asked confused, patting his flat pockets.

"Do you have a gun on you?" Adon rephrased his question.

"No."

"Empty your pockets and put e'vrythang you got on this table," Adon demanded, not taking any chances.

Doe complied.

"Now lift up your shirt and lemme see your bare chest, and do a 360 turnaround for yo boy." This way Adon checked for both a concealed burna and a wire.

Doe had neither.

Adon compared his close-up view of Doe's face with the photo. He had no doubt this was the same man. Adon reached for Doe's ID that was placed on the table.

"Tell me your name, cuz."

"My name is Donald Brooks, but I've long went by the nickname Doe."

"Have a seat," Adon said and slid the old photo across the table as Doe sat. "Who is that infant child you holdin' in the picture?"

Doe instantly smiled.

"What's funny," Adon asked in a distasteful tone and sat up in his seat.

"Nothing's funny, I just can't believe that you don't recognize your-self as a baby. Haven't you seen any baby pictures of yourself before?"

"What!?" Adon said and snatched the photo and put it close to his face. And the answer was no, he had never seen a picture of him so young.

"I'll never forget that day," Doe said. "It was the day your father asked me to be your godfather. It was on a Sunday, and just after we posed for that picture we went and got you baptize," Doe seemed to be reliving the day.

"Wait, you knew my pops?" Adon asked attentively.

"Did I know your pops?" Doe repeated his question in a sarcastic tone. "I cannot find words adequate enough to describe your pops and my relationship. Your daddy and me was like brothers in the real sense of the word.

"On the day you were born I was there along with Macklin and Loretta. I nicknamed you Smiley because you came out the womb smiling. Your father fell in love with you the very second you entered

201

this world, we all did."

Doe paused when he felt himself becoming emotional. He regrouped and began again.

"If you look close there's your dad on the other side of the camera snappin' the shot."

"Where?" Adon asked excitedly, staring at the photo.

"Right there in the mirror behind you and I," Doe pointed to the photo. "The flash from the camera was so bright you could barely see him, but that is definitely his reflection. If you look real close you would spot the side of his face."

Adon did just that and he saw his father. He used all the mental strength he had to fight back his emotions. With a blank stare he said, "After all those years of thinkin' that I was alone in this world. I got a godfather?"

"Yeah, son, you do and I'm so sorry that I let you down," Doe said with sincerity and before he knew it, Adon reached across the table and pulled his body from the seat and embraced him. He was startled. Once his heart rate dropped to it's normal rhythm he wrapped his arms around his godson, returning the embrace.

"Boy, you have really grown to be a big strong dude," Doe said while experiencing Adon's bear hug.

"Now it all makes sense! I knew there was somthin familiar about your voice and the way you talked. And you haven't aged a bit," Adon said releasing him.

"Well," Doe began, "prison has this funny way of preserving a person. Adon, before we go any further it's somethin' I must tell you."

"What's that?"

"Nitty killed your father," Doe came straight out with it and Adon plopped onto his seat like Doe had zapped the very life out of him.

Adon stared in a daze. Everything around Doe became pitch black. His eardrums shut down although Doe's mouth was moving steadily. Over again the words ran its course inside his mind: *"Nitty killed your father, Nitty killed your father."*

"You're lying!" Adon bellowed and smashed the side of his fist onto the table, but Doe refused to back down. He had to convince

Adon of the truth; his very life depended upon it.

"Listen, I know how you feel about Nitty, but for years he's been feeding you nothin' but lies and did everything in his power to ensure that everyone around you was in accordance with his deceits and cover-ups."

"How did this shit go down?" Adon seethed.

"First, what you must understand is that you were born in the middle of a war. And I mean that literally. Although you were delivered in the comforts of the most expensive hospital in Chicago, the entire city was a battle zone and your father had to have around the clock security in your room, outside your door, and on both ends of the hospital's floor just to keep you safe."

"Who did the war involve and why?" Adon asked, Doe had his full attention.

"It involved only two organizations. Two of the most powerful underworld organizations of Chicago: the High Supreme Gangsters, who have since converted over to the Gangster Disciples, and The Great Convolution, who is now known simply as The Convolution. And to answer your last question as plain as possible. It all began when Nitty was exposed as an imposter who infiltrated our organization and betrayed us all, particularly your father."

"And that's why Nitty and The Convolution want you dead, because other than Agent Karpe, you the only one who could unveil the truth?" Adon asked.

"Exactly."

"I wanna know how my father was killed?" Adon asked with austerity.

"It was midnight on October 10, 1989, you were only four then. We received an inside scoop that the key men of The Convolution, including Nitty, were on the north side of the city attending this war strategy meeting inside a warehouse. So myself and fifty of our best men rushed over to the location only to find that it was a trick. No one was there and twenty-seven of our men died from an explosion that occurred from one tug of the warehouse's door.

In the meantime, at your father's home, Karpe deactivated Macklin's house alarm with the help of one of his electronic technical colleagues. Nitty entered the home alone and discovered that Macklin was asleep in his living room. Before he could defend himself, Nitty threw a cord around his neck and strangled him to death.

"Wait a second. Did you say Karpe tapped into his alarm system?" Adon asked as the wheels inside his head began to turn.

"Yes, I did."

"Karpe, as in Federal Agent Karpe?" Adon asked again only to be sure. "Would he know you when he sees you?"

"Yep, that's the one, and he could pick me out of a thousand faces. Oh, yeah, he knows me," Doe confirmed and Adon immediately reflected on the Grand Cherokee he thought might have been tailing him on his way to the Plaza, but when the SUV broke off his course he brushed it off.

"What is it?" Doe asked as he sensed a shift in Adon's demeanor.

"Be quiet and don't move," he said in a low tone. From where they sat Adon visually scoured the mall area just outside of the Starbucks and spotted something strange at a concession stand.

"Oh shit!" he bellowed as a silent projectile punctured the paper cup that Doe was drinking from.

"Get down!" Adon yelled, and yanked Doe under the table with him.

"What's going on!?" Doe asked confused.

"Somebody clappin' at us!" Adon answered and pulled his Desert Eagle.

"I didn't hear any gun shots!"

"They're using silencers, now stay down!" Adon suggested.

"Who could it be!?"

"I'm not sure, but I believe it's Agent Karpe."

"Agent Karpe!" Doe yelled and attempted to flee. The instant he was seen ten silent projectiles were shot in his direction. Adon grabbed onto the back of his shirt and pulled him out of harm's way just as the bullets cut into the wood that made the booth.

"What the fuck you thinkin'? STAY DOWN!" Adon commanded.

"That man has a license to kill and it's been that way since before you were born! The way I see it, if we stay here he's going to mosey right over and exercise his license!" Doe yelled and tried to escape again, but he couldn't break Adon's grip.

"We need to get out of here, godson!"

"Look, you ain't goin' no where 'cause soon as he gets the opportunity he's gonna treat you like a candle and blow yo' lights out. Now, he won't be too quick to bring his ass over here 'cause he knows I'm here wit' you," Adon said.

"And?" Doe asked only because he didn't catch the point.

"And, he knows better," Adon said. "Now relax."

He released Doe's shirt, wrapped both hands around the burna, and barely poked his head outside the other end of the booth. No one in his view appeared to be out the ordinary. No Agent Karpe, or anyone with a gun. Only bargain hunting consumers and their small children who continued to shop and walk leisurely about. No one had any idea of what was occurring.

"I don't see nobody, man," Adon said.

"Maybe he's gone," Doe said wishful thinking.

"Naw, he ain't leavin' 'til he finish what he started. That much I do know about Karpe," Adon stated the truth.

Adon turned to Doe and said, "Trade places wit' me."

"Huh?"

"Just do it." Adon went over the top and Doe crawled under. "Now, I'm finna make a move. So take this," he said, handing Doe the burna.

"Man, godson, this sonavabitch got the weight of a dumbbell," Doe said, referring to the bulkiness of the .44 automatic.

"Now you stay put. Don't try to follow me or run from under this table. This is the safest place for you right now and if that fool does become restless then you slump his ass. Straight up like that, aiight?" Adon said and before Doe could respond he bolted from under the table.

Without thinking, Doe attempted to watch where Adon was going and exposed just enough of his head to get Agent Karpe's attention. Agent Karpe tore up the wooden panel trying to get at his dome. The hissing sounds from the projectiles scared the living shit out of Doe. He jumped back and scooted as far as he could under the table.

He wondered was Adon out there somewhere laying flat on his face dead.

"How can this shit be taking place inside a mall filled with people?" he thought aloud and edged back to the front of the booth with his finger on the trigger.

Without warning he heard a loud crashing noise. Shattered glass and pieces of aluminum framing slid across the mall's open floor. The revving sounds of an engine pierced his eardrums. People screamed and ran away from the mall's entranceas a set of motorcycle tires screeched to a stop right in front of him.

"Give me the burna!" Adon yelled and reached down as Doe threw it to him. He caught it with his left hand and let loose in Agent Karpe's direction, who was now visible and diving clear from the bullet's path.

"C'mon! C'mon!" Adon yelled to Doe and continued to shoot while innocent bystanders ran in hysteria.

"Put this on!" he said and Doe squeezed his head into a matching Suzuki helmet and hopped on the back of the bike.

Adon put one foot on the peg, revved the engine, and did a complete in-place turnaround on the waxed floor, then sped for the mall's exit.

Agent Karpe jumped to his feet and let loose with two .45 autos in their direction as people screamed and ran aimlessly.

Adon put the RPM in the red and released the clutch, raising the front end of the Suzuki and floored it straight through the battered aluminum framed doors.

Agent Karpe ran for the exit where his Grand Cherokee awaited in the police/fire zone parking, only a few feet outside the mall's doors.

Adon zigzagged through traffic on 95th street when he realized Agent Karpe wasn't alone. There were now two silver H2 Hummers hot on his trail.

"Hold on!" Adon yelled after encountering a narrow escape with an oncoming CTA bus.

Doe was startled from the voice that vibrated throughout his helmet, and nearly caused Adon to lose control of the bike from jumping abruptly.

"Doe it's me, Adon. Your helmet is equipped with a built-in microphone and speaker and so is mine. That's why you can hear me so clearly."

Adon weaved through cars but the Hummers were still in his side view mirror.

"Shit!" Doe shouted after Adon made an unexpected turn that dipped the bike so low his knee nearly scraped the pavement.

"My bad," Adon said. "Hold on!"

Agent Karpe was closing in and Adon pulled back on the throttle, taking the Suzuki to 100 miles per hour up a residential block. Agent Karpe hung his burna outside the window and shot eight rounds in their direction.

"Fuck!" Adon cursed at the sight of a busy intersection up ahead. Ironically, the streams of traffic were partygoers leaving his picnic.

He turned on 87th Street and was forced to idle down. Agent Karpe gained ground and continued to open fire. Adon quickly turned the handlebars and detoured onto the sidewalk. One of the Hummers came down a side street and appeared in front of them with burnas blazing.

"Oh shit!" Adon said and raised the front end, literally putting Doe's backside inches from the ground and blocking the bullets as each one bounced off the carbon fiber bottom. He made it pass the Hummer unharmed, and brought the bike down just in time to see a fruit stand blocking the sidewalk.

Adon took it to the streets and quickly reached 70 miles per hour. Doe dipped back and forth right along with him as Adon maneuvered miraculously around and in between unyielding obstacles that motocross riders wouldn't dare to attempt.

"You doing good Doe, just hold on!" he yelled and made a sharp turn up a side street and it freed him up a little, but by this time the second Hummer had finally caught up and bullets were exploding from several directions.

"I'ma get you to safety, Doe. I got'cha!" Adon encouraged, refusing to give up.

Doe looked ahead at the oncoming congestion and then behind him at Agent Karpe and the relentless Hummers. He felt pain in his back and suddenly wasn't as optimistic.

"Adon I just want you to know," he began, "you were always considered the future, the Prince; that's why Macklin named you Adon. You were genetically predispose to be a Don. And that's why The Convolution drafted you, godson. You're the chosen one."

Bullets hissed passed and Adon continued to zigzag in his pursuit of safety. "Is you still wit' me, Doe!?"

"Godson, I went to prison for murder. That was me in the hooded raincoat. I killed your mother," Doe confessed.

"WHAAT!" Adon let out a loud guttural roar as Doe's grip loosened around his waist and body weight pressed heavily against his back. Adon glanced in his side view as Agent Karpe and the Hummers slowed their pace and made separate U-turns. He knew then that Doe had just made a dying confession.

Adon pulled the bike to the curb, kicked out the stand and caught Doe's body as it slumped over. He kneeled down, eased the body to the ground, and removed the helmet from Doe's head. Doe's face was wet from tears. Suddenly the normal functions of Adon's mind shifted into reverse:

"So my little prince," Loretta said. "Are you ready to go inside and eat some strawberry pancakes?"

Little Adon was too busy studying the characteristics of the school kids to even have noticed that his mother had said anything. Loretta turned to look in the backseat.

"C'mon now, boo-boo, I'm sure Miss Muffet will be so thrilled to see her little man," Loretta tried to persuade as the rain started to come down harder upon the roof and windshield.

Little Adon turned to his mother and suddenly became frightened by the man in the hooded raincoat. The evil man opened the car door, catching Loretta by surprise.

She screamed, "You don't have to do this! Be your own man and let go of me, Donald! Let me go!"

The evil man struck her in the face with a closed fist.

"Get the fuck out of the car before I kill you in front on your boy!" the evil man threatened and dragged Loretta out of the car.

Little Adon, restrained to his car seat, reached out his hands and cried, "Mamaaa!"

A short time later, three loud gunshots fired in the distance.

That was the last time Adon saw his beloved mother alive. That was the familiarity in Doe's voice that Adon remembered.

Police sirens broke Adon out of his daydream. He looked down at Doe one last time and hopped on his bike as squad cars closed in on either side. Adon revved up the engine, blue lights reflected off his helmet.

"Turn off the motorcycle," a cop said over the loud speaker while fellow officers had Adon at gunpoint.

Adon held his front break and pulled back on the throttle, peeling rubber in place. In mere seconds, his back tire had the entire area filled with a thick white smoke that was impossible to see through. The police officers were distraught, and like a lightening bolt Adon sped out of their reach.

Before the smoke cleared, he was three blocks away and counting. The officers quickly picked up chase in a ten squad car pursuit, but they were far too late.

Adon made it to an on-ramp that descended to the Dan Ryan Expressway. That's when he really opened up the valves on the Suzuki Hayabusa 1300R. At 170 miles per hour, he placed miles between him and the po-pos in no time.

CHAPTER 33

Nitty, along with his security personnel, were in downtown Chicago inside of his newly purchased five-star deluxe penthouse unit that sat on the 89th floor of the Trump International Hotel & Tower, the world's highest residence above ground level.

While his five-man security crew discussed the number one draft pick Derrick Rose and the Bulls, Nitty walked over to the 10-foot window overlooking the legendary Magnificent Mile. He removed his fedora and caressed his temples.

Donned in an Italian-cut suit and Fratelli loafers, Nitty's status in the game had been identical to the symbolic meaning of the penthouse he was standing in, "On Top Of The World." But after nineteen years the shit was coming to a head. He could sense it.

Although he'd like to think otherwise, he was convinced that Doe managed to tell Adon the truth before he took two to his back. He tried to call his wife countless of times only to get no answer. He looked down at his diamond-studded wedding band and caught a sick feeling that she, too, suffered the same fate as her son. His oldest friend, Casey, was no longer living, and to add to that, no matter how close his men got, Shamrock was still out there.

His security personnel grouped around the 42-inch LCD flat-panel watching ESPN. Their voices started to rise as they debated on who was the toughest point guard in the league. Nitty was disgusted. He could give two fucks about their discussion. He walked into the Limestone bathroom and shut the door.

Having secured her a room at the last minute, Natasha was on the 26th floor mezzanine where the hotel condominiums and executive lounges were situated. With the help of Killa Mike, they tracked Nitty's last steps to this location.

She was sitting at a table, finishing the cleaning of her .45 ACP.

This was one night she wasn't going to take the chance of it jamming. She got up and walked over to the DVD player and popped in *Shamrock, The Edited Copy* for the first time. She began to view the exact version that Adon watched on the dreadful day he found out his closest homie was a fuck nigga. She listened to the audio, and due to her college studies in Electronics and Communications Engineering Technology, she knew right off the bat it had been tweaked.

She removed the DVD and replaced it with the one that read *Shamrock, The Unedited Copy,* and experienced a totally different visual of events. Not only did Shamrock threatened to sue the federal agents inside of the white Dodge Charger for harassment, but he was hostile and cursed them non-stop. And the Spiagga Restuarant scene wasn't all what it appeared be neither. As the original footage showed, Shamrock *was* there with a fly young lady.

When she got up from her chair to use the powder room is when a different white male approached. In a result, Shamrock coughed up a gob of mucus and spat in his face and cursed him as well. Shamrock was anything but a snitch.

"Conniving bastard," she said referring to Nitty.

She shut off the TV and gave herself a once-over in the mirror just to make sure her evening attire was Trump Towers worthy. She looked undeniably breathtaking in a hand-sequined corseted dress and a pair of Chanel slingback pumps.

"Let the games begin," she said and placed the burna and DVDs inside her Prada clutch and walked out her room.

Draped in an upscale suit and Cazal eyewear, Shamrock blended well with his high-class counterparts. He was currently on the 16th floor inside a signature restaurant named Sixteen. Besides the bottle of Cabernet that was a quarter full, his companions tonight were two young Caucasian ladies who favored the likes of Jessica Simpson and the tennis star Anne Kournikova. The two of them were sisters and the heirs to a fortune.

"Isn't this so beautiful?" she said in reference to the 30-foot, dome-shaped ceiling made of West African wood.

"It sure is, Snow Flake. Welcome to the Trump Towers Chicago," Shamrock said after biting down on the last of his haute cuisine.

"Are you a native of Illinois?" the other asked.

"Naw, Snow Bunny, I was born in New York, and that's the place I call home today. I'm just here on bidness," Shamrock explained.

"Are you a gangster rapper?" Snow Flake asked. "Because you look identical to that DMX guy."

"I guess the jig is up, you blew my cover," Shamrock said and poured himself another glass of bubbly. "But I want you to keep that on the low."

"Can I rub your bald head?" Snow Bunny asked.

Shamrock glanced beyond the 30-foot floor to ceiling window and captured a clear view of the Wrigley Clock Tower. It was about that time.

"Hold that thought," he said, and grabbed his briefcase and bounced, leaving the young ladies with the bill.

Natasha had a seat over by the window in the hotel bar named Rebar overlooking the Michigan Avenue Bridge. She sipped on a cocktail while gazing at the lights that sprinkled the city. She touched the rim of the glass with the gloss on her lips and tossed back what was left. She said a silent prayer, grabbed her clutch, and aimed for the exit.

Adon pulled up on Wabash Avenue in his Cadillac Escalade ESV, directly in front of the Trump Towers grand entrance. He opened the door and let his Belvedere crocodile shoes descend to the even concrete and clasped the top three buttons on his jacket of a Zanetti eggshell suit.

"Here you go," he said to the valet and tossed him the keys.

Adon tilted his brim and walked inside and through the lobby undisturbed. He boarded the elevator and pressed the button for the eighty-ninth floor.

Nitty walked out of the bathroom drying his hands with a towel. He reached the front room when a knock sounded at his penthouse door. His men quickly posted up with their weapons drawn. The African looked over at Nitty for a signal. Calmly, Nitty tossed the damp towel atop a table, over his .357 Magnum, and skewed his head toward the door. The African heeded the order and walked over to the door. He pulled the hammer back on his burna and turned the handle.

"How's it hanging boys?" Agent Karpe said as he walked in without waiting for permission to enter. "Mr. Calhoun, just the man I come to see," he said and went straight over to the mini-bar and poured a glass of Merlot.

"Everybody out," Nitty said to his security personnel.

"What?" The African wasn't sure he heard him correctly. "Are you sure?"

"Leave the penthouse. Hell, leave the floor; go down to the mezzanine level and have some drinks, I don't give a damn. Just get the fuck out of here, and turn off that ESPN bullshit before you leave."

"Well, well, well," Agent Karpe started. "I see someone wants to have a private meeting. Don't I feel special."

Nitty watched his last man leave and shut the door before he turned to Agent Karpe. "What do you want?"

"As usual I delivered, so as usual I'm here to collect," Agent Karpe said.

"You didn't deliver," Nitty shot back. "As *usual* you fucked up!"

"What are you talking about? Doe is dead. I saved your ass, again," he said and took another sip of his wine.

"You allowed Doe to get to Adon before you got to *him*."

"Uhh," Agent Karpe uttered and waved his hand. "We were so far up their asses I doubt the two of them had a chance to talk about the weather much less matters of the past."

"And I doubt that you're right," Nitty said and grabbed a remote, and closed the electronic curtains.

"Not to mention," Agent Karpe said. "Do I have to remind you that I unveiled the identity of the new undercover operative?"

"And you let her get away."

"Well, she's a crafty little bitch. The important thing is that I know who she is. She'll bite the dust," Agent Karpe assured and narrowed his eyes. "Are you trying to stiff me out of my money? Because you know Nitty, I am the wrong man that you'll want on your bad side."

"Let's address another topic," Nitty said as he walked over to the table where the damp towel sat on top. "About the tangible evidence that was supposedly left in Shamrock's Mercedes trunk by the feds."

"Yeah, what about it?"

"In nineteen years there have never been tangible evidence of any kind that could've linked me to Macklin's murder. But you were there on the scene the night I took Macklin's life, so I didn't think twice that maybe after all these years you've held onto something that could prove my guilt. With that in mind, I never hesitated to pay your money-starving ass for botched performances. The point of the matter is there was never any evidence left behind for Shamrock to view."

Nitty pointed the same remote toward the stereo, and cranked the music sky high.

"What are you doing? You don't want to do this, Nitty!"

"You lied to me MUTHAFUCKA!" Nitty reached under the damp towel.

Agent Karpe dropped the wine glass and went for his weapon but was a tad bit slow.

Nitty upped his .357 and exploded two slugs, ripping Agent Karpe's chest to peices. He fell to the floor.

Adon approached the Penthouse door in haste, and with much force he kicked it down on his first attempt. He charged in and immediately sent two bullets into the stereo and quickly turned the burna on Nitty as he walked over Karpe's body without a care. He smacked Nitty across the face with the Desert Eagle.

"Give me dat!" Adon snatched the gun from Nitty's grasp and filled his other fist with it. Now Adon was double-breasted. He pressed the burna against the front of his chin and Nitty slowly held his hands up.

"Adon, let's talk about this," Nitty said calmly.

"You a dirty-weasel muthafucka!" Adon fumed. "Before I decorate this room with your blood, I wanna hear it from you. Did you or did you not kill Macklin!?"

Natasha walked in unnoticed and said, "What's wrong Nitty, the

214

barrel of that gun got your tongue? Tell my brother why you killed my father."

Adon looked over and saw Natasha with her burna aimed in the same direction as his. "Tasha, what the fuck is you doing with that gun? And what the fuck is you doin' here!?"

"This is my fight just as much as it is yours," she said mellow.

"I got this, sis!"

"Adon, she isn't as innocent as you think—"

"Shut the FUCK UP!" Adon bellowed.

"Speaking of innocent, I paid your stately home a visit and I found this."

Natasha tossed the DVDs at Adon's feet.

"Bruh, he's been deceiving you this whole time. Shamrock never betrayed you, snitched you out, or anyone else. Nitty copied the original footage and had it altered, audio and all."

"What?" Adon turned to Nitty with the Desert Eagle still in his face.

"NFL, remember that?" Shamrock said as he walked into the penthouse with his twin .10mms pointed out in front of him. "No matter the weather, you my 'nigga fo' life.' Whatever happened to that, A?" Shamrock asked with one burna aimed at Nitty, the other trained on Adon.

Adon looked back at Shamrock. It was like a cross between seeing a disgruntled ghost and reuniting with a best friend all at the same time. There was so much going through his mind that he didn't no where to start. He reverted his attention back to Nitty.

"So is it true? Did you alter the DVD!?" Adon demanded to know.

"Yes, I did. But before this go any further let me explain, because apparently Doe didn't tell you everything," Nitty said and Adon put the burna under his chin and slightly raised his head.

"If you're not going to kill him get out of the way, bruh," Natasha warned.

"He's already a dead man sis, but before I can put my nightmares to rest I gotta hear what he gots to say." Adon then turned to Nitty. "Now talk."

"I loved Macklin. He was a mentor to me. But I loved your mother more. I couldn't stand the way he was treating her—"

"Don't listen to his shit bruh, he's only trying to deceive you again!" Natasha said.

"I would come around occasionally and see her marked with bruises—"

"Shut up, Nitty!" Natasha demanded.

"And then the black eyes and cigarette burns became constant—"

"He did that only because she was a whore and sleeping with every dick that pointed in her direction!" Natasha yelled.

Adon jerked his head her way with angry brows. "What the fuck did you say, Tasha?"

"Bruh, it's true! Ask him, he knows first hand!"

Adon looked at Nitty and said, "Continue."

"Your mother was not a whore, Adon. She was a sensitive, caring, and loving mother. She loved you two to death," Nitty said sincerely.

"Did you sleep wit' my mother," Adon asked looking him square in the eye.

"We had an affair before you were born, yes. We were planning to run off together."

"So why didn't you?" Adon asked.

"She didn't wanna leave your sister. By this time Macklin found out about the affair, and he and I fell out big time. Only then, did I join The Convolution and the city was virtually captivated by the deadliest street war Chicago had ever seen. It made the St. Valentines Day Massacre that took place in the 1930s look like child's play.

"Then she found out she was pregnant. And for four long years she led Macklin to believe that he was your father, but in her heart she knew she was living a lie. Until one day she confessed," Nitty explained.

"So what is you tryna say?" Adon asked, his burna still under Nitty's chin.

"I am your father," Nitty said catching Adon off guard. Adon's forehead furrowed before looking away.

"Move out the way lil' bruh, and I'm not going to say it a third

216

time," Natasha threatened.

"Just wait! Give me a minute and let me think," Adon said. "So that's why Doe murdered my mother because she betrayed Macklin?"

"That's right, son," Nitty confirmed as Adon was gradually lowering his burna from Nitty's chin.

"That's it, no more!" Natasha barked and started to walk up to Nitty with her burna aimed.

"Got dammit I said wait!" Adon drew down on his sister with the .357 and stopped her in her steps. She stared at him in dismay. "There's no need for any mo' blood shed, this is my fuckin' father!"

"Man, mafuck dis!" Shamrock broke his silence. "Both of you mafuckas can go."

"Stop right there, Shamrock!" Natasha said and turned her burna on him. "Now I don't give a damn what you do to that piece of shit, but the gun you got aimed at my brother, I suggest you drop that before I drop you!" she said adamantly as Nitty gradually extended his hand under the front of the table.

"HE REACHIN'!" Shamrock yelled and suddenly the lights went out and the penthouse went completely black. It resembled Grant Park on the 4th of July as it was strafed with a hail of bullets.

After the shooting had ceased, Adon scrambled for a light switch. His forearm was burning like fire. He ran blindly to the walls and ran his hands over them. He gave up there to search another angle of the Penthouse when he tripped over Agent Karpe's body and fell to the floor. He felt an object. It was the remote. He pressed down on all the buttons.

The entire penthouse lit up with bright lights, ESPN appeared on the screen of the flat panel, and the electronic curtains pulled back.

The first person he saw was Nitty, slumped over the table and bleeding profusely from a number of fatal wounds. Adon felt some irritation on his forehead. He rubbed his hand over it and saw blood. A bullet had grazed his forehead. He darted his eyes around for Shamrock, but he was no longer there. He placed his hands underneath him and jumped to his feet. He grimaced in pain from the gunshot wound in his forearm. He turned in haste to the last place he saw his sister standing.

"NOOO!" he screamed and ran to Natasha's side.

He fell down to his knees and lifted her upper body, putting the back of her shoulders on his thigh while he cradled her head.

"Tasha, stay with me. Please stay with me!"

He looked down into her face as blood oozed out of her mouth. Her beautiful dress was soaked with her own blood.

"Now I know ho..how you felt whe..when you got shot as a kid," she said weakly.

"But don't trip, it's nothin. I pulled through so you will, too."

"Lil' bruh, you know I've always loved you, right?" she said softly.

"Stop talkin' in the past tense, sis. You gone be aiight." Adon declared.

"I'm sorry for everything. Sor…sorry for not spending more quality time with yo…you when we were young. Sor…sorry for not being there for you when we were separated. Sor…sorry for—"

"None of that was yo' fault, Tash."

"I don't have much time left, so please le…let me finish."

After a pause Natasha said, "I've knew since we were little, that Daddy wasn't your biological father. I over heard Mama on the phone telling Big Mama about it. I knew that Nitty was your real father, and for the longest time I held this hate in my heart for what she caused to happen to my daddy. And that hate trickled down to you and that wasn't fair. I'm sorry,"

"But how did you know that Nitty killed Macklin?" Adon asked.

"Because I was there, A," she said spitting up blood. "After Daddy kicked Mama out she came back for you a couple of days later and left me behind. On the night that Daddy was killed, I heard a minor struggle coming from the livingroom. I left my bed and walked up in time to witness Nitty choke Daddy's last breath. I wasn't seen. I ran back to my bedroom and hid. After I heard Nitty leave, I watched him from my window as he got inside a car and drove away. The man that was driving was that white man who's lying dead on the floor," she was referring to Agent Karpe.

Adon's bloody tears fell to her face.

"Lil' bruh, Charlotte and Joy never left the city."

"What?" Adon asked confused.

"They're being held on the west side, go get your baby," she said and handed him a bloody piece of paper with an address. "I'm sorry." Natasha stopped breathing.

"NOOO! God, nooo!" Adon wailed, holding Natasha's lifeless body in his arms.

CHAPTER 34

"What da fuck is you hesitating fo'? Put my dick in yo' mouth bitch!" Mario stood over Charlotte with his manhood in his hand. Due to Natasha's need for Killa Mike's presence in the field, his opportunities to get at Charlotte had since doubled. He had gotten so bold with it that assaulting her in front of Joyous became commonplace.

Charlotte was on her knees in front of him. Her eyes were dry, her body numb.

"Get to it, ho!"

Joyous watched in silence from the corner of the room. Her face was marred with tracks of dried up tears. She, too, was all cried out and numb.

Charlotte gently grabbed a hold of Mario's dick and wrapped her lips around it. Slowly she bobbed her head back and forth, stopping at the midpoint of his shaft and coming up each time.

"Yeah bitch, keep it going," Mario moaned with pleasure. "Rub my balls ho. You know how I like it. Ohh!" he murmured at Charlotte's caress.

Charlotte glanced down at his pants that puddled around his ankles. His butterfly knife hung halfway out of the back pocket. She picked up her pace, taking him in deeper and jacking him simultaneously.

"Yeah, tramp!"

He grabbed a fist full of her hair and began to thrust wildly. He grabbed the back of her head with both hands and buried her face into his pubic hairs, disregarding the gagging noises that she was making.

"I bet cha never sucked Adon's dick like dis before!"

He tossed his head back and released in her throat. Charlotte grabbed the knife and bit down on him, severing his dick head.

"AHHH! You bitch—"

Charlotte rose up from the floor, drove all eight inches of the knife in his chest, and spit the head of his mangled dick on the floor. He reached for the knife's handle and collapsed across the bed.

"C'mon baby." Charlotte reached for Joyous' hand and they ran out of the bedroom and to the only door that led to the outside. She struggled with the heavy wood, it wouldn't budge. Charlotte saw a shadow on the wall coming from the bedroom.

"Get over here, Joy."

She brought her daughter closer to her while her back was against the door.

"Where you think you goin', bitch!" Mario bellowed from the room.

Charlotte wasn't about to give up now. She turned to the door and gave it her all and managed to pull it a foot from the post.

"C'mon, baby!"

She sent Joyous out first and then she squeezed between the tight space.

Adon bent the corner of Lake Street and Central Park like a lunatic, and sped up the block. He scoured the block as he approached the apartment building, and spotted Charlotte running with Joyous in her arms. He pulled over and stomped on the breaks.

"Charlotte, it's me!" he hollered and met them at the curb.

She threw her arms around his neck as her legs gave in. He held them both up.

"Who did this to you!?" He asked after he got a good look at her face. He stared at his daughter's sad eyes and his heart broke. "Where da muthafucka at!?"

Charlotte pointed toward the apartment.

"Get inside the truck," he said and escorted them both to the passenger side, opened the door and helped them in. He pulled his burna and ran for the apartment. He saw that the door was opened.

"Awww!" He kicked it halfway off the hinges and stormed in. He made his way to the bedroom. Mario laid face-up on the floor dead; blood still oozing from his ripped penis. Adon checked around the apartment and ran back out to the truck, joining his family.

"Was there anybody else?"

Charlotte nodded while she held on to Joyous.

"Who and where they at?"

Charlotte shrugged her shoulders, rocking back and forth.

"FUCK! FUCK!" Adon punched his dashboard and Joyous started to cry. He looked over and realized that he was scaring them both.

"Daddy sorry," he said and kissed their foreheads. He reached in his backseat and retrieved her Burberry scarf. "Here," he wrapped it around them, "we gotta get goin'." Adon put the ESV in drive mode.

Killa Mike and Mick had just turned on Lake Street on the way back to the apartment. After seeing the Chicago Police Department flood Trump Towers, they immediately got ghost. Killa Mike thought the worst, while Mick's only concern was getting his money.

Killa Mike stopped at a traffic light in deep thought. He questioned his abandonment of the scene, and wondered if he would've stayed just a little bit longer maybe Natasha would've walked up out of there unscathed. He played with the idea of going back. The light turned green and he pulled off when a blinding light charged for his side at an alarming speed, so quick he couldn't react.

A thunderous crash sounded, and in a blink of an eye their Lincoln was pent-up against a light pole.

The driver of the wrecked '72 Deuce and a Quarter stepped out. He wasn't sorry for having sped through a red traffic light and crashing into a car that had the right a way. Instead, he was irate that they were in his way. He walked through the radiator's smoke as it filled the air, and continued until he stood at the driver window of the Lincoln.

Killa Mike groggy from the crash, looked up and saw two .10mms at his dome.

Shamrock filled their upper torsos with burning hot lead.

"Wrong place, wrong time," Shamrock said unaware that he'd just murdered Charlotte's and Joyous' kidnappers. He walked off, feeling the chest part of his vest where he felt three holes embedded by Natasha's .45 ACP. He could still feel the sharp pain.

The BlackBerry chimed.

Adon released his interlaced hold with Charlotte's hand and picked up his cell. He saw Vanity's name on the screen. He looked over at Charlotte and Joyous. He tapped his forehead with the tip of his phone, as he was indecisive. He then pressed the forward option and tossed the cell on the dashboard, and noticed a sheet of folded paper that he didn't see before. He reached for it as he drove up the Chicago Loop. There was writing on it and he recognized the penmanship right away.

It said, *For your info', Nitty was nothing more than a pun. The Ruthless Dictator goes by the name of Nefarious. No matter the weather, you still my NFL, my nigga. Don't ever forget that!*

AUTHOR BIO

Rumont TeKay was born and raised in Chicago, Illinois. While his back was against the wall and hope was bleak, he found solace in the elements of another writer's storylines. His inspiration flared and Rumont TeKay put his mighty pen to paper and hasn't let up since. Through it all, he has learned that hope never dies just as long as one breathes life into it. He is currently hard at work on his next book while building his publishing company. Visit him online at www.murrayparkpublishing.com.

"Second To None!"

Name: _____

Address: _____

City/State: _____

Zip: _____

QTY	TITLE	PRICE
	The Ruthless Dictator	$14.95
	Shipping & Handling	FREE

TOTAL $ _____

To order online visit
www.murrayparkpublishing.com

Send cashiers check or money order to:
Murray Park Publishing
4230 East Towne Blvd, Suite 114
Madison, WI 53704